Bamboozled

Trapped in poverty, tricked into slavery

Merry Carroll and Carol LaDuca
in collaboration with
Victoria VanHorn

ISBN: 979-8-9894522-0-0

Bamboozled

This is a work of fiction, based on a true story. With the exception of Soleil, names, characters and events are used fictitiously.

Cover art photography by Carol LaDuca
Cover design by Merry Carroll

Contact info:
MerryCarroll.author@gmail.com \ CarolLaDuca.author@gmail.com

Preface
The Backstory

The first time we met her, we were astounded to learn that Soleil, a young, vivacious Filipina woman who is now part of our extended family, had been a victim of human trafficking in the Middle East. The more we learned about her journey, the more intriguing her story became. Although we have only known her as Soleil, she told us that Soleil was not her given name. We've fictionalized the younger version of Soleil and called her Edith. Our main character, Edith, exists only in these pages.

Bamboozled highlights the struggles Edith and others endure as women born into poverty. It is the story of how desperate women can easily be duped into believing they will make a fortune by signing a contract to serve as professional housekeepers or nannies in places like the Middle East. Instead they are often signing up to become domestic slaves subject to abuse, loss of freedom and inhumane treatment.

Bamboozled is a story of endurance, courage and love. When Edith ultimately escapes her enslavement during the onset of the Syrian Civil War and returns to the Visayas, she changes her name to Soleil. Changing her name had the happenstance of changing her life.

Once we authors became enlightened about the prevalence of human trafficking and the atrocities happening to enslaved people, we were compelled to share what we learned. Although this story is fictionalized, real stories like this are still happening. Enticing, but deceptive ads for Overseas Filipina Workers (OFWs) are even more prolific today. Stories like this need to be told.

Carol LaDuca, Merry Carroll, Victoria VanHorn

For more information about domestic slavery and labor exploitation, we encourage you to visit the website of the Global Fund to End Modern Slavery at https://gfems.org/reports/overseas-filipino-worker-voices/

Part 1
Poverty in Palo

"The opposite of poverty is not wealth.
The opposite of poverty is enough."

—Anon

Chapter 1

The Backpack

"Holy guacamole!!" Ana Lopez exclaimed. "This is one slippery baby! Hang on tight, Liezel, she's quite squirmy!" she advised, as she carefully laid the wriggling newborn on its mother's chest.

Ana was the community's unofficial, untrained, self-taught but willing midwife who delivered Edith in 1989 on the first day of May. "I've delivered almost every baby in this barrio and not one of them has been as spirited as little Edith here," Ana told the new mother who was now holding on to her for dear life. "She's going to be full of surprises, this one. You mark my words, Liezel," she prophesied. Ana claimed all the babies she delivered as her personal gifts to the community and never failed to include upbeat predictions about each baby's future as part of her service. Some of her delivered babies were now in their twenties and many of the town's parents had raised these children with Ana's prophecies in mind.

This town was Palo, the home of hard-working, impoverished people in the Philippines. Palo is on the coast of Leyte, one of the larger islands in the Visayas, a region comprising several hundred islands. It's a far cry from the prosperity that exists five hundred miles to the north in Manila.

Edith was the first of ten Santos children born into the poverty that characterized the marriage of Liezel and Carlos Santos. She came into the world tumultuously, wriggling and crying, as if the circumstances into which she was deposited were not going to suit her.

The roof over the Santos' heads was corrugated metal, the floor beneath their feet was well-trod dirt. The parents spent their days coaxing corn, sweet potatoes or taro out of their dry half-acre and sold what meager products they produced. Most days they piled the vegetables up on dilapidated crates in their front yard, hoping to make a sale or two to passersby. But on Fridays and Saturdays, they loaded a wagon and dragged their produce by bicycle to the market in Palo where sales were somewhat brisker.

Other families in their barrio, with better locations in the Visayas, owned or rented small paddies that provided rice to eat and rice to sell. Not so for the Santos family. Their rented half-acre plot was dusty and dry. It was no miracle that this arid square could produce a living for Liezel and Carlos: it was sheer determination.

The Santoses spent most of their mornings attacking the weeds that grew faster than the corn they cultivated. After breakfast, Liezel would tuck baby Edith into a handbasket and head to her field. She'd survey her tiny patch looking for a cornstalk that might be high enough to provide the most shade where Edith could follow the clouds curiously while her mother battled her nemesis.

By the time Edith was two and toddling behind her mother among the cornstalks, there was a sister in the handbasket. Edith hovered over baby Betsy as if she were a doll. A scant year later a brother, Albert, made his entrance.

Day after day when Liezel was not in the garden weeding, she stood by her doorway with a wiggling child on her hip, hoping to sell a yam or two. Although sales to tourists or other adventurers were rare, the neighbors in their barrio were quick to support the young couple. "Go to Liezel's and bring me some of her delicious mangoes," they'd tell one of their own children. Or "Run over to Liezel's and get me six of her sweet yams." So between what they could grow for themselves and with the support of neighbors and sometimes strangers passing by on the dusty road to Tacloban, the Santos family managed to stay afloat.

With each new baby Liezel brought into the world, Edith's list of chores grew longer and when her mother's hip could no longer support an infant (as another infant from within was demanding the space), Edith's hip became the surrogate, first one hip, then two. One after another these babies became as much hers as her mother's. She gave them baths in the aluminum wash tub that shared duty with the laundry, kissed the scrapes, and mediated the siblings' squabbles when they happened.

When Edith was four she had a glimpse of her future. Two girls, hikers, came backpacking down their dusty road chattering away in English. Liezel was in her garden when she heard their voices. She hurried to her stand in hopes of selling a yam or two. Edith followed closely behind.

"Hello," they called when they spotted Liezel. "Can you tell us where Hill 522 is?"

"You're almost there. It's right behind you," Liezel replied pointing. The girls looked up and then at each other.

"That's it? But it's just brush and bramble and palm trees. And it's really, really steep!" one of them gasped.

"And it's probably full of snakes, Linda," said the other, "I am *not* going to climb it. I don't care how historical it is!"

The girls looked so Filipino that Liezel had to ask, "Are you from around here?"

"No," said Linda, "we're students at Berkeley." Then added, "Oakland," and finally, "California," when they noticed Liezel looked puzzled. "We're on winter break," stated Kathy.

"College students?" Liezel asked in amazement, "What in the world are you doing here? Wait. You two must be dying of thirst on our dusty road, let me get some waters," she added as her eyes danced over a basket of purple yams.

"That'd be great," said Kathy, the girl who wasn't about to climb. When she noticed the little girl squatting in the door frame, Kathy waved and Edith gave a shy wave back.

As Liezel returned with a pitcher of water, the taller girl said, "Thanks so much. I'm Linda Phillips and this is my roommate Kathy Richards. We're Filipina Americans." She went on to explain, "My parents were born in San Francisco but my grandmother was born here in Leyte, somewhere around Guinhangdan Hill. My grandma tells me stories of her childhood in Palo where she met my grandfather. Her stories are sometimes frightening: how the Japanese invaded Leyte during World War II, how they marched through Palo threatening and frightening everyone. That's when my grandparents fled to America and they've never come back. I'd heard their stories for so many years that I wanted to come and see for myself. So I decided to backpack through these parts on my winter break and bring them news of their childhood home," she said, adding, "and I talked my roommate into coming along. My grandma suggested we visit Guinhangdan Hill, now known as Hill 522. But now that I see it, I'm not sure why."

"I know it's not much to look at," Liezel said, "but it has significant historical importance to us. Didn't your grandma ever explain its story?"

Linda replied, shaking her head, "Not too much. I wasn't too interested in stories of war when I was growing up. All I know is that it was named Hill 522 because it's 522 feet high."

"Really?" Kathy interrupted. "Now I'm *definitely* not climbing up. It would just be 522 feet of brambles, vines and God knows what else," she announced to the chagrin of her roommate.

"You don't have to worry about brambles and snakes," Liezel

informed, laughing, "there are actual steps if you go around this hill to the other side, 522 of them. I'll briefly tell you why it is so important to us Filipinos," Liezel continued, as she began to explain with great pride. "It is on this hill in 1944 that the Americans, led by General MacArthur, defeated the Japanese who had invaded our island. It was a pivotal moment in helping end World War II. I do hope you'll make the climb, both of you. It will give you a good idea of how difficult it must have been to re-take this hill, given the challenging terrain. You will understand why we are eternally grateful to General MacArthur and the Americans, and you should be doubly proud. Not only is your heritage American but it's Filipina as well. To this day, many grateful Filipinas give their babies American names. Just like my Edith here."

Edith had been listening silently the whole time. Although she didn't understand the conversation, she was mesmerized by the Americans and their backpacks. Her face lit up and she smiled at the girls when her mama mentioned her name. Linda walked closer to the child, leaned down and looked directly into her eyes. "Edith, when you grow up, you should go to school at Berkeley. You would love it," she said, hoisting her backpack over her shoulder.

"Hey Linda," Kathy called out. "We better get moving if we're going to climb that hill."

"You're willing to climb? Great! What changed your mind?" Linda wanted to know.

"I just realized how proud I am to be a Filipina American."

The girls were heading back to the dirt-encrusted road when Linda turned around and walked back toward Liezel. "I want to buy two of those great-looking purple yams," she said, handing over a $10 bill to Liezel.

"Sorry, but I don't have any chan ..." Liezel started to protest.

"Don't need it," Linda said, winking at Edith. "Put it in the little one's Berkeley College fund."

Edith watched intently as the yams were dropped into the

backpack and Linda rejoined her friend.

"What the heck are we gonna do with two yams in the middle of a jungle?" Kathy said laughing, totally impressed by her friend's thoughtfulness and generosity.

No sooner had the hikers disappeared down the road when Edith tugged at her mother's apron. "Mama I want one of those," she declared.

"One of what?" Liezel asked, now delightfully distracted by the ten dollar bill in her hand.

"A backpack."

Liezel laughed in surprise. "Whatever would a four-year-old do with a backpack? Are you planning to travel?"

"Yes, that *is* my plan," the child answered resolutely and went off to get Betsy up from her nap.

Chapter 2

Barking Dogs

Education had not been a strong point in the Santos family. Liezel and Carlos had completed only third grade before they were needed to work Carlos' uncle's paddy. What few words they knew how to read then were soon forgotten, replaced by the snapping of rice stalks and the slap of feet padding along in the monsoon-fed waters.

"Mama," said Edith on her fifth birthday, "I want to go to school."

"Iha, my sweet," her mother replied, "school is not for us. We're all needed in the field or the weeds will win."

"No, Mama, the weeds will not win and I simply must go to school. If I don't go to school, I'll never have a chance to go to Burglary School, like those hiking girls said I should."

Liezel was momentarily dumbfounded. "Ohhh!! You mean *Berkeley*!" she finally said when she caught her breath. Liezel couldn't remember the last time she had laughed so hard.

"Yes. So you see, I have to go to school and I must learn to read and write in English. But don't worry, I have a plan."

"A plan?" Liezel said laughing. "A plan! Five-year-olds don't have plans. They help their mamas and they learn to cook and sew and sell produce at the stand."

"I can do it all," Edith insisted, "Watch me. I'll get up so early and do my chores. I'll learn to cook *and* I *will* go to school."

"We'll see what Papa has to say about this nonsense," Liezel conceded, knowing the battle had already been lost. Unlike Liezel, Papa was no match for his daughter's wiles and on the first day of school he put on his best shirt, took his daughter's small hand in his and together they started the long walk down the dusty road to the schoolhouse where Carlos enrolled this insistent firstborn.

"I'll see you at 3 p.m. when school's over," he told her as he hugged her goodbye in the school yard. "But starting tomorrow you'll have to walk to here by yourself. I'll be helping the neighbors with the pigs and there'll be no time to walk you," he explained.

"I know that Papa. I can walk by myself. I'm not afraid." But she was. Papa had shooed away three large dogs that had leapt off their stoops when they passed. Papa had calmed them but she was much smaller.

I can do this, she told herself in the silence of the walk home with her hand securely in her Papa's. She really believed it.

Each school day morning she'd mold a tablespoon of rice into a ball in her hand. When the dogs came bounding and barking she'd sing to them, "I have a treat for you today. Good boys!" In no time pit bulls became pups in their affection for her and began sharing a portion of her walk.

When Miss Ramirez gave her a notebook with every page lined in light blue but otherwise blank and a pencil whose point she could sharpen in the grinder on the wall near the classroom door any time it dulled, she knew she was going to love school. The notebook seemed to be waiting for her. She would fill it with all the important things Miss Ramirez would teach. Already she had memorized the alphabet and E was her favorite letter.

She opened the notebook and on the very first page she drew

a vertical line attaching three short horizontal lines to it.

E.

E is for Edith. E is for Eventually. E is for Everything, she mused.

As she put that first E in her notebook, she knew she'd be the one to break the Santos' curse of being uneducated. She'd be the one to do better than her parents had and make it past third grade. And she'd be the one to insist all her siblings went to school.

"But I don't want to go to school," cried Betsy the following September when it was her turn to enroll. "I want to stay home and help Papa."

"Papa doesn't need you today," Edith replied. "Isn't that so, Papa?"

What choice did he have with this resolute girl? Carlos would look up from his breakfast bowl with a reluctant nod.

By the time she was in fifth grade she had all her school-aged siblings enrolled in the public school. With Edith it wasn't a choice.

"Get up, time for school," she'd sing before dawn as she'd shake nine-year-old Betsy from her cozy blanket. Then she'd move on to the others tickling them and singing as those still under the covers pretended they hadn't heard her. Eventually Edith had all the school-aged children up, washed and fed a bowl of rice in time for the first bell.

"Look at that Edith," their neighbor Luiz would say, nudging his wife and pointing as Edith led a parade of the less willing down the dusty road of their haphazard neighborhood. "Carlos must be so proud of his children."

"Pfft," his wife replied with a puff of disdain. "Who's home helping Liezel and Carlos? Not those kids! No, they go to school while the parents work their knuckles to the bone. What kind of thanks is that?

"Pfft," she said again.

Chapter 3

The Trouble with Kissing

Fortunately for Edith, not all the neighboring adults begrudged Edith for wanting to be educated. Next door, less than a few acres away lived papa's older brother by ten years, Jacob, and his wife, Agnes. Their three children were grown up and the youngest had just entered the university in Manila. Agnes was a firm believer in education and although her family was slightly less poor than Carlos' crew, their land was slightly more productive. Having only three extra mouths to feed enabled Agnes to see her children through grade and high school. Agnes was not a fan of babies. "All they do is cry and demand food," she used to say. But by the time Edith was three, her Aunt Agnes took a real shine to Edith, performing many of the duties Liezel was usually too overworked to perform: consoling her over bruised knees, teaching her to play cards, and always, always reading to her. Whenever Agnes discovered that Edith could read a book by herself, she sent that book home with her. "That Edith of yours," she said more than once to Liezel, "she's a smart one."

Over the course of her childhood, Edith became a voracious reader who never tossed away any book she could get her hands on. Her mother sometimes complained that Edith's pile of books was taking up "too much real estate" in their already cramped home, but not too often. Liezel was happy to have a few moments of peace and quiet when Edith would pull out a book and read to her siblings, which she did almost daily.

One night Edith was searching through her book pile looking for a kids' book she knew the three youngest would enjoy. At the bottom of the pile, she spotted the notebook she had written in when she was starting school. *What ever happened to that five-year-old dreamer?* she wondered. It was then she decided it was time once again to start writing down her dreams. She stashed the notebook under her straw-filled mattress. *If only I had kept writing in this notebook over the past six years, who knows what I would have discovered about myself!* she mused.

Birthdays weren't a very big deal in the Santos household but were usually marked by a special dinner. Quite often the birthday child also was assigned an additional chore or two. Edith's thirteenth birthday was no exception. "Edith," her mom began, "now that you're a teenager, I think you are mature enough to handle the vegetable stand in Palo by yourself. With this pregnancy, I just don't have the energy to take the cart to market and stand all day anymore. You'll be in charge of the stand after school ends next month and I'm sure you will do a great job. You're getting so pretty, I bet you will outsell me by miles. Happy birthday."

Edith groaned inside. Ever since she was eight, Edith had accompanied her mom every weekend at their vegetable stand. They would load up the wagon early on Friday morning and drag it by bicycle to their spot in the market on the outskirts of town. During the school year, Edith joined her mother after classes on Fridays. On Saturdays, she helped out for a full eight hours. As tedious as the job was during the school year, Edith really dreaded working the stand in the summers when the heat was oppressive. She was constantly jealous of her two friends who spent the weekends swimming at the beach in Palo.

Great, just great, she wrote in her notebook the evening of her thirteenth birthday. *Not only will I have to haggle with cus-*

tomers all by myself, but I will have to miss school on Fridays.
Mama says it's my last year of school so it doesn't matter. But it
does matter! There has got to be something more for me than a
lifetime of selling vegetables in this poor, sad place. I'm already
thirteen! I want much more than this.

With those words, something shifted in Edith's soul. It was
not a subtle shift. Within a short time, the entire family had noticed her changed attitude, her rebellious spirit. They had witnessed quite a few outspoken disagreements with her parents, especially her mother.

"Why were you and Mama arguing again?" Betsy asked.
"You are making her very upset, what with a baby on the way and
all. You're not being very nice."

"All I did was tell Mama that I would only work the vegetable
stand until high school starts in the fall. She had a fit and said that
high school was out of the question. Said she needs me to run the
stand, especially once the baby arrives. I asked her for how long.
She said, 'For as long as I say.' I got really mad. Wish I hadn't
told her I hope that baby dies at birth. She slapped my face. I
apologized, but I couldn't take back my words. Mama ran outside
sobbing. I don't know why I said that."

"I'll tell you why she said that," Agnes said to Liezel who had
arrived moments earlier at her door in tears, relating the argument. "Hormones," her sister-in-law said simply. "This is new
territory for you, but I endured the puberties of both my daughters
and my son. I cried too, the first few times my once sweet children started being bold and obnoxious. At thirteen, Edith's hormones are taking control, or better yet, are out of control. She's
growing into a woman and the last vestiges of the umbilical cord
are dissolving. She's not your sweet obedient little girl anymore,
but a teenager trying to grow into her adulthood. My advice: be
prepared, be patient and don't take her rebellion personally. Bless
your heart, I don't envy you. You've got a rash of puberties coming
up. But you'll get used to them," she promised cheerfully.

After the terrible confrontation with her mother that after-noon, Edith was ashamed of herself. Sitting in the shade behind the house, she found some solace writing in her notebook. *I won-der what's going on with me,* she wrote. *I've never in my life said such awful things to my mama. But I couldn't help it. I've been talking and thinking about high school since the fourth grade. I just assumed that that is what was next for me. How can I ever be somebody or do something wonderful if I'm stuck selling veggies in the dirty, dusty market for the rest of my life? I don't want to become my mama. I don't want her life, but that's all she's ever known. I'm beginning to see how her life really is. Endless cook-ing, cleaning, and coaxing veggies to grow where they don't want to. One pregnancy after another. That's not for me. I feel that I already have had my share of raising children, with another on the way. I must find a way to get to high school. Maybe I should talk to Papa.*

It was nearly dark when Papa came in from the fields, his hands blackened with earth and his face burned by the sun. Edith was filled with dread when Mama, instead of gathering the kids together for their family dinner, slid her arm into Papa's, saying, "We need to talk."

Edith could hear their murmuring voices coming from the dirt path behind the house, and Mama was doing most of the talking. Betsy whispered, "Oh, oh, Edith, sounds like you're in big trou-ble." Edith wished she had a bed to crawl under.

When her parents returned, Papa sat at the head of the table as he customarily did. Mama brought the usual large bowls of rice and small plates of chicken to the table and the entire meal was eerily quiet except for the scraping of spoons and loud burps from the four-year-old. Edith retreated to bed as soon as she could be excused and no words were spoken that night about this turning-point day.

"Good morning, Papa," Edith said shyly. "I need to talk to you just for a minute before you go to the fields. It's about what happened yesterday."

"Oh yes, yesterday. I'm having trouble believing such evil words came from the mouth of my sweet, considerate eldest child."

"I apologized as soon as the words flew off my tongue, but I'm not sure Mama even heard me. I have no idea what snapped in me. I am so ashamed of myself."

Papa said he understood, saying he had his share of shameful moments when he was a teenager, not so long ago. His words gave Edith hope. "Papa, I need your help," she began. But Papa interrupted. "I know how much you wanted to go to high school," he said with a sadness in his voice. "I wish I could help. But your mama has made up her mind. This is one battle I just can't win for you."

Then fate intervened. Edith awoke one morning with a heightened sense of discomfort. Her abdomen was achy and even sometimes painful. As she stood up, she was horrified to see a reddish color staining not only her thin bed sheet but also her nightshirt. She took a few steps only to discover blood running down her legs. *What the heck is happening to me?* she wondered. Then she began to cry. Her thoughts were terrorizing her.

She was sitting in the kitchen with one of the few family towels stuffed between her legs when Mama came in to start making breakfast. "Mama, I'm not going to be able to take over the stand," she said flatly. Mama whipped around from the oatmeal she was stirring and angrily said, "You really don't have a choi…" but before she could finish, Edith calmly interrupted. "Mama, I'm dying."

Mama's eyebrows shot up a few inches. "And *I'm* dying to know why," Mama retorted, only just then noticing the tears running down Edith's cheeks.

"My insides are falling out. Down there," Edith said, pointing in the direction of the family towel. "There was blood all over me and my bed this morning. My belly hurts, really bad sometimes. I think my stomach is falling out, or something even more horrible. I'm sorry, Mama. I really didn't mean to die on you."

Liezel was instantly ashamed that she had never taken the time to explain this female phenomenon to her eldest daughter. "Oh, Edith," she said, wrapping the dying crying child in her embrace. "Oh, no, my dear. You are not dying. Only your childhood is. This morning you became a woman. I apologize for not telling you about this sooner. Here's what's going on."

After Mama's talk, Edith was relieved of her morning terrors, but still found much of Mama's explanation quite unbelievable. "Does this mean I have to work the stand, even when I'm gushing blood?" she asked.

"I'll show you how to deal with it," Liezel replied. And she did.

The week after school was over, Edith was alone, wobbling on the family bicycle heading to market with a wagon full of the summer's early harvest of yams and corn. She had learned how to arrange the produce appetizingly after watching her mother do it for many years. She easily set up the stand on this first day (*of the rest of my life,* she moaned). All day long she had to answer many queries from familiar customers. "Where's your mama, little one?" and "Is your mama home with the newborn?" It was all Edith could do to keep from retorting, "No, I'm here alone from now on. It's my punishment for being mouthy one time."

As the summer went on and high school, for some, was about to start, Edith grew more and more discontented. Her notebook started to fill up with the resentment she was feeling.

Why does that stupid Cruz kid get to go to high school? He can't even read the shopping list his mother sends with him to my stand every Saturday. Sometimes I feel like messing with him. "Oh, it says here on your list you should pick up five yams and a dozen ounces of intuition," is what I'd say to the big dummy. He'd probably say, "Forget the intuition, Mama knows it gives me headaches." Ha! There just has to be a way to have some fun at this job. Oh, how I wish it were me heading off to high school next week. I've gotten to the point where I don't even bring it up to Mama anymore. It makes her snappish at me and I never want to snap back again.

Eventually, Edith gave up being angry with her fate, but within months, fate was handing her something much better. Edith started to physically change. Her teeth now fit perfectly into a face that had filled out, accented by deep dimples and high cheekbones. The rest of her body followed suit. She grew nearly three inches taller, and now at 5'6" she literally towered over many of her customers. As the early days of spring grew warmer, Edith's t-shirts grew smaller and tighter. "Mama needs to take you for new clothes," Papa said one evening as he suddenly noticed his little girl wasn't a little girl anymore. "You've outgrown your shirts. Run over and ask Aunt Agnes if she has any you can borrow until we can get you new ones."

When Agnes opened the door, she gasped. "Is that you, Edith?" she teased. "Oh! How you've changed, so grown up! I haven't seen you in quite a while, you're so busy these days, but, wow, you have gotten even more beautiful. I didn't think that was possible."

"Oh! Aunt Agnes, you always make me feel so good," Edith said, disengaging from the woman's delightful embrace.

Agnes was more than happy to rummage through her clothes for something more appropriate than Edith's too-tight t-shirt. As low on the poverty rung as she was, Agnes always had a flair for dressing well, even a little exotically. "What do you think about this one?" she asked, flashing a bright yellow sundress in front of Edith's mesmerized eyes. And so it went. In a short time, Agnes had a nifty pile of interesting clothes for Edith to take home and try. "Oh, thank you, Aunt Agnes. I promise to take care of them and return them as soon as Mama takes me shopping."

"You'll do no such thing. They are yours to keep. I can't fit into them anymore and I doubt I'll be crash dieting anytime soon," she said laughing. "But wait, I have something else I think you'll be needing." With that, she pulled a large straw hat out of a box and plopped it on Edith's head. "You need to keep the sun off your beautiful face and gorgeous hair this summer. Oh! One more thing." Agnes rummaged around in a paper sack and pulled out a tube of lipstick. "It's called Sultry Summer, and it really goes with the hat."

Edith's mama never wore, or had time for, makeup, so holding this little tube in her hand felt like a luxurious gift. "Let me," Agnes said, taking the tube and expertly applying it to Edith's full lips. "Just ignore the crack in the glass," she suggested, holding a small hand mirror in front of Edith. That moment was the first time in her life that Edith saw more possibilities than she'd ever dreamed about. She saw her real beauty. Now she just had to figure out how to use it.

It wasn't long before that opportunity came. The very next day, she chose the yellow sundress and straw hat to wear for her stint at the market. She stopped pedaling the bike once she rounded the bend from her house and retrieved the tube of lipstick stashed in her pocket. "I hope this all lands on my lips," she mused as she applied the Sultry Summer even better than she thought she could.

It took fewer than two weekend markets before word spread through town about the hot chick running the Santos' vegetable stand. Or, more precisely, before word spread through the high school's male population. Soon nearly every boy in town was begging bewildered mamas to let them go to market to buy the week's necessities.

Edith's life of resentment and despair changed overnight. She began to enjoy getting dressed up and going to market. In fact, she began to thrive on it. After the first month, she had a long list of regulars who spent much more time at her stand than necessary and who also spent quite a bit more money just to see her smile at them. She was selling veggies to adolescent boys who previously wouldn't even touch them, let alone taste them. She quickly discovered that batting her eyelashes turned high school boys into blithering idiots. She was having the time of her life and her family noticed.

"Why are you so happy lately?" Betsy asked one afternoon while they were out picking vegetables for the next day's market. Edith didn't hesitate to tell her that she was having a blast running the veggie stand. "It's gotten to be really fun. I meet so many nice people, the work isn't hard at all. I just get to stand around smiling, joking and hearing lots of juicy gossip," she quipped. "To say nothing of the cute boys I get to talk to!"

Her words of praise for the veggie stand spread like wildfire through the household and soon all her siblings believed that running the veggie stand was a much better assignment than pulling weeds from the fields. Especially Betsy.

"I have a birthday surprise for you this year," Mama said in late April just before Edith's fifteenth birthday. "I'm not that great at giving good birthday gifts but this is one I know you'll like."

Mama was right about giving terrible gifts. It made Edith wonder what it could be that Mama guaranteed she'd like. But she didn't give it much thought. Her thoughts lately were centered around a boy named Mateo who came both Fridays and Saturdays to the veggie stand. "Looks like I forgot to get some carrots when I came here yesterday," he'd say by way of an excuse to see her. This had happened every weekend for the past six weekends and became their little joke. He always offered to help her reload the cart for the trip home after the market closed on Saturday. She happily accepted his help and when one Saturday he planted a small, sloppy kiss on her full lips, she accepted that too.

Gee whiz, she wrote in her notebook that night. *I just don't get it. What's the big deal about kissing? I remember last year reading a few pages of Aunt Agnes' Harlequin paperback that she mistakenly gave me. I was sure that kissing would be a lot more exciting. Sara in the book got kissed and went on and on about a strange tingling sensation she began to notice happening under her skirt. Before I could find out what happened next, Mama swooped into the room and zeroed in on the sexy cover. I never did see that book again. But it does seem to me that kissing could possibly lead to pregnancy and that's something I really want to avoid. Mama and Papa are always hugging and kissing. That's proof enough. I think I'll lay off kissing for quite a while.*

As her birthday drew closer, Edith started to anticipate the gift she was guaranteed to like. What could it be? Eyeliner? Mascara? (Mama had noticed Edith's lipstick the one time she forgot to wipe it off before returning home.)

As was customary on birthdays, the Santos' dinner menu was pretty much the same as any other day, except the portions were larger. So the family was quite delighted when, on Edith's fifteenth birthday, the menu changed. Mama had gone to town and had come back with bags of hamburgers and french fries from Palo's newly-opened McDonalds. Edith was thrilled, thinking this was the great present Mama had promised. All her siblings were ecstatic. "I want to have the same meal for my birthday in August," Albert said. "Best food I've ever tasted!" he exclaimed more than once.

"We'll see," Liezel said. "But now it's time for your special present, Edith. As you know, Betsy's turning thirteen this summer, same age as you when you started running the veggie stand." *Where is this going?* Edith wondered. Mama continued, "Betsy is insisting that she is old enough to take over the stand and seems very excited about it. So once Betsy has her birthday, no more veggie stand for you, my dear. In September, you are going to high school. I wanted to make your wish come true."

Edith couldn't believe what she was hearing. Her first impulse was to rush to hug and thank her mother, which she did. Looking over Mama's shoulder, she saw Betsy wearing the smuggest

smile as if all *her* wishes also had just come true. Her second reaction was unexpected, even to herself. Edith suddenly realized
how much she'd miss the overwhelming attention the stand was
bringing her, to say nothing of the pleasure she got from flirting.
"Mama, I know I hated working at the veggie stand at first, and
bugged you endlessly about high school, but I've gotten used to it.
I'm not sure I still want to go to high school."

Mama was flabbergasted. "You're going to high school if I
have to take you there myself!" she threatened.

Papa may have walked five-year-old Edith to her first day of
grade school with loving compassion, but Mama marched the
fifteen-year-old Edith to her first day of high school with steely
determination. Mama was more fearsome than the long-dead pit
bulls ever were. In any case, Edith knew that there was no way
she could stop her mother, even if she threw rice balls at her.

It didn't take Edith long to discover that high school was way
more exciting than even the veggie stand. She recognized many
of the students from her vendor days and was reunited with old
friends from her grade school days. As much as many of the boys
hoped to stimulate her interest, Edith was much more stimulated
by her classes. She was determined to excel at school and by the
end of the first quarter, her teachers recommended she be promoted to second year. "That Edith Santos, she's a smart one," her
teacher Miss Ortiz said to the principal. "She aces every exam, is
truly invested in learning and is probably the best and smartest
student I've ever had. The other teachers all agree. She must be
bored stiff being in the same classroom as Cruz and his ilk."

Miss Ortiz's words worked wonders and Edith sailed through
high school in just three years. She avoided being distracted by
boys dying to kiss her. Although she finished high school with a
lot of useful knowledge, her naivety had hardly changed at all. A
dozen classmates received their diplomas with swollen bellies.
"Next time, watch out for that kissing stuff," she teased her pregnant best friend, Gloria.

Gloria wasn't the only one into kissing. Shortly after graduation, she had a strange request from her sister Betsy. "Can we talk?" she asked one afternoon while the two were paring the vegetables for dinner. "That's an odd question, Betsy. You're a blurter. So do what you do, spit it out," Edith responded.

Betsy couldn't suppress her huge grin. "I think, well, I know I'm pregnant," she said with a happy giggle. "I am so excited, I can't keep this secret any longer. You're the first to know, well, almost the first. Ethan knows too. Yes! I'm in love! I met him at the veggie stand a few months ago. He's very cute and lots of fun. Ethan and I have talked about getting married and now we're gonna have a baby!"

Edith's already big eyes doubled in size. "What? Are you kidding? Who is this Ethan? You've been kissing, haven't you?" Edith was shocked that her sister seemed so delighted about being pregnant. "You're going to end up just like Mama," she blurted out without thinking.

"You don't understand, Edith. That's exactly what my dream is. I want Mama's life. A loving and kissing husband, a bunch of kids, happiness and love every day. It's gonna be awesome!"

Just three weeks later, it was clear that Ethan was no longer in the area, perhaps not even in the Philippines. Betsy was determined that she could manage without this kissing boyfriend, but Edith could tell she was scared and worried. Mama and Papa would surely not abandon Betsy and her newborn, but that meant more expenses for the already strapped household. Edith knew she had to help out.

"Mama, Papa," Edith said a few months before Betsy's baby was to be born, "I'm eighteen now. I can help. I plan on getting a good job and give you the money. The family will need it. Now that your knees are bad, Papa, the fields won't be as productive. And Mama, Betsy's baby's going to need food and diapers and ..."

"Where can you get a good job around here?" Mama interrupted, already anticipating how much a little extra money would help.

"I need to go to Manila. That's where the money is. I can get a good job in Manila," she said, relating how she'd heard three of her former classmates had already moved there and were sending "big money" back to their families.

"Manila! Edith, that's so far away! It's a big city, lots of bad things happen in big cities. Manila! Oh, Edith, no, I can't agree to that. You have to stay here."

"Mama, I can't stay here and watch our family suffer. I have to help. This is one way that I can. Besides, I'm an adult now. I have to help. I love my family and whatever it takes, I will do."

Liezel was resolutely resistant as Edith continued to badger her parents about moving to Manila.

Betsy's baby arrived prematurely a month later. Everyone knew the medical bills would eat them alive. Mama finally relented. "You're right, Edith," she said. "You should go to Manila where there is good pay. I can help. I have a childhood friend, Maria, who lives there now. I'll write to her and ask her to help you get find a job and get settled."

Chapter 4

The Guy on the Bus

The bravado she felt in the months and weeks leading up to her going to Manila dissipated the moment the bus came into view at the Tacloban stop. She had never been on a bus before. As it neared and grew in its perspective size, she wondered if her legs were going to lift her up its three steps or bolt her to the spot she was on.

The bus door opened and a gust of bus air filled her nostrils. She was about to turn and run when the image of her father walking her to school, her small hand in his big, well-worn and callused one reminded her she could do this. She smiled at the driver hoping to get a welcome, but he couldn't care less about who was getting on or off as he checked her ticket. Without looking up he gave a slight nod toward the rows of the seats behind him. As her eyes adjusted to the gloomy interior her next decision loomed. Every seat already had a rider. Her eyes darted from row to row as she wondered which one of the passengers who was now giving her the once-over would entice her to choose their seat.

An old man looked up over his newspaper; she thought he might be trouble. An abuella glanced from her knitting; boring. How about the cute guy with the Walkman headphones? No, she had seen smiles like his on the boys in the market who ogled her. The lady with the baby on her lap? *Oh no, not there,* she warned herself. Then she spotted the backpack. Ever since those American girls, hiking through Palo, stopped at her mother's stand, backpacks had a lure she found hard to resist.

"Excuse me," she said, "is this seat taken?" Obviously, it wasn't, but the occupant didn't seem to mind such an evident observation and slid to the window seat.

What a stupid thing to say, she admonished herself as she swung her own backpack to the floor at her feet. He closed the little leather notebook he was apparently writing in and said cheerfully, "Happy for the company." He was older, maybe 30. He balanced the leather notebook on his knee and extended a hand, "Michael Peters."

Her parents had warned her at least a hundred times in the last few weeks to beware of strangers, and here she was, ten minutes into her Great Journey, chatting with one. *I can do this,* she told herself.

"Edith, Edith Santos," she said bravely.

It was his notebook that created her first impression of him for she, too, kept notebooks, only hers were not quite as elegant. She wondered what he wrote in his. Hers were filled with dreams and plans even though the path to any of those was never clear. She pondered the leather cover on his and felt she already knew this Michael Peters, that they had something in common. She made a mental note to get herself a leather bound notebook just like his when she got to Manila. *Great Journeys, the likes of which she was now on, needed leather,* she mused.

As the bus rumbled along, she learned that Michael was a nurse with the Peace Corps and was on his way back to the States after serving two years in the western Visayas. His volunteerism had been rewarding, and now, still in the glow of that work, he was brimming with happiness and delighted to have a willing listener with whom to share his stories. His job in the Peace Corps, he said, was to travel among the provinces monitoring and remedying health issues not only of the people of the Visayas who were mainly without any health care opportunities but to attend to the well-being of his fellow Peace Corps volunteers who were serving as educators, engineers and agriculturists throughout the region.

His enthusiasm set a fire in the soul of the eighteen-year-old sitting next to him. If she, too, could be a nurse she would know what to do if her father got cut on some scrap metal while he was repairing their roof, or she'd know how to help her youngest brother, now two, whose nose never stopped running. She could know things that mattered. Yes, she could be a very good nurse. All the impossible steps that must happen between now and then were of little concern.

Five hours later when the bus pulled into the ferry terminal in Allen for the next leg of their 500-mile journey to Manila, Michael and Edith were still in animated conversation. She was listening intently to every word Michael Peters was sharing and whenever he'd take a breath she'd ask a small question. She stored his answers in memory so she could later add them to her notebook. She didn't want to forget any details.

The two-hour ferry ride across the San Bernardino Strait was the fastest in history to the girl with the questions. By the time the vessel was tied to the wharf and passengers had scurried off toward the awaiting bus to Manila, she was still quizzing Michael, picking his brain of all that it knew about nursing, and he was loving the audience.

"Hurry," said Michael when he noticed they were last off the ferry. He pulled her by hand as they rushed toward the bus, "or we won't get a seat together on the bus."

There was one row still unoccupied at the back of the bus, no one's favorite row to be sure, but they took it deciding they had come this far together, together they'd see their journey to its end. Soon the drone of the motor from the back of the bus made their eyelids grow heavy. They both fussed in their seats trying to get comfortable. Edith drifted off first, her head bobbled a few times then settled on Michael's shoulder. Michael let it be and soon his head fell into her hair. He dreamt of his homecoming while she envisioned an angel pinning a small white cap onto her silky black hair on the stage of a large auditorium.

"End of the line," the driver grumped, waking the last two passengers in the back of the bus. "Manila," he added.

Both happy and sad their journey had ended, they tried to say something meaningful as a good-bye that concluded their nineteen hour friendship.

"Will you be okay here?" he asked, suddenly aware of the iffy neighborhood surrounding them.

"Yes," she assured him, showing him an address she pulled out of her backpack. "My mother wrote to a childhood friend who lives here in Manila and this friend has invited me to stay a few days until I find work. I'll be fine."

He had a plane to catch; she, a taxi to find.

"What a nice coincidence it was to meet you, Michael Peters, on the bus from Tacloban."

"There are no coincidences, Edith Santos, they're signs." He gave her a hug and was gone.

As Michael vanished into the crowd of passersby, the cacophony of the city which she hadn't noticed when she was standing next to him, suddenly became clamorous and daunting. The only thing standing between her and a panic attack was the slip of paper in her hand. *I can do this*, she told herself, recalling the pit bulls of kindergarten days that once snarled at her from their stoops. She hailed a taxi.

Her mother's friend wasn't as eager to meet Edith as Liezel had predicted. Mrs. Chin, as Maria Santiago was now called, and Liezel had been inseparable childhood friends. Maria had the gift of convincing conversation. One day when they were teenagers in the '70s, Maria, whose father owned a profitable rice paddy in Tacloban, invited Liezel to vacation with her on Kalanggaman Island where rich tourists came from all over Asia to sunbathe on its white sand beaches. "Maria! What are you doing?" Liezel cried out as Maria took off her t-shirt. "You know we don't wear bikinis! Ever!"

"We're not in Palo anymore, girl, we're tourists now. Look around. Only the local girls are wearing cover-ups," she sang as she stuffed her shirt into her beach bag. Maria was on the hunt.

Liezel was the prettier of the two girls and within minutes she had attracted the handsome young Wa Chin, whose father owned a factory in Manila, to their beach blanket. Chin had his eyes focused on Liezel, but Maria, the cleverer of the two, held him spellbound with her juicy compliments and somewhat bare body. Two years later Maria was Mrs. Chin of Manila and Liezel hadn't heard from her since, except for their annual Christmas cards.

Chapter 5

Silkworms and Sweatshops

The maid opened the door and led Edith to the dining room. Mrs. Chin didn't look up when the maid announced Edith's arrival. She was caressing a bolt of magenta mulberry silk that had just arrived from Suzhou and was lost in the luxurious softness of the yards she had unrolled from the bolt.

As Maria lovingly smoothed the fabric across the dining table she was already imagining the design this silk would be fashioned into, the gown she would wear to the Caritas Ball and Art Auction this fall. At long last the aspiring Chins were now receiving invitations to Manila's most prestigious social events. In fact the Chins, along with two other couples, were to be recognized at the Caritas Ball as this year's "Angels of Manila." And the day after the Ball they'd be featured in the society section of Sunday's paper. This did not just happen to happen. Maria had worked hard to climb the ladder of the elites.

She had volunteered in the charities run by women who matter. She had fed the urchins of the streets, solicited donations for the museum and held fundraisers for widows and orphans in her beautiful home. Ostensibly generous, Mrs. Chin, the former Maria Santiago of the poor Visayas region, was finally recognized by the elite. The event to which she would wear a magnificent magenta mulberry silk gown proved her triumph of effort. She would be at the Caritas Ball to see and be seen, just like Imelda.

Maria had come to her wealth and position through her husband's fortune in inheriting the garment factory his father had owned in the heart of Manila. Twice a year, late summer and early spring, Wa traveled to China to select and buy the hundreds of bolts of fabrics he would be needing for the upcoming season. He kept current with the trends and had an eye for what the U.S. market would be demanding come spring. He bought commonplace fabrics, cottons and polys, nothing too pricey, nothing too cheap. Maria never accompanied her husband on these buying treks because she found the manufacturing facilities in China to be dirty and disgusting, and the haggling he'd be engaged in to be crude and lowbrow.

Last winter, though, she had changed her mind about going. She had read an article in *Global Fashion* that discussed the most prestigious silk in the world. For 4,000 years the Chinese had been making it. The Bombyx mori moth silkworm only ate leaves of the mulberry tree and it took 2,500 silkworm cocoons to produce a mere 17 ounces of thread. "I want that," she determined. "I will wear a gown of Bombyx mori moth silk to the Caritas Ball." She told Wa she would go to China with him this year and to put the silk farms of Suzhou on his itinerary.

Now the bolt had arrived. She wondered how many ounces of silk were in it then tried to multiply how many silkworms had given their lives to make her the most beautifully dressed woman at the Caritas Ball. "A lot," she concluded without giving it another thought.

Edith sensed she was interrupting a mystical moment as she stood in the door frame. Although Mrs. Chin was not facing her, Edith noticed the woman's shoulder blades elevate then suddenly drop, accompanied by a disgruntled exhale of air, as if she was greatly irritated by the intrusion. She finally detached herself from her exquisite fabric and turned toward the intruder, looking annoyed.

A moment of first impressions filled the room. On seeing

Edith, the exact replica of her childhood friend, Mrs. Chin had a fleeting moment of sadness. She was remembering her friendship with Liezel like it was a lost treasure, not one stolen from her but one she chose to discard. A feeling of loneliness momentarily overcame her but she managed to squelch it. She would deal with Edith, this intrusion from her past life in the boonies of the Visayas, as soon as possible. Tomorrow perhaps.

Edith, too, was silently evaluating. She wondered how Mrs. Chin could have been her mother's best childhood friend. They seemed so different from one another. It certainly wasn't because they had similar auras. Her mother's aura was warm and welcoming. Standing here, now, in this doorway she felt neither a warmth nor a welcome. Edith had expected Maria would be as youthful looking as her mama, Liezel, who worked hard in the fields and was still fit and trim. Edith guessed that Maria's pudgy face was the result of opulent living and no hard work. A faint smile crossed Edith's lips as she considered describing her first impression of the former Maria Santiago in her notebook. She would call it: Mrs. Chin's Chins.

Maria Chin quickly composed herself in front of Edith, as she had taught herself to do in the early days of her marriage to Wa when the Chin family was considered a scourge on Manila because of the conditions in old Mr. Chin's Garment Factory. Wa had gone to the university where he learned how to make favorable impressions out of less than favorable realities. Although Maria had gone to the college of hard knocks, she studied the talk and the walk of the well-to-do ladies of Manila, for her goal was to become one. She had become an exceptional mimic.

"How is your dear mother?" she now was saying. "I must get back to Palo the next time I'm in the Visayas. We have a vacation house in Cebu and I keep meaning to skip over to Leyte to see her and your dad. But it's so beautiful in Cebu, I just can't seem to break away to go slumming."

"Mama's fine," Edith replied, wishing she had gone to a hotel instead. "She looks forward every year to your Christmas card."

"And I to hers," Maria added. "Liezel's cards are always so newsy. I'm so glad she felt comfortable enough to ask me to look after you briefly while you find a job here in Manila. We're like sisters, you know. Now that you're here, I feel like I'm part of the family again, like an auntie," she smiled and for the moment she wished it was true.

That moment passed as quickly as it came and both Edith and Maria were considering what direction their conversation should take when the front door opened and Wa called out, "I'm home." As he dumped his briefcase on the hall chair he looked into the dining room and the first thing he saw was the beautiful bolt of silk. "Wow!" he exclaimed as he entered the room and gently caressed the material between his thumb and finger, tactically embracing it as if beauty could be touched. Then he turned. "Wow," he said again as his eyes met Edith's. "Liezel!"

"It's her daughter," was all Maria could manage to cough out.

She had seen that look on Wa's face before, thirty years ago on the beach at Kalanggaman Island. Liezel had been the reason the young Wa had flirted with the girls from Palo. Liezel was the one with the silky hair, the golden skin and the saucy breasts of an emerging woman pushing against her cover-up. Liezel was the pretty one, and to be frank, the reason Maria chose her for a friend. Liezel was her bait.

Before Wa could indulge in his memories of that day on Kalanggaman beach, Maria rushed in with the purpose of today's visitor. "Edith is job hunting here in Manila," she explained.

Wa's face brightened. "I certainly can use more help at the factory. In fact, I've just put out job opening notices. You could start tomorrow. Are you willing to learn to sew, Edith?"

Fire flashed across Maria's face as her eyes darted between her husband and Liezel's beautiful eighteen-year-old daughter. She knew she should squelch this idea immediately. "Edith certainly wouldn't want factory work, Wa. Why, she doesn't know a thing about sewing. She wouldn't like repetitive work. She'll hate being in a hot, dirty building all day. No, dear, my best friend's daughter should have a better opportunity than the one you can offer. I will find her a more genteel job, one where she'll be introduced to the elites of Manila, one where she'll learn the manners of people with influence." Even as these words were spilling out of her mouth Maria had devised her solution.

"Edith will make an excellent au pair," she went on. "She's experienced in caring for children, and look, my dear Wa, doesn't she have such a pleasant demeanor?

"Why just the other day at a luncheon, Carmella Ramos was lamenting that despite the many interviews she has had with young women, she's not found a suitable au pair for her two lovely children. She says the girls she has interviewed are very demanding, asking about days off, wanting ridiculous pay, one even asked for use of a car. I think Carmella will love Edith. Not only that, dear, but the Ramoses will be forever grateful to us for having recommended her. I'll call them first thing in the morning," she crowed as if Edith was not even in the room.

"No, Mrs. Chin," the usually demure Edith retorted. "I have not come all the way to Manila to babysit. That's what I've done all my life and although I love my sisters and brothers, and certainly had a great part in their upbringing, I'm done with that job. I want something new. Mr. Chin, I'd love to learn to sew."

"Then it's settled," said Wa. "Come to work with me in the morning. I'll get you set up and introduce you to your supervisor."

Maria was not pleased. If she had any outstanding gifts, it was the gift of perception. She looked again at her husband, again at Edith. She perceived trouble.

Chapter 6

Sweat in the Sweatshop

One hundred and forty pairs of eyes immediately noticed when Mr. Chin entered the garment factory the next morning, accompanied by a tall stunning young woman in a yellow sundress. "Ooh la la, does Mr. Chin have a new girlfriend?" one worker whispered to the girl at the next sewing machine.

"Ladies!" Mr. Chin's voice boomed throughout the cavernous work space. "Get back to work immediately!" All eyes quickly darted back down to their sewing machines which had gone momentarily silent.

Edith was stunned by what she was seeing: row after row of women sitting at sewing machines crammed closely together. The din from the sewing machines was amplified by their sheer number and the factory floor was already stiflingly warm at eight in the morning.

"Follow me," Mr. Chin said to Edith as they climbed the stairs to his air-conditioned office. "You're way overdressed to work on the floor. I think you belong in an office. This one, in fact. I really need a new secretary," Mr. Chin said, wondering how soon he could tell old, dowdy Mrs. Pauli he was letting her go. It wasn't going to be easy. She'd been his very efficient and loyal secretary for more than fifteen years.

Edith was taken aback. "No offense, Mr. Chin, but I have my heart set on learning to sew. It will be a very useful skill for me to learn. Tomorrow I will wear jeans, like the others. I just didn't know what to expect." Mr. Chin hadn't known what to expect either when he noticed how pretty Edith looked as they rode to the factory that morning. "I'm afraid that Maria would find it unacceptable to assign her best friend's daughter to the sewing floor," he replied, adding to himself, *and so would I.*

"No, Mr. Chin. I want to learn to sew. It's why I came all the way here," she said, standing very tall and staring directly into his eyes. He immediately recognized that 'I intend to get what I want' look on Edith's face. It was the same look his wife wore on countless occasions over too many years.

"Well, okay," he relented. "I'll put you on the floor for a few days. But the minute you find it tedious or boring, my offer for you to be my secretary remains open. I think you'd make an excellent secretary," he said, adding once again to himself, *especially how you look in that dress.*

Mr. Chin led Edith back down the stairs to the whirring, stifling factory floor. He walked directly to an unoccupied sewing table, its previous occupant fired just yesterday for taking too many bathroom breaks. He didn't know, or perhaps didn't care, that the poor girl had a medical condition.

"Rosalie," he said to the woman busily stitching endless red buttonholes onto polyester jackets at the adjoining table, "This is Edith. Today you will teach her how to sew." Rosalie was mad. This would really play havoc with her daily buttonhole quota. But disagreement was not an acceptable option in Mr. Chin's garment factory. "Of course, Mr. Chin, sir," Rosalie said most agreeably.

Edith was a quick study and had learned how to thread the machine and adjust the settings by the time her section was given its ten-minute morning break. Usually the break room was a cacophony of bored chatter and gossip, but this day it suddenly became eerily quiet when Edith walked in. At first, all their attention was focused on Edith, but quickly their attention shifted to Rosalie who was now being peppered with questions and gossip about "the new girl."

Meanwhile, upstairs, Mr. Chin had accomplished very little so far. He had spent the morning at his office window staring down at the factory floor. More specifically, he was staring at what looked like a bright yellow sunflower planted amidst drab, dusty garden weeds. His interest in Edith was intense and his thoughts were racing, including the thought that Maria would probably kill him if she knew.

Just then his intercom buzzed. "Mr. Chin, sir, your wife's on the phone," Mrs. Pauli said in her slightly cracked voice.

"Wa," Maria began, "how's it going today? And how's Edith working out? Just thought I'd remind you she needs to find a suitable place to live. She just can't stay with us forever, you know. Maybe we can put her up in a hotel for a few nights until she finds her own place. What do you think? She'd probably jump at the chance for two nights in a hotel."

Their conversation brought Wa back to the reality of his life. *I really need to get that order placed today,* Wa thought as he moved from the window to his desk where papers were piling up.

The next day, there was no bright yellow sundress beckoning to distract him and some work got done.

During the afternoon break, there was a tentative knock on his office door. "Edith! What a nice surprise. Are you liking your job? Is there something I can help you with?" he asked, noting that she looked mighty fine even in drab, well-worn jeans.

"The job is going just fine, but I hear from other workers that they have to meet certain quotas. I want to know what my quota is, Mr. Chin."

"Oh, please call me Wa," Mr. Chin said.

"Oh! Okay, Wa," Edith said hesitantly because it felt weird.

"It just so happens you don't have to fill any quotas. I just want you to learn to sew and be happy doing it. It's a perk I give to all my special friends and family members," he lied. "But since you're here, I've been wanting to tell you that Mrs. Chin and I want to help you get settled into your own place. We've decided that you can stay with us until Saturday and then we'll move you into a hotel for two weeks until you find a place," he said, lying again.

"That's very generous, Mr. Chi ... Wa. Thank you. In fact I've already met two girls whose other roommate is moving away soon. But I do appreciate your generous offer. You are so sweet," Edith replied with a deeply dimpled smile that lit Mr. Chin up.

"If there's anything you need, anything at all, I want you to know you can come to me. I'm almost like family, you know," Wa said, hurrying back behind his desk. It wouldn't do to let Edith notice just how excited he was to see her.

With only a few minutes remaining on her break, Edith hurried down to the break room smiling as she recalled Mr. Chin's kind offer. "Ooh," Lucy said in a singsong voice as she sidled up to her new friend. "You sure look happy. Did something exciting just happen in Chin's office?"

"Not really," Edith said, "but he did offer to help me get settled into my own place. That was so sweet of him."

"Wanna know why?" Lucy quizzed. "That's because he is so sweet on you. We've all noticed the *special* attention Chin is giving you. And don't think we don't notice him all day long with his tongue hanging out staring directly at you from his office window."

Edith was more than surprised at this assessment. "You've got it all wrong," she said. "Wa's—I mean, Mr. Chin's—wife and my mother were best childhood friends. They generously have taken me under their wing while I get settled. Even gave me this job."

"Oh, it's Wa now, is it?" Lucy said with a gleeful laugh. "We all see it with our own eyes. Chin has the hots for you. Just beware that he's married to a conniving bitch. I've seen her in action a few times. She always gets what she wants, no matter who she has to trample on. But not to change this awful subject, Analyn and I are hoping you'll still move in with us. Lyka is leaving for Lebanon tomorrow so there's a bed for you tomorrow night."

"Great! I'll move in tomorrow then," Edith said, knowing she'd be missing her first chance to spend some nights in a hotel.

By the end of her first month working in the factory, Edith's skills were rivaling workers who'd been in the factory for years. At the same time, Mr. Chin's horniness was rivaling that of men thirty years his junior. "Mrs. Pauli," he'd say at least once a week, "go down and tell Edith to come up to the office." At least once a week, all the girls would look up knowingly, as Edith's departure for the office always left them in giggles and gossip.

Maybe Lucy is right, Edith thought to herself, the third time she got called upstairs. This is beginning to creep me out. The next time it happens, I'll inform Mrs. Pauli that I'm just too busy. But despite her feisty thoughts, Edith did no such thing. Once or twice a week, Edith went upstairs when requested and smiled at Mr. Chin's flimsy reasons for her presence, and it wasn't long before she finally noticed that Mr. Chin really was excited to see her.

Chapter 7

A Devious Plot

Maria Chin's vibes were on alert. Ever since Edith showed up in Manila, old feelings came back to put her on guard. She thought about the day on the beach thirty years ago when Wa desperately wanted to attract the attention of Liezel and she, Maria, had to divert and distract. She surprised herself, even then, that she had the power to win what she wanted.

Then she thought of the first Mrs. Chin, her mother-in-law. Maria knew it would be a battle weaning Wa from his mother and she was right. The first Mrs. Chin was not about to surrender her son to what she considered a Visayas pariah and she turned out to be a strong competitor. The battle was fierce. Maria had to kiss up to this woman in ways that tested all her creative malevolence. The more Mrs. Chin complained to Wa about Maria, the more love and kindness Maria displayed toward the woman until Wa began to think his mother was at fault. Wa never knew what hit him and *still doesn't,* she chuckled to herself thinking about it.

Now this troubling issue of Edith. Edith, per se, was not the problem. It was Wa. Maria noted how spellbound Wa became on seeing Edith in the dining room on the day she arrived in Manila. It was the same besotted look he had given Liezel that day on the beach. It was by sheer cunning that Maria had claimed Wa for herself and now her vibes told her she might have to do it again.

But how? Edith would be at the factory all day as would Wa. Maria wished she had a spy at the factory, someone she could trust to keep an eye on Wa. But anything to do with the factory was so far beneath her. Her lifestyle demanded she not know anything about sweatshops. She felt no connection to the source of her opulence, same as her friends whose husbands also ran 'factories.'

As she mechanically arranged a vase of fresh flowers on the circular table in the foyer, she thought only about how she could get the information she wanted. Then, as she was laboring over the dinner menu for the evening's guests, she had what she called 'a most brilliant idea!' Dinner on Sundays. She'd invite Edith to dinner on Sundays. She didn't mean some Sundays, she meant all Sundays.

Once a week would be enough time for Maria to ascertain and evaluate what, if anything, was going on between the two. And there would be a great upside to this idea as well. Wa would be impressed with his wife's kind empathy for her best friend's daughter; her many lady friends will be impressed to learn the lengths she's willing to go to support the daughter of a destitute friend from the impoverished Visayas; and "even if Edith doesn't want to come on Sundays," she smirked to herself, "she can't refuse. I'll simply insist and she'll infer that her employment demands it. I'll see to that." Finally, Maria decided to write a quick note to Liezel saying she was enjoying the task of looking after her daughter. Nothing would be left to chance.

Maria's plan worked well for a while as she built a mental dossier of minor offenses mostly against Wa. For instance at Sunday dinner Wa would pull out a chair for both Edith and her to make sure they were comfortably seated. That was new. The Sunday sports pages no longer came to the dinner table. That, too, was new. Lately he had taken to telling interesting stories about his days at the factory.

"Who knew he was such a conversationalist!" Maria said side-glancing at Edith as if her rolling, smiling eyes were saying "who *is* this guy?"

Wa would quiz Edith on her goals and dreams and she told them she wanted to become a nurse. "But I have a long road ahead before I can pursue nursing school," she added.

"Maybe I can help," Wa offered as part of one evening's small talk. Maria red-flagged that remark immediately. "And what do you mean by that, dear?" she asked as casually as he had said it.

"Oh, I don't know. Edith has become very proficient at the kind of sewing jobs I have her on: collars, buttons, zippers, those kinds of things. She uses the machine like she's been sewing all her life." A look of concentration came across his brow. "A new position might be suitable," he weighed out loud, "perhaps the pattern department."

"The pattern department!" an astonished Maria said a little too incredulously. "Why? It takes your employees years to obtain that proficiency. Certainly Edith hasn't reached that level. I'm sure you wouldn't be comfortable in that demanding department," she said, turning to Edith with a quizzical look of horror.

"I think I could handle it, Mrs. Chin. I love sewing. Doing things upside down and inside out seems to come naturally. At first I was terrified of those machines. Now they are part of me," she laughed, "or maybe I've become a machine myself,"

Maria now knew her plan of Sunday dinners was about to run its course. She had gotten what she needed from them: yes, Wa was showing too much interest in his young employee. She was grateful Edith didn't seem to recognize what the walls of the dining room seemed to be screaming: I Want Her!...*No, You Can't Have Her!*...But I Want Her!...*And I Say No!*

Maria needed a new plan.

The doorbell rang and her next idea was standing on the other side of the door. She opened it to her good friend Lin Wang. But before Maria could give Lin a welcoming embrace, she looked out toward the street as Lin's son, Jun, sped away on his scooter. Lin turned and looked too, shaking her head. "I appreciate Jun giving me a ride, but I really don't like going that fast," Lin said as she entered the hall, dropping her purse on the table with the vaseful of flowers. "I have to hang on for dear life. If I say anything or scream, he'll go even faster, and laugh, thinking he's delighting me."

She was complaining about her favorite son when she spied the rosettes on the table that Maria had already made. She had come so Maria could teach her how to make them for her daughter's upcoming wedding.

"I used to make these as a child in Leyte," Maria said, her hands already forming a new rosette. "We made them for festivals. We had wonderful festivals back home in our nearby town of Tacloban. The adults tattooed their bodies with paint depicting the bravery of our heroes and we danced in the streets. The children of Tacloban made these rosettes and we applied them to every surface we could find, including our bodies. I could make them in my sleep. See? I haven't forgotten."

Lin's daughter, Ting, was about to be married. The reception would be held in the grand ballroom of the Mundo d'Oro Resort and Hotel. The hundreds of rosettes they are making will decorate the grand ballroom of the hotel completely covering the arched walkway through which all guests would enter the room. Then as guests emerge from the arch, they'd be in an explosion of flowers both real and hand-made that would magically transport them into a fairyland garden.

As the two women's fingers twisted the crepe paper, these best friends chattered away. They talked of all sorts of things, even troubling things like Edith's arrival, Wa's interest in helping Edith, Jun's quarrel with his girlfriend.

"Doesn't Jun graduate this year?" Maria asked as part of their ongoing conversation.

"Yes, there's so much going on this year," Lin said. "Did you know he just broke up with Binday, or I should say Binday broke up with him? That surprised me. I thought for sure they'd be getting married."

"Binday broke it off with Jun? I don't believe it!" Maria replied. "He's such a catch. She's making a terrible mistake."

"She came crying to me the other day," Lin went on. "She calls me Mama, you know. She said 'Mama, Jun says he loves me and someday wants to marry me but when he goes out with his friends from college he posts pictures of himself with other girls and when I ask him what he's doing with other girls he says they're just friends. But in the pictures, Mama, they look like they're way more than 'friends.'"

"I told her to give him more time. But she says he likes fun too much and she's ready to be more serious. She was sobbing into my shoulder. I was holding her and petting her hair. We hugged but what can I do? Nothing."

The bell at the door began ringing and ringing and ringing, annoying both women. Maria was about to give whoever was at the door a piece of her mind when Jun swept in, "Hi Tia Maria," he sang as he gave her a hug. Maria wasn't really his aunt but she loved that he felt such affection for her.

"Your mom was just saying you broke up with Binday."

"Yeah, she's kind of a stick-in-the-mud," he said recklessly. "She never wants to go out to the bars and have fun. Besides, I'm not a serious kind of guy, right Mama?" he said, picking his tiny mother off her feet and twirling her around. "Ready to go home?"

"I'm not going to get on that thing with you unless you promise to go the speed limit."

"I'll go the speed limit," he was saying as they left the house.

Maria watched as they sped off. She could hear Lin screaming, "Slow down!"

While Maria was finishing the last of the rosettes, her mind was concocting a plan that included Edith and Jun. "Jun likes pretty girls," she reminded herself, "and Edith needs to meet someone her age. Hmmm."

The following Sunday before Edith arrived for dinner, Maria called Jun and asked him to drop by at 6 p.m. to pick up the rest of the rosettes. Edith and Maria had just put the last of the dishes away and Edith was gathering her things when the doorbell started ringing and ringing and ringing. Startled, she looked at Maria. "Oh, that's just Jun," Maria said as he burst into the room, "my friend's son."

"Edith, meet Jun, my friend Lin's son," she said.

Jun just stood there.

"Cat got your tongue, Jun?" Maria teased for she had never before seen Jun at a loss for words.

"No, Tia Maria, I didn't expect you'd have a guest. I didn't, I thought, I ..." his words stumbled out chaotically, while his eyes remained totally focused on Edith.

Edith reached out to shake hands. "Edith. Edith Santos," she said but when her hand touched his, neither was in a hurry to let go. The hesitation was not lost on Maria.

"Hurry on, Edith," Maria urged, handing Edith her jacket, "it's almost dark, I don't want you walking home late." Jun, unaware that he had just been played like a violin by his aunt, quickly offered, "Would you like a ride, Edith?"

"Sure," she said, but she was unsure if it was the ride home that she wanted or to sit behind Jun on scooter and wrap her arms around him.

Maria watched Edith climb on behind Jun, hugging him tentatively. "Drive carefully," she cautioned, waving as Jun drove away.

"Problem solved," she chortled as she closed the door behind her.

Chapter 8

The Dress

As they turned the corner, Jun gunned the scooter, and was instantly delighted when Edith clung tightly to his back. *Oh, man, those are some awesome boobs,* he thought to himself as he pushed the throttle a bit more. Edith was terrified. "Stop!" she shouted into the wind. "I want to get off. Stop. I'll walk home. Stop! Now!" she screamed into his ear. Jun never took orders from a woman before, but this time was different. As much as he rued the thought of losing the pressure of her body against his, Jun slowed down and stopped. His reasoning was skewed in his favor. *I'll do what she says or I'll never get my hands on those breasts,* he thought as he pulled to the curb.

"You scared me to death," Edith said. "You drive too fast for me. I'll walk from here. I don't intend to die from fright." Jun became uncharacteristically apologetic. "I don't want that to happen either," he said. "Get back on. I promise to slow it down. I'll make it up to you by taking a nice slow scenic drive through some of our prettiest neighborhoods."

By the time they arrived at Lucy's place, Edith's terror had transformed into delight. "Thank you, Jun. That turned into the best first scooter ride I've ever had," she said laughing. The sound of her laughter, coupled with her astonishing boobs, prompted Jun to say, "I'd love to see you again. Can I pick you up Thursday at 7 p.m.?"

"He asked you out on a date? How exciting! Especially if he's as gorgeous as you say he is," Analyn said after listening to every detail of Edith's evening.

"Ooh, better be careful," Lucy cautioned. "Mr. Chin's gonna rage with jealousy. This will break his heart, to say nothing of his stiffy!" she said, laughing uproariously.

On that Thursday, Jun arrived promptly at 7 p.m. and drove cautiously to a restaurant in the ritzy part of Manila. A few days later, they spent an evening at a popular disco, with Edith wearing party clothes borrowed from Analyn. She was growing more and more impressed with Jun and his flashy lifestyle. "I think I'm in love," she exclaimed to her roommates when she got home from her second date. She had just found out that kissing was quite exciting, nothing like the wimpy smooch she got from Mateo some time ago.

"My sister Ting is getting married in two weeks. I'd love to invite you as my guest. Actually, as my girlfriend. Please say yes," Jun surprised her by saying on their third date.

"You've got to be kidding us!" Analyn exclaimed when Edith told them her news. "The Mundo d'Oro? Oh my god, that's the fanciest place in all of Manila. I'm so jealous. I couldn't even get hired as a bathroom cleaning lady there. They said I looked too poor. Yikes! You are so lucky! You need to look ritzy. Looking poor is not an option at Mundo d'Oro." Lucy nodded in total agreement.

"Gosh, I should have told Jun no. I have nothing to wear! This is about as ritzy as I ever look," she said, pointing to another dress she had borrowed from Analyn."

"Wait! I've got it!" Lucy said excitedly, dashing off to their bedroom. "I think I have the perfect dress for you!" Moments later she emerged holding a long, sleeveless apricot gown trimmed with sequins and pearls. "Oh, wow! That's gorgeous!" Edith exclaimed.

Analyn was also impressed. "Have you been holding out on us, Lucy? Did you have another life I've never heard about?" Analyn teased. "Wherever did you get such a dress?"

"I used to work as an au pair for a lady on the other side of town. She gave this to me one day saying I could have it because she couldn't be caught dead wearing the same dress twice. I kept it because it was so exquisite. Go ahead, Edith. Try it on!" Lucy urged.

Moments later Edith emerged from their bedroom, eliciting gasps from her stunned roommates. "Thanks, guys, but I don't think this is me," she said. "First of all, the dress has no back, but most of all, the dress has very little in front. I'm literally hanging out."

"Are you crazy? It fits you perfectly. Shows off curves I did not know you had. You look gorgeous!" Lucy said excitedly. Analyn, much more practical, chimed in with, "If you want to run in high society, you have to dress the part. You say you love Jun and he probably feels the same, but this dress will clinch it. This dress could be your ticket to a well-to-do life. Like I always say, if you got the boobs, flaunt them."

"Wouldn't it be a sin to wear this backless, low-cut dress in church?" Edith asked, squirming under the pressure of her roommates. "Don't worry," Analyn said, "I have a shawl you can wear in church that will make you moderately modest."

Two weeks later as the bride walked down the aisle, Maria poked Wa in the ribs. "Well, well, well, look who's here," she whispered to Wa with concealed glee. She had just spotted Edith and Jun sitting a few rows behind them. *Oh my!* Maria said to herself. *That was one of my best plots ever!*

"She has a boyfriend?" Wa whispered incredulously as he spied the couple, completely overlooking the bride's entrance.

"Sure looks like it. Isn't that wonderful for Edith? She hooked herself up with one of the wealthiest families in town," Maria stated with false admiration. "That's Lin's oldest son, Jun. I'm so happy for Edith. But it's kind of sad that she probably won't need us much anymore," she said cuttingly, piercing a hole in Wa's lustful old heart.

Chapter 9

One Cosmo Too Many

"Wow!" was all Jun could say repeatedly when Edith deposited her shawl in the cloak room at the reception. "You are by far the hottest woman I've ever seen," he blathered, his eyes stuck on her cleavage. "You make other women look boring. I'm so proud you are mine." Edith was beaming.

Maria's intention to make the wedding banquet room at Mundo d'Oro look like a flowery fairyland was fully realized, especially for Edith who had never experienced such opulence. As she and Jun walked through the rosette-enshrouded archway, it seemed every masculine eye was upon her. That was certainly true of Wa who was seated with Maria near the head table. He was still in shock to discover Edith's love interest was not him. Still, he couldn't take his eyes off her or notice how alluring and sexy she looked.

"Would you like a Cosmo?" Jun asked her as soon as they found their table. "What? You've never had one? They say there's nothing hotter than a girl with a Cosmo. You're quite hot already, but would you like to try one?" he asked hopefully.

As Jun was getting the drinks Edith noticed that the mother of the bride, Lin, had stopped at the Chin table, pulling up a chair to talk. The two women seemed to be in an animated conversation and wore serious expressions, which transformed into strained smiles when they caught Edith looking their way. Edith gave them a little wave which was acknowledged by two nodding heads.

She couldn't know from her distance that Maria was boasting about the success of her little ploy to matchmake Edith and Jun, a ploy that Lin hadn't known Maria had orchestrated.

"You did what?" Lin was saying through her teeth.

Maria was stunned at Lin's reaction. "What did I do that was so horrible?"

"You have a lot of nerve introducing Jun to your niece."

"She's not my niece," Maria was saying, "Edith is just the daughter of my childhood best friend from Palo. And yes, I introduced them. So?"

"I can't have my son falling in love with someone from the provinces. How would that look!"

"Lin, I'm from the provinces and you and I are best friends."

"That's different," Lin fumed, "you've proven yourself. You've done what it takes: tirelessly volunteering, chairing committees, being so generous with Wa's money ...."

"What!" Maria exclaimed, realizing for the first time that their friendship had been built on Wa's family fortune. "What are you saying, Lin? Why, you little ..."

"Ladies," Wa interjected in an attempt to cool the escalating conversation.

"Shut up, Wa, this is between Lin and me."

"You know how much I love Binday," Lin spewed as if Wa wasn't even there. "I want Binday in my life, not Edith. I'm waiting for Binday to come to her senses. I know Jun loves her and will marry her someday. To me, Binday is already family," she snarled. "Imagine how distasteful it would look if Jun married this poor waif from the Visayas."

Edith noticed both women stiffen. She glanced at Wa and

saw that he didn't like what he was hearing. He was learning about his wife's matchmaking contrivance for the first time and realizing Maria had hoodwinked him again. He had been under a delusion that he had a chance, albeit slim, with the beautiful girl from the Visayas.

When Jun returned with her Cosmo, Edith positioned herself where she could still look over his shoulder to see what might happen next at the Chin's table. She saw Lin abruptly get up and turn to other guests while Maria and Wa, now alone, seemed to be snarling at each other having words.

Jun distracted Edith momentarily and the next time she managed a glimpse toward the table she caught sight of Maria stomping out of the ballroom, purse and shawl in hand, with defeated Wa trailing behind.

Before she could finish her first Cosmo, Jun summoned the waiter for a second one. By her third Cosmo, Edith was beginning to feel and act like the life of the party. Just then the music started and Edith quickly stopped wondering about the Chins.

"Let's dance," Jun urged. Within minutes they were spinning and gyrating to loud rock music. "Oh, you're such a great dancer," she hollered out to Jun during the first dance. "I'm having so much fun," she said, putting her mouth close to his ear during their second dance. "I think I'm getting a little dizzy," she said during their third dance in a voice that was getting slightly slurry. "Can we sit this one out?"

Finally! This was the moment Jun had been waiting for. "I've got a better idea," he said, putting his hands on her cheeks as if rearing up for a kiss. "It's really loud in here and I think you could use a break and a bit of quiet. Come with me, beautiful," he said as he led her out of the ballroom and started punching buttons on the lobby elevator. Edith shot him a questioning look. "My sister won't be needing the bridal suite for a while yet. She won't mind that we've gone up to take a little breather.

"Oh, honey," he said to Edith as he closed the door to the suite, "did I tell you how absolutely gorgeous you look tonight? That dress! Your hair! Your face! I'm such a lucky man, what did I do to deserve someone like you?" he wondered, before giving Edith his knock-your-socks-off kiss. That she returned the kiss with enthusiasm bolstered his resolve.

On the very next kiss, she felt Jun's hands caressing her bottom and completely missed the fact that he was simultaneously walking her backward toward the bed.

"Oh my god," he said, breathing heavily, "I want you so bad. I've never felt this way before. I've got to have you. You're driving me absolutely crazy." By this time, they had reached the foot of the bed and just a tiny bit of pressure caused Edith to fall back onto it.

It had been all fun and games up to this point, but Edith became instantly clear-headed when Jun fell right on top of her with his hands reaching up her dress to yank at her panties. "Jun, no!" she said quietly, "I'm not ready for anything to happen." Her panties were now at her knees and his free hand had traveled north. "Jun!" she said more forcefully, "let's get out of here and back to the wedding. I do not want this."

"Oh, don't be teasing me, baby. You know you want it. Just to be clear, I'm not taking 'no' for an answer."

Edith finally became frightened of this man she thought she knew and began to use all her might to push him off her. He just laughed. "I said NO! Get off me!" she was now screaming and crying. Neither of which had any effect on Jun.

A few horrible minutes later, Jun rolled breathlessly off Edith.

"You hurt me!" Edith said in tears. "You really hurt me bad." She could barely look at him as she got up and dressed, checking in the mirror to make sure she hadn't wrinkled Lucy's dress. "What the heck? What's that on the back?" she wailed.

"Oh my god," Jun said in shock. "You were a virgin! I didn't know. I'm sorry. I didn't mean to hurt you," he said sheepishly, recognizing the spot on the dress as a bit of blood.

"I'm going home. Take me home right now," she demanded. "On second thought, no, never mind. I don't want you near me. I'm leaving." And with that she left the bridal suite and left the newlyweds with semen and blood on the pure white bedspread.

How will I get home? she wondered as she stepped into the elevator with her back to the wall. A solution popped into her head. "Hi, it's Edith," she said into the telephone at the lobby's check-in desk. "Remember you once said if there was anything I needed, I just had to ask? Well, I really need a ride home, Wa."

Chapter 10

All My Fault

The Chins had driven home from the wedding in silence letting the liquor they had consumed at the reception forge their issues against one another. By the time they reached the threshold of their lovely home, the liquor was ready to speak. Maria started.

"Why you bag ng dumi, couldn't you leave my best friend's daughter alone?" she barked as she mounted the curved staircase toward their bedroom.

"What are you talking about? You have no reason to call me a dirtbag," he yelled from the bottom of the stairs. "What did I do now?"

"You think I'm blind? I see how you look at her."

"Who do I look at?" he said, playing innocent, not knowing if she could actually read his heart.

The bedroom door slammed shut with such vehemence the huge oil painting of themselves at the Caritas Ball that hung in the foyer crashed to the floor, twisted. Maria opened the door, "See! See what you made me do?" her tirade continued.

"That's right, blame me. Blame me for inviting a stranger into our home without even consulting with me. Blame me for putting in long hours in a factory so you can live in one of the best houses in Manila and slam its expensive door in my face. Blame me for taking you away from the slums of the Visayas. Maybe my mother was right," his voice trailed off as he turned toward the kitchen where they kept the bourbon.

"I'm not done speaking with you yet, Mr. Chin," she said, narrowing her eyes and setting her jaw. "Do I need to remind you of what I said I'd do the next time I caught you ogling?"

"I wasn't ogling," he said weakly with his back to her.

"That's right," she continued. "Ogle is not the right word, more like leering, or better yet, lusting. You better not be having sex with your newest employee," she said, finally spitting out what she was getting at. "Don't say I haven't warned you. If you love your house, your factory, your trips to China, your Rolls, you'll never be able to afford to ogle again because all of these things will be mine. I'll see to that. And now here's what you're going to do on Monday: fire Edith."

She turned to go back into their bedroom when the phone in the foyer rang. She stopped, stood in the bedroom doorway and strained to hear who was on the line.

"Yes," Wa said into the receiver. "I know I said that. This is just not a good time." He listened for a few seconds and then said, "I'll be right there. Wait outside."

"Who was that?" Maria called from the top of the stairs but he was already gone. "Anak ng aso" she spewed. It wasn't the first time she'd called him a son of a bitch.

Wa found Edith in a crumpled mess sobbing on the steps of the hotel's service doorway. He got out of the car and pulled her up. She sobbed into his chest, "Please take me back to my apartment." He had a decision to make as he held her and said, "Now, now," not knowing what the problem was.

With Edith in his arms, where he had been picturing her for months, his dilemma became real. Should he risk everything that Maria had threatened to take from him: his home, his factory, his not-always-business business trips to China, his Rolls? Should he declare his love for Edith, taking the chance she'd feel the same? Or should he back away and keep his stuff? Wa knew what he had to do. He was not a gambler.

He drove Edith to her place consoling her as best he could, offering up his neatly folded handkerchief, 'now, now-ing' her when he couldn't think of what else to say and behaving as fatherly as Edith had expected.

Still woozy, she stumbled as she got out of his Rolls then immediately puked on the sidewalk.

"Are you okay?" he called through the car's open window as she wiped her mouth on her arm and ran into the apartment. He knew he had just dodged a bullet. "What if she had puked on my carpet?" he worried. "My life would have gotten even worse, as if that's possible."

"Where did you go? Who called?" was the reception Wa got at home.

"It was nothing," he responded.

"Nothing doesn't happen late on a Saturday night. You were with her, weren't you?"

"If you must know, as of course you always must, I was at the factory. The call was about an attempted break-in. I had to check the security system. Kids tried to jimmy a door. That's all. I'm going to bed."

The last thing he heard as he burrowed his head deep into his pillow was "fire her."

When Lucy came home from her night at the disco, she found Edith doubled over on the couch, sobbing. "Are you drunk?" she asked. Edith's head went up and down.

"Was that your puke on the sidewalk?" Again her head bobbed.

"Are you crying because you're feeling sick?" Edith shook her head the other way.

"Okay, then, what happened?"

It took a while before Edith could control her voice enough to speak. She pointed to the dress, now on the floor, that Lucy had lent her for the wedding. "I tried to clean it," she bawled, "but it won't come out."

Lucy picked the dress from the floor inspecting it. It was certainly ruined.

"What happened?" she said calmly, knowing blood stains on the back of a dress usually meant one thing.

"Did you have sex?" Lucy continued quietly.

"No," Edith answered. Then slowly added, "Yes."

"Well, Edith, what is it? No or yes?"

"I didn't have sex. He did."

"What?" Lucy bellowed. "Who did? Jun?"

She shook her head yes.

"Jun forced you?" Lucy asked, shocked.

"I told him no. I begged him, no." Edith's body was now convulsing with uncontrollable tears.

"You were raped, Edith! That's date rape!" she exclaimed as she began pacing the room wondering what to do next. "I think we should go to the police."

"We can't go to the police," Edith cried. "They won't believe me. If I tell them I've been raped by Jun Wang, they'll say 'not one of the Wangs!' They'll tell me the Wangs are one of Manila's finest families, that girls my age are always vying to snag one of the Wang boys. They'll say I lured him on and when he dumped me I cried 'rape.' They'll blame me, not Jun."

"Don't be silly," Lucy said consolingly, knowing that Edith was probably right.

Suddenly Edith jumped up off the couch. "Oh my god!" she screamed. "This was all my fault. I'm to blame for getting raped, Lucy. It was how I was dressed! If I hadn't worn that sexy gown, this wouldn't have happened! I led him on! I was asking for it!"

"Don't be silly," Lucy said a second time, knowing that Edith was positively wrong. "Don't you dare blame yourself for getting raped. Too many women do that. Jun's horrifying deed has nothing to do with what you wore, or how you looked. Don't you ever say, or even think that again. Hear me?" she said, shaking the sobbing Edith by the shoulders.

"I'm sorry," Lucy relented. "You've had an awful time tonight. Look, take a bath then crawl under the covers and hopefully you'll be able to sleep off your drunk. We'll deal with the 'what ifs' tomorrow."

"Your dress is ruined," Edith whimpered.

"I can always get a new dress," Lucy smiled, "but it's not that easy to find a friend like you."

Edith went to work as usual on Monday and again on Tuesday and Wednesday. She had no idea she was supposed to be fired. But Maria had not forgotten her ultimatum to Wa. "Well," she said to Wa on his return from work Monday, "did you fire her?"

"Yes," he lied, "I hope you're happy."

"Oh yes, I'm very happy. You're a good man, Wa Chin," she fawned.

With the threat of an affair satisfactorily removed she became her old self once again. She was somewhat kinder to Wa and much kinder to her domestic staff. It seemed life went back to normal.

All was calm for the next several weeks. Wa stopped favoring Edith at work and the girls on the floor, noticing, felt sad about losing their source of gossip. Edith was now making patterns, even taking books home to learn more. The only person counting days was Lucy.

Three weeks and no bad news, she thought, watching Edith thumb through a pattern book on the couch. Maybe Edith will get lucky.

Four weeks passed without incident, but in the fifth week, she found Edith retching in the bathroom. "I can't go to work today," Edith told her roommates. "I've got the flu. I hope you don't catch it. I'll try to wipe down everything I use."

"I'm sure it was just something you ate last night," Analyn said, "I thought that satay we had yesterday had an off-taste, didn't you? Don't take the day off, your family's counting on the money you send."

"You're not sick, Edith. Eat a few of these crackers. It'll calm your stomach," Lucy told her, pretending that what she suspected wasn't true. Lucy just wanted one more calm day before the shit hit the fan.

The next morning Edith was vomiting in the bathroom again, "I know what's happening," she cried as she closed the toilet seat and sat down on its lid. "I'm pregnant! I must be. I'm Oh my God, I'm having a baby. His baby. I don't want his baby. I hate his baby."

Then an unrecognizable voice came out of her mouth that sounded like there was a devil in her throat, "I HATE HIM! I HATE HIM! I HATE HIM!" it shrieked. The voice was so other-worldly that it scared her roommates. They backed away from the bathroom door and put their hands over their ears. When Edith was finally exhausted from screaming and the devil seemed to have left her, she rolled herself into a ball and slid to the bathroom floor, inconsolable.

Edith was too distraught and too nauseated to even think about going to work. "Tell Mr. Chin I have the flu, would ya, Analyn?"

While her stomach finally settled down, her thoughts were anything but quiet. For the first hour, she lay in a fetal position on the couch in tears feeling sorry for herself. *What am I going to do? How can I take care of a baby? What will my parents say? Why was I so stupid to think I was in love with a guy like Jun? How was I so wrong about him?* Her last frightening thought before falling asleep was *I'm doomed to live my mother's life.*

When she awoke, she felt surprisingly clear-headed and feisty. She got up, found her notebook and began to write.

Okay, now what? Who can I depend on to help me through this? My roomies are great, but this is not their problem. I can't rely on them to tolerate my throwing up and crying for the next eight months. And a newborn in the house would cramp their style. That would be unfair. No, I can't depend on Lucy and Analyn. My parents? I certainly can't depend on them. They already depend on me. I can't bear to see my mother's face when she finds out. Maybe I could confide in Maria. She'll know how to best handle my parents and my dilemma. Maybe even give me some emotional support. But I'm not sure about her. She has suddenly stopped inviting me to Sunday dinner where we always had time to talk. And I can't forget the ugly face she wore for Wa at the wedding. No, not Maria. I really don't like her much. Wa? He's definitely a possibility to support me. He was so nice to give me a ride home when I needed one. And he never even pried about my tears. He's a nice man. If I asked, I'm sure he would help. Well, maybe he would help. He's been kind of avoiding me at work. I haven't been up to his office for our little chats in weeks. But, yes, I still think I could depend on Wa. I know for sure I can't depend on Jun. That scumbag stole my virginity and gave me this baby in return. He hasn't even tried to contact me since that night. Not even to apologize. Nothing! After what he did to me. I don't know why people like sex so much. It's horrible.

Who else is there? There's nobody. There's only me and this bastard baby.

Edith stopped writing for a moment to reread and her heart stopped when she read her last words: bastard baby. She picked up her pen with fresh resolve and wrote: *I'm going to get even with the bastard who gave me this bastard baby,* she vowed.

Chapter 11

The Ultimatum

When work resumed the next day, Wa was happy to notice Edith was back at work in the pattern department. Truth was, he still couldn't help but notice everything about Edith.

"Mrs. Pauli," Edith said, calling up to the office. "Could you ask Mr. Chin if I could see him for a moment?" When he heard the request, Mr. Chin enthusiastically agreed and automatically prayed that today would not be the day Maria would pop in for a surprise visit. It was hard enough keeping Edith hidden away in the pattern department.

"What's up, young lady?" he asked brightly. "What can I help you with?" *If only he knew*, thought Edith. "I'm sorry for missing work yesterday. Had a flu. I thought I was over it this morning, but I don't think I am. I'm so very tired right now that I hope it's okay with you if I leave a little early. Like, now," she said.

Determined as she was to keep her pregnancy secret for now, Edith felt really bad about lying to Wa. She felt worse when she heard his response. "Sure, absolutely, Edith. Go home and get some rest," he said, just then noticing her red-rimmed eyes. "I don't mean to pry, but you look sad. You've been crying, haven't you? If there's anything I can do to make you feel better, please let me know. You can count on me."

At his kind words, suddenly all the tears that were just a blink away came cascading down Edith's cheeks. "Oh, Wa," was all Edith could moan before those tears on her cheeks became sobbing wracks in her chest.

Wa was so stunned by her crying, all he could do was repeat "Now, now, it's going to be okay."

"It's never going to be okay, Wa," she sniffed, and before she could stop the words from spilling off her tongue, she blurted, "I'm pregnant."

"Jun?" Wa asked incredulously.

Edith nodded. "I didn't mean to tell you. Promise me you won't tell anyone else. Promise me, please," she begged.

"I promise," he vowed, as she darted out of his office.

"Oh, God," Wa said to himself, collapsing into his chair moments later. "She's pregnant! If Maria finds out, or should I say, *when* Maria finds out, she'll accuse me of fathering a baby she herself never could produce. There will be more fights, more accusations, paternity tests and in the end, Maria will take everything I have, especially since I've already lied about firing Edith. For my own sake and sanity, I will actually have to fire Edith. This is all too much."

It hadn't taken Wa but a second to guess who the father was. He'd seen the way they were dancing at the wedding; he'd noticed how possessively and often Jun was kissing her: on her lips, on her neck and at least once on her décolletage. "That son of a bitch," Wa muttered to himself. "I'm gonna go have a talk with Jun. I'll kick his ass." If only he had known Edith had been raped, he would actually have done so.

The next day, Wa fired Edith. "But why? Did I do something wrong?" she asked. "Is it because I'm you know what?" she asked, reluctant to even say the horrible word aloud.

"Let me explain," Wa said with a heavy heart. "Maria and I, well, we don't have the best relationship. She thinks there's something going on between you and me and has been insisting I let you go. Matter of fact, she thinks I fired you weeks ago. Hope she never finds out! While it's true I am very fond of you, it's not like that." *Anymore*, he thought to himself. "But I have good news. My friend, Mr. Chue, who also owns a garment factory, has agreed to hire you. I spoke so highly of your design abilities that he's going to put you in the pattern department. He pays even better than I do. You can start tomorrow if that's agreeable."

Edith was upset about losing her job and her connection with Wa and the few friends she had made at work. But at the same time, she was thankful Wa had found her a new job and that he was still looking out for her. Later that night, her roommates were really surprised when she told them her news about being let go. "I must really be naive," Edith lamented. "I had no idea Maria and Wa were having troubles and that I was the source of it. That explains their strange behavior at the wedding."

Analyn had to know. "Did you tell him you're pregnant? That you were raped?"

"Yes and no. I didn't tell him Jun raped me. He never has to find out. I thought you girls were just teasing me about him having the hots for me a while back. But apparently, Maria thought so too. I really feel bad that this has caused problems for them." Edith told them she needed to make things right and clear things up with Maria.

"I don't know if that's such a good thing," Analyn worried. "It could backfire."

As Lucy was about to agree with Analyn's assessment, a pile of mail fell through the slot in the door. "Girls! Girls! A letter from Lyka," she yelled excitedly as she picked out the one with the foreign stamp and ripped open the envelope. "Let me read it to you."

Dear Analyn and Lucy, the typewritten letter began. *"I am so sorry for not writing sooner but I have been very busy learning my new position in this wonderful and gorgeous home, or should*

I say, mansion. The family is awesome to me and I love the missus and master. Every day, I play with their two children, a boy, four and a sweet little girl, almost three. Some days, we go to the park for a picnic and then spend the afternoon splashing in the backyard pool (which is incredibly huge!). I get two days a week off and they let me use one of their cars to go to the city or wherever I want. They are so generous. Plus! I am making nearly three times what I earned at the garment factory. I couldn't have landed in a better place. I just love what I'm doing. Hope you (and your new roommate) are doing well. Please understand if I don't write more often, but know that I am well and happy. Miss you guys. See you next year when I get my three weeks' vacation!

"The letter is signed in Lyka's notoriously illegible handwriting," Analyn commented.

"It's a relief to finally hear from her," Lucy added. "You would like her, Edith. She's the life of every party. So glad she's doing so well. And the money she's raking in! Wow!"

"Sure, the money's good," said Analyn, "but she had to sign a two-year contract and the job is in Lebanon. I'd be too scared to go." Lucy and Edith agreed with Analyn, admitting they'd probably be too scared to go as well.

When the three girls were together, Edith half forgot her anger but when she sat alone in her room a million confused thoughts rushed through her mind. With no one except her friends to advise her, she decided to confide in her notebook and trust in the words she wrote.

Here I am again, notebook. This time I'm in real trouble. I need to know what to do next. My friends insist I've been raped and until they said that very word 'rape,' I couldn't believe that happened to me. I thought it must have been the way I dressed or the way I let him kiss me while we danced. So let's get this straight, notebook, I no longer believe any of it was my fault and Yes, I've been raped.! Good! I got that out. Now let's move on."

The notebook was slow to respond. Edith kept picking up the

ballpoint pen and putting it back down on the bed. It just didn't want to spell out the obvious. Eventually, though, it came down to three little words. She picked up the pen and wrote *Tell Jun Now*. Then she tenuously lifted the receiver from its cradle and held it to her ear for a long time. "I can't do this," she said aloud.

Yes you can, her subconscious responded. *What should I say when he answers?"* she wondered.

Say hello. Say this is Edith, how are you Jun?

"Then what?" she said out loud to herself.

Tell him you want to meet. Pick the place so he's away from his school and his friends. You need to meet him face to face so you can read what his face says compared to what his mouth is telling you. You'll know what to do next, trust me, the words on the page said. *Just dial the damn number.* And so she did.

To her great relief Jun was happy to meet her, excited even. He must have figured she finally got over her shyness about having sex for the first time, and that maybe she was ready for another romp. He liked her enough to encourage it. He was still chuckling about the shocked look on his mama's face when he showed up at his sister's wedding with his date, "that poor Visayan waif." *I got Mama good that time!* he said to himself, smiling at the memory.

He's going to meet me Saturday near the lagoon in the Chinese Gardens, she wrote in the notebook. *Now what?*

First off, keep your cool. Don't lose your temper and above all, don't cry. The object is to get support for your child. Your child, Edith. This is your child.

Edith stopped in the middle of the words she was writing. My child. Until this moment she considered it Jun's bastard baby. For the first time she realized, no, this life within her is not Jun's bastard baby. It's her child, her very own child. The realization startled her.

Oh baby, she wrote in her notebook, *I am so sorry I called you that awful name. I'll never call you that again. You are all mine right now, not his. We'll give him his chance on Saturday when I'll tell him about us and then we'll know what kind of a papa he's going to be. Don't fret, baby, I'll figure things out.*

Plan A. The obvious, she wrote. *I need money. As soon as my new employer finds out I'm pregnant, I'll be let go. That gives me three, maybe four months if I'm lucky, to hide you, little one. You will not grow up in poverty. I solemnly promise you that right now, right here on these pages. I won't let Jun abandon us.*

So when I meet him on Saturday I'll calmly say: "Jun, I'm pregnant with your baby—our baby." I'll tell him I can't do this without his help. Whether he wants to be in our child's life or not, I'll insist that he support us. Perhaps he'll be a good guy and step up but that's not likely.

Plan B, I'll threaten to go to his parents and say their grand-child needs support. Perhaps they're good people and will do the right thing. We'll cross that bridge when we get to it.

When Saturday finally came she vacillated between strength and cowardice but quickly discovered if she patted her tummy, she could call up her Dragon Lady spirit. She took the bus to Rizal Park, and on the walkway toward the pavilion kept patting her belly for courage.

Jun had his back to her, looking out over the lagoon, as she approached. He had one foot on the concrete bench, one elbow on his knee and with his free hand, was smoking. He looked like an Adonis. No wonder she was so captivated by him. *Don't let him know you're scared,* she reminded herself, *and whatever you do, don't cry.*

"Hi Jun."

He turned as she called. He was definitely happy to see her. "Great idea meeting here at the lagoon. I have forgotten how real and good life seems when you're surrounded by nature."

Life is real all right, she mused.

He suggested they walk around the lagoon but she said no. She needed to watch his face as she told him the news.

"What's new with you, Edith?" he asked, casually taking her hand in his.

"Well, I've got a new job in a better factory. I'm a pattern maker now and you're going to be a father. I'm carrying your baby." She said all that in one breath and watched his smile flatten as he put all those pieces together.

"You're pregnant?" was his quiet response. "And you think I'm the father? Come on, Edith, get real," he retorted, adding "is this some kind of joke?" as he swiped at the sweat forming on his upper lip. "We only had sex once *and* it was your first time. Nothing ever happens the first time. How can you say I'm its father?"

"Our baby is not an *its*," she replied without flinching. "Little Jun is not an *its*."

"Stop it," Jun said angrily. "Don't call it Little Jun! How do you know it's mine? It could be anybody's. Guys are always looking at you. I've watched them. It could be any one of them."

He flicked his cigarette into the lagoon.

How disgusting, she thought as she watched it fizzle out.

There was no trace of Mr. Nice Guy in his voice when he finally spoke again. He was saying she should get an abortion, of course. "So, what do you want from me? To go with you to the clinic? To pay for it? What? What do you want, Edith?" he barked in a voice tinged with fear.

"First of all, an apology for raping me would be nice," she replied in a voice just loud enough to catch the attention of passersby. "And, of course, money. It's expensive to raise a child."

"Money!" he laughed. "If I give you money, it'll be for an abortion."

"But I'm not having an abortion, Jun, I'm having Little Jun. It's not your choice. It's mine."

"Where do you think I'll get money," he sneered. "I'm in school. I don't have money."

She shrugged. "I don't care how you get it. Rob a bank for all I care. Just get it."

"Or what?" he said, at this point realizing she had very little control.

"Perhaps your parents will behave more responsibly than you. After all, they are our baby's grandparents. I think I'll pay them a visit."

"Be my guest!" he laughed. "You think my mother will give a damn about a grandchild from the slums of the Visayas? Ha! She'll laugh in your face. You can't imagine how disappointed she was in me when I brought you to the wedding. She said I embarrassed her."

Edith hadn't planned on that response. Her bravado was slipping away. Once again she patted her stomach then said, "I'm not going away, Jun. I haven't told Maria yet that I'm pregnant. Maria will be angry with you if you don't support me. You know Maria, she can be quite vindictive. She'd love to rub this in your mother's face."

Jun did know Maria, knew she could make trouble. He put his face in his hands and sighed, "How much do you need to just go away, to leave me and my family out of this?"

Edith thought it might come to this and she had spent time calculating how much she thought it would cost to raise a child back home in Palo. She had decided $500 would be enough. Her parents had never seen a sum that large in their entire lives but at the last minute she doubled it. "$1,000," she blurted out.

"$1,000!" he exclaimed, "that's extortion!" She shrugged.

He threw himself around the pavilion for a few minutes punching his fist into his other hand and in general acting like a spoiled brat. He finally stopped inches from her face and spit out, "Okay. $1,000 and never contact me or my family again." Edith accepted the terms.

Edith was pleased with her bargain as the bus rattled through the streets of Manila. "Baby," she said, "we're going to be okay. Today your mama's Dragon Lady spirit came to the rescue. I was powerful! And don't worry that I'll name you Little Jun. I never want to hear that name again."

Pleased with her negotiations with Jun, Edith was now eager to get home and tell her roommates of her successful achievement. Analyn and Lucy were working together in their kitchen threading chicken onto skewers, making a mound of satay they would bring to a party that evening when Edith walked in bubbling with news.

"Guess what?" she exclaimed, as they stopped threading. "I met Jun today. I gave him an ultimatum. I said he had to do his share of the cost of raising this child. He was shocked when I told him he was going to be a father. First word out of his mouth was abortion. I told him there'd be absolutely no abortion."

"And?" the girls said in unison when Edith stopped to catch her breath.

"And in the end I talked him into giving me monetary support. He's going to give me $1,000," she happily added. "That's a lot of money!"

The girls looked at each other. Edith saw the disbelief in their eyes. "You said you gave him an ultimatum," Lucy said. "What kind of threat did you make?"

"That I'd tell his parents they'd soon be grandparents and if they didn't respond, I'd tell Maria what happened. She'd love to make trouble for the Wangs."

"And just when is Jun going to get you this money?" Analyn asked, wiping her sticky hands on her apron so she could plant them on her hips.

"Um, well, I'm assuming soon. I mean, he wants to have this whole thing behind him. I don't have an exact time. I'm sure he'll call soo ..."

"Oh, Edith," the friends cried in unison, now surrounding her in a hug. "Oh, Edith."

"What?" Edith said. "WHAT?" she said again, her eyes darting in fear between the faces of her two best friends.

Chapter 12

Maria's Revenge

A whole week went by before Edith accepted the fact that Jun was not going to be true to his word. There would be no money to support her baby if she didn't get smart. She patted her belly and said as she was dialing the phone, "Watch out, world. Dragon Lady is pissed and ready to fight."

"Hi Maria, it's Edith. We haven't talked in quite a while. Invite me for coffee and I'll tell you all my exciting news." If she was anything, Maria was a nosy shrew. She could not deny Edith's request. 'Exciting news' sounded too irresistible.

"That would be wonderful. But let's make it lunch. I want to hear everything," Maria responded. "Wa's out of town on business, so it will be just you and me. How about Sunday, noonish?"

"I can't wait," Edith said truthfully.

Maria couldn't wait either. *I wonder what her news is*, she mused. *Is she going to tell me she's marrying Jun? That would surely give old Lin a kick in the ass ... her son marrying a Visayan waif! I can't think what could possibly be more exciting news than that!* After their phone call, Maria was smiling and chuckling to herself all day long.

Finally noon on Sunday arrived. Normally, Edith would have felt awkward and uncomfortable showing up at this house on Sunday, as she had so often in the past. As she rang the bell this time, there was not a trace of discomfort. Edith was on a mission to provide for her baby and she didn't feel the least bit bad about using Maria and her vicious tongue to take care of the details.

The two women chit-chatted their way through the salad, but by the time the last leafy vegetable was gone, Maria was salivating. "So, Edith, you simply must tell me your exciting news," she blurted. "Does it have anything to do with you and Jun?" she projected.

"As a matter of fact, it does," Edith answered smoothly. "I'm pregnant. I'm a mama and Jun's the papa."

The look of shock and surprise on Maria's face confirmed that Wa had kept his promise not to tell anyone her news. Maria was truly flabbergasted. "Pregnant? Did you say pregnant?" she repeated, as if her big ears weren't working. "Oh my god, there's a wedding coming up! When's the big day? Details! Details!"

"Well, Jun hasn't proposed yet," Edith said simply. "He must be planning one of those awesome proposal events. When I told him I was pregnant, he looked so cute, bewildered and even a tiny bit scared. He was so sweet. He doesn't seem very excited yet about parenthood, but I certainly am," she lied. It was time to plant the bug in Maria's brain. "And I'm hoping that this news is as exciting for the first-time grandparents. I don't think Jun told his parents yet about our baby. I think he'll be telling them soon. I'll bet they'll be thrilled."

Edith's fabricated fib hit its target squarely, right in the center of Maria's revengeful and nasty soul. Maria barely heard their remaining conversation; her mind was racing about how to best use this big 'exciting news' as a weapon against her former best friend, Lin. *This will show her my power as a vengeful Visayas waif*, she imagined, her eyes dancing.

Edith felt her mission accomplished as she hugged Maria on her way out the door. She patted her belly on the walk home, amazed at her Dragon Lady prowess.

Maria wasted no time at all dialing up Lin's number. When Lin glanced at her caller ID, she almost didn't pick up. Lin was still quite furious that her wonderful son was dating the poor waif from the Visayas all because of Maria's deviousness. It was more than two months since the wedding and she had just assumed the two were still dating. Occasionally she would ask Jun if he and Edith were still a couple, and every time Jun couldn't resist teasing his mother, and never truly answered. Instead, he'd taunt her by saying, "Edith's such a beautiful woman, don't you agree, Mama?"

I wonder what that bitch wants, Lin thought maliciously as she picked up the phone and primly announced, "The Wang residence. Lin speaking."

Maria swallowed the starchy retort she would have preferred and instead made her voice all sweet and sugary. "Oh, Lin," she began in a singsong falsetto. "I'm so glad to reach you. We haven't talked in a while, but I just had to call you and say congratulations. I'm so thrilled for you and your husband. How exciting!"

"Why, thank you," was Lin's unexpected reply.

Does she already know about the baby? Maria wondered. *I was sure she'd be screaming at me instead of thanking me. How did I get this so wrong?* But seconds later, Lin continued by saying, "Yes it was such an honor for the Wang family to be named 'Manila's Most Prominent Family' in the paper this week. We are quite excited. Anyhow, I'm in the middle of something, Maria, so let's chat again soon."

"Wait! Hang on!" Maria shouted in mounting desperation. "That wasn't why I was calling. I just wanted to congratulate you on soon becoming a first-time grandmother. It sounds like a Jun and Edith wedding is in your future. Should I start making rosettes?" she added snidely.

Lin wailed a long, painful "Nooooo!" into the phone before the line went dead. *And maybe Lin went dead too,* Maria thought gleefully.

Chapter 13

Baby Talk

Edith was confident that Maria immediately phoned Lin to gloat over this devastating news. She pictured Lin anxiously confronting her favorite son who would smoothly mollify her with a lie. The next thing she expected was to hear from an angry Jun. So Edith was perplexed when three days went by without a word from him. Her roommate Lucy was giving her the old "I told you so" followed by unsolicited advice on how to properly avenge evil-doers. "No, I don't want to get any more deceptive than I was with Maria," Edith fired back. "It didn't work anyway. Haven't heard from Jun or his mama at all."

Analyn took a different approach. "Look, Edith, if I were you, I'd do anything I could to provide for my baby. Besides, don't you think your baby's grandparents have a right to know their grandchild, to say nothing of an obligation to help you provide for him? If Jun won't come through, that scumbag, you need to take it up with his mama. You simply must take a stand. And you can't do it by being deceptive, but by being truthful. Tell scumbag's mama what really happened."

Edith knew Analyn was right. She had to keep in mind what was best for her baby, not what was less stressful for herself. Stressed is what Edith was as she rang the Wang's doorbell the next day. "Please tell Jun I'm here to see him," she told the maid who came to the door. "Oh, Jun is not home. He's on holiday in the Alps. He'll be home next Monday," the maid said, trying to dismiss Edith by closing the door. "Wait! In that case, I'd like to speak with Mrs. Wang, please," Edith said, using her foot to keep the door open. "I'm afraid that's not possible without an appoint ..." the maid started to say. Just then a voice rang out behind her. "Who's at the door?" Lin asked in a polite voice which turned ugly when she spotted Edith. "What the hell are you doing here? Go away. Now!"

"I just wanted you to see me carrying your grandchild. I have some business with Jun, but he's been avoiding me," Edith said calmly.

"Been avoiding you? But I thought he was about to propose. Least that's what I heard. That you two were planning a wedding."

"Maria has a funny way of putting things, doesn't she?" Edith said smiling. "There will be no wedding, in fact, no way in the world would I marry that son of yours. May I come in for a few minutes? There's something I think you should know."

Lin was elated to hear there would be no wedding. The waif from Visayas would not be jeopardizing her family's prominent standing in the community. "Yes, of course, please come in," Lin said in a voice that oozed graciousness and relief.

"My dear, what makes you believe Jun is the father?" Lin began tepidly. "You must be mistaken. I can see why you'd like it to be Jun who impregnated you. After all, we are the most prominent family in Manila," Lin said, still unable to stop gloating about that honor. "But, it could be anybody's."

"This is what I have to tell you," Edith began. "Listen carefully. I will only speak the truth. I am eleven weeks' pregnant. Eleven weeks ago was your daughter's wedding. That night, Jun took me up to the bridal suite when I told him I needed a break, that my feet hurt from dancing in heels."

"Oh, so that's when you think you got pregnant?" Lin said.

"No, that's when I got raped. By your son. I was a virgin at the time. Ask your daughter if she noticed the blood I left behind on the bedspread."

All the color drained from Lin's face and she looked like she might faint as Edith continued. "Once I realized that he wasn't going to take my repeated nos for an answer, he ripped off my panties and pinned me to the bed. The whole awful thing was over in seconds. I left the wedding in tears, never wanting to see that awful boy again. Once I realized I was pregnant, I contacted Jun because I'm in no position to provide for this child on my own. I need help. He promised help, but never came through. Now I hear he's off playing in the Alps. Breaks my heart."

"Indeed, it's a heartbreaking story," Lin conceded. "But my Jun is not a rapist. He would never do anything like that. Not my sweet Jun."

"Now I understand why he wouldn't listen to me screaming 'no!' Your spoiled brat never heard that word from you."

At this point, Lin had had enough. "I'll get to the truth when Jun returns Monday," she said indignantly as she ushered Edith to the door. "You've made some shameful accusations."

Edith couldn't resist a parting shot. "Know what else would be a shame? If Manila's 'most prominent family' was found to be prominent for all the wrong reasons."

Chapter 14

The Right Thing to Do

Jun's papa was not anywhere near as mushy and soft on Jun as Mama was. He'd seen enough of Jun's behavior to know that his son was little more than a bully, a braggart and an obnoxious brat. When Lin told him about Edith's claim that Jun had raped her, he had no trouble believing it.

On Monday when Jun returned from the Alps, Mama greeted him at the door before he had a chance to set down his skis. "Welcome home, sweetie. I missed you. Did you have a good time?" she asked, before launching into what was really on her mind. "You didn't rape Edith, did you? She says she's pregnant with your baby. She came here a few days ago trying to extort money from us. Tell me you didn't rape her."

Jun, for once, did as he was told. "I didn't rape her, Mama." He then proceeded to embellish how Edith had lured him up to the bridal suite where she was very naked when he came out of the bathroom. "She grabbed my you-know-what and it was impossible to resist her. It won't happen again, I promise, Mama."

"I believe you, sweetie. However, your dalliance did result in her becoming pregnant. I guess Papa and I will come up with some money to help her raise this child."

Jun inwardly smiled. "Yes, Mama, that's the right thing to do."

Papa wasn't so easy on him. "Jun, come down here, we need to talk," was the first thing he said upon returning home from work. Jun did not like the tone of his father's voice. When he arrived in the living room, the look on his father's face was even more threatening. "Did you rape that girl? Edith?" he said menacingly. Jun was at a loss for words, trying to decide which was worse: lying to his father, or raping Edith. "Well, not exactly. I mean, technically, she was sort of asking for it, well, not in so many words. I wouldn't exactly say it was rape." Jun was stumbling badly.

Papa grabbed Jun roughly by the shoulders, shaking him. "I asked you if you raped Edith. Yes or no," he shouted, forcibly throttling Jun until his teeth chattered. Jun had never seen Papa so furious. He feared he was about to be beaten bloody. "Yes or no, Jun? Answer me!" Papa screamed in his ear. Jun knew his father already knew the truth. "Yes, Papa. I did do that."

"You lowlife. You disgust me," Papa yelled before shoving Jun halfway across the room where his shoulder hit the china cabinet, rattling Lin's prized dishes.

"Rape is not just a crime, it's a sin and you must atone for it. Here's what's going to happen next, Jun. Here's what we'll do for your baby and for our grandchild. I understand Edith wanted your help, asked for a mere $1,000, and you took off to go skiing. We're, meaning you and me, are going to give her enough to raise that baby properly. I think $3,000 is an appropriate amount to soften the crime and atone for the sin you committed. Half that money will come from you. Where will you get that much, you wonder? First off, you will sell your motor scooter and that gaudy gold jewelry you like to wear. Then you will go to work in my factory until you earn the rest of what you owe me. That means college will have to be postponed until you're mature enough to have learned your lesson. If you ever rape another woman, I will find you, and you'll wish I hadn't."

Lin had been eavesdropping on their conversation ever since

she heard her fine china rattling. *He really did rape her,* she thought, stunned. *How foolish I have been all these years!* She ran upstairs crying. She could see the headlines already: "Prominent Wang Family No Longer Prominent; Son Rapes Visayan Girl."

Chapter 15

A Grandfather's Hug

The following Saturday morning, early, Edith answered a knock on the door with an audible gasp.

"You recognize me, then," the visitor said.

"Yes, from the wedding, you're Jun's father."

"May I come in?" he was asking as she just stood there paralyzed with fear. Edith opened the door wider and waved him in without a word.

"Can we speak privately?" he asked expecting roommates to appear from behind closed doors.

"Roommates are out for a run then they'll stop for a bagel. I'm alone," she tenuously answered.

"May I sit?"

She nodded toward the couch and sat across from him on a chair she pulled away from the kitchen table. She waited.

"This is not an easy visit for me," he finally began. "My son has disgraced me. And harmed you. I am devastated. Our family is in tatters over this. Lin cries all the time, Jun only talks to his mother now that I've given him my ultimatum and, me? I'm so disgusted with Jun that I can't stand being in the house when he's home. And you are carrying my first grandbaby.

"Lin sent me here to try and bribe you into getting an abortion," he continued. "She thinks if no one knows about this scandal it will save the Wang family name from the snickering busybodies. That's important to her, but on the way here I realized this is my grandbaby, my precious grandbaby. What if this baby is the only grandchild I will ever have? Probably not, but it could happen. How would I feel then?

"It breaks my heart that I have to tell you that we, well Lin, really, will not accept this child into our family. I will never be able to hold him in my arms and coo to him and teach him how to ride a pony and ...." Mr. Wang stopped imagining. He didn't want the tears to well in his eyes. He needed to finish stating his reason for coming. He needed to get back to his life as if nothing had changed.

"Edith," he finally said. "I know what sum of money Jun and you settled on. That is not enough money. I need to know that you and my grandbaby will be fine, more than fine, that you both will thrive. I am giving you triple what you asked of Jun. I know it's not nearly enough to raise a child, but it's a good start. By the time this amount runs low you will have become an amazing mother and have created a wonderful life for both of you. I will pray every day that this is true."

Edith didn't know what to say. She hadn't expected Mr. Wang to be so sympathetic. At last she said, "That's very generous of you."

"No," he said, "I'm not being generous. I'm trying to do what's right. You can't imagine how sad I am that my son has shamed me in this way ... and catastrophically changed your life. I am so sorry. What will you do now, Edith? Will you stay in Manila?"

"I'll stay here until my employer learns of my pregnancy and then, of course, he will have to let me go. I'll go back to Palo where my family is. I only came to Manila to earn money to help support my family. I'm one of ten, did you know? And I'm so lucky, I have the best family a girl could ask for."

"One of ten!" he whistled. "Then my grandbaby will have plenty of aunts and uncles and lots of cousins. That makes me very happy. I wish you well, Edith. May God go with you." He reached into his pocket for the check he had written as a bribe but now gave as a gift. He stood, thought about giving her a hug, wanted to, but couldn't decide if that was appropriate. Edith noticed his dilemma so she tentatively put out her arms and an embrace confirmed their mutual sadness. "This hug is from your grandpa," she told her baby bump.

"Thank you for that," he smiled ruefully. "Now all that's left is the lie I'll be telling Lin."

Chapter 16

One-Way Ticket Home

As she watched Mr. Wang drive away, Edith was overcome with the strangest emotions she had ever experienced. She was torn between jumping for joy and wallowing in empathy for the saddest man she had ever met. As she looked at the figure on the check, she couldn't help but cry as a way to relieve both odd emotions.

"Baby, we're going to be fine," she declared as she patted her belly. "We're going to be more than fine. You and I are going to have quite an interesting life." Little did she know how true her prediction would someday become.

She was still smiling when her athletic roommates burst through the door. "You have cream cheese on your upper lip," Edith pointed out to Analyn, before exploding into delirious laughter. "And you, Edith, have a shit-eating grin on *your* upper lip. What gives?"

"I just had a visitor. No, change that. I just was visited by a real live angel."

Both Analyn and Lucy rolled their eyes. "And did this angel have wings? A halo, perhaps? Golden harp?" Lucy teased.

"This angel was Mr. Wang. He gave me this," Edith revealed, waving the check in the air. Her roommates' eyes stopped rolling, followed instantly by hoots of delight and excitement. "Oh my God, how wonderful for you! Did he give you enough to make up for everything?" Lucy asked. Edith had already decided not to tell her roommates the size of the check. It was for her and her baby and, really, nobody's business. "It was more than enough," she said simply, still wearing the shit-eating grin.

That night, after her roommates had left for the evening, Edith paperclipped the check to a page in her notebook and began to write.

Today is a day I will never forget, she wrote. *In a matter of a few minutes, all my anxiety and despair about having this baby, well, it just went 'poof'. I never really expected to get any help from the Wangs, but Mr. Wang, who will always be thought of as my angel, surprised me with more help than I could have imagined. He is my baby's grandfather and I will never forget him. I intend to pray for him the rest of my life. He has saved me, or rather he has saved us , me and my baby. What's next for us?* she wondered as she patted her belly and took another look at the check. *I could send half this money home and still have plenty to get me through this pregnancy, but then I'd have to tell Mama and Papa how I happened to have so much. I'm ashamed to tell them that I had been raped. I still can't help blaming myself for being so naive and stupid to have let this happen to me.*

Thoughts of her parents brought up memories of how wonderful it was to have been raised in such a loving family. Money or no money, there was always understanding, forgiveness, and kindness surrounding their home in Palo. It was a far cry from the cruelty, snobbery and vindictiveness she experienced in Manila. She picked up her pen once again.

I'm going home, she wrote decisively. *I want us to be where love is.*

Finally Edith had decided on her course of action. She'd continue working at Chue's garment factory for another two months or until she was fired for her obvious pregnancy. That would give her time to earn more money to bring home and the time to adjust happily to her condition. She'd go home with joy.

As the weeks wore on, Edith wore baggier and baggier shirts to camouflage her rounding belly. Her relief at knowing her baby's future was financially secure brought out Edith's talents as a pattern maker at Chue's. She began experimenting with unusual fabrics and trims, creating patterns that translated into novel eye-catching apparel. Her creativity quickly caught Mr. Chue's eye who began to think about how much more money he could make with her avant garde designs.

"Today's the day," Edith said to her roommates one morning as she headed out to work. She was nearly five months' pregnant and no matter how hard she tried to hide her bump with Lucy's largest shirt, there was no camouflaging her condition any longer. "I had such a restless night," she told them, "and when I woke up this morning, my belly seemed to have doubled in size. Today's the day I'm going to be fired," she announced, not unhappily, to Analyn and Lucy.

"You're going to leave us?" Analyn said quite unhappily. "Hope you won't forget us once you get home. We're really going to miss you."

"And all this time, I thought you'd be one of those pregnant women who never look pregnant and just pop out a surprise baby in nine months," Lucy said. "I really hate to see you leave. But, yeah, you do look especially pregnant today. Hope Mr. Chue doesn't chew you out!"

That morning as she entered the pattern department, Edith realized that she no longer walked, she waddled. "Yup, today's the day," she said to herself as soon as she was summoned to Mr. Chue's office.

"Edith," he said, "I have some bad news. I'm afraid ..." he began.

"That you have to let me go," Edith finished for him.

"Yes, I'm afraid I do. That's just the way it is in the garment industry. I'm really sorry. I hate to lose such a talented pattern maker," Mr. Chue said, mentally mourning the loss of the big money he'd been anticipating from Edith's designs. "When's the baby due?" he politely inquired. "In three or four months, you say? Well, you had me fooled for quite some time then. I wonder why Mr. Chin didn't tell me of your condition when I hired you. He must have known. Anyway, you can finish out the day and pick up your final check from my secretary on your way out. Good luck, and thanks."

The next day Edith bought her one-way plane ticket home.

The busy-ness of the Manila airport was staggering. So many people of so many colors and cultures, all looking like they knew exactly what they were doing. She was astounded at the amount of luggage most people were lugging through long lines. With the exception of her notebook, now nearly filled with sketches, pattern ideas and written thoughts about Manila, her backpack did not hold much more than when she arrived in Manila nearly two years ago. *Except for the check,* Edith thought, smiling.

"Well, you certainly look happy," a woman behind her in line remarked. "Huh?" Edith said, not sure the woman was addressing her. "I said, 'you sure look happy.' It's nice to see someone smiling in an airport. Going off to meet your husband?" she asked presumptively. "Are you planning to surprise him with your pregnancy? How exciting ! When is your little bundle of joy due?"

Edith was caught off-guard by the stranger's barrage of questions, but was happy to have someone distract her from her first-time-flying anxiety, as the line inched closer to the jetway. "He or she is due in about four months, I might even have a Christmas baby," Edith responded. "I am thinking about how happy I am about going home again. But I am also a little anxious. This is my first time on a plane."

"Oh, yes, I can remember my first-time flying jitters. You just need to keep a smile on your face and those happy thoughts and you'll be fine. If we sit together, I'll keep you distracted and you'll be home in no time. I'm Sue, by the way. Sue Tomei." Sue was the perfect distraction. The woman was a talker and spilled all kinds of details about her life, her family, her work, even details of what the family dog ate for breakfast. "My sons love that dog," she added, before stopping to take a breath.

"So, do you have any daughters?" Edith inquired as a matter of politeness. "No, unfortunately, just a sister, Anna. She's very eccentric and artistic. She has one daughter, Pieta, whom I just love. Pieta's an adventurous soul if there ever was one. In fact, last year, she moved to Syria to be an au pair for a very rich family. Anna called and read me the letter Pieta sent her a few months ago. Sounds like she loves working for this family, is making great money and has a lot of perks. Even said she has use of one of the family cars on her days off. Sounds unreal, doesn't it?" Sue said. Edith was having trouble keeping up with Sue's deluge of information. "It sure does," she replied, happy to be seated next to this talker. It made the flight seem quick and in no time at all, the plane landed. "Best of happiness with your new little one," Sue said as she scurried off to baggage claim.

The bus from the Tacloban City Airport to Palo dropped Edith off in front of the town square. The sleepiness and shabbiness of Palo was a far cry from the hubbub and opulence of Manila. Edith momentarily wondered if she'd made the right decision. Within a few minutes, her mind was catapulting her into doubts and distressing thoughts. *Don't go there,* she admonished herself. *Do what you always do. Write these feelings down. It's how you become rebalanced.* "That's it!" she said, sitting down on a nearby bench and reaching into her backpack for her notebook.

She began to write. *How strange I feel to be sitting here in my town square, excited to be home after nearly two years away, yet at the same time, I'm suddenly feeling worried and anxious. I wonder if I should have warned my family that I was pregnant, or at least told them I was coming home. Life in Palo is very predictable and big surprises are not the norm. How will my family react? I'm so scared that this pregnancy will especially hurt Mama. I don't think I could stand seeing a look of dismay or disappointment when she sees me. I'm sitting right across from the market where Mama and I sold our produce together for several years. I remember how she used to always tell me what a smart and sensible girl I was. Working the market with her felt like drudgery at the time, but when I look back now, that was the time when I really got to know my mother. It was also the time I vowed I never wanted to live my mother's life. It looked to me to be nothing but pregnancies, endless sacrifice and hard work from dawn to dusk in a dirt poor corner of the world. Now look at me! Here I am, back in my dirt poor corner, pregnant and scared to death Mama will think poorly of me when she sees the mess I've gotten into. I don't think I'll be welcome.*

Just then, she heard her name being called from across the square. "Edith! Edith Santos! How nice to see you back home, Welcome back!" shouted the voice of a former classmate, waving to Edith as he continued his jog. That was just what she needed to hear. She picked up her pen again with a totally fresh outlook.

That was a sign, she wrote. *I don't need to worry what my family thinks about my situation. Deep down, I know that I will be absolutely accepted and loved no matter what. I paid a price for this check paperclipped here in this notebook, but I don't intend to tell my family all the sordid details. I don't want their sadness and sympathy to stalk the remaining months of my pregnancy. Yes, I am coming home pregnant, but I am also arriving with the means to help in a way I never dreamed possible. This is where I need to be at this time. This is where my people are. Okay, baby girl or baby boy, let's get moving. We have a joyful homecoming to get to.*

With that, she hoisted up her backpack and excitedly walked the very familiar road leading her home.

Chapter 17

Special Delivery

Edith had barely set foot in the front yard when she heard an electrifying squeal. "Mama, come quick! Edith's home! Edith's here! Where's Papa? Oh, come quick!" It took Edith a moment to realize the squeal was coming from her now much taller sister, Angie, now thirteen. "Oh, Edith! You're back! I've missed you, really missed you," Angie said, rushing into Edith's open arms. "You feel different. Oh my goodness! Are you pregnant? Are you having a baby?" Liezel came rushing out of the house with tears of joy in her eyes. "Edith, it's you! What a wonderful surprise. I see you have another surprise for us. You're having a baby! How exciting!" Mama said with warmth. There was not the slightest look of disappointment or dismay in Mama's eyes.

Their embrace was long and full of happy tears. "Yes, I'm finally home!" Edith exclaimed as they began to untangle from one another. "Come in, Edith, you need to sit and rest. I'll fix you a cool drink." As Mama fussed with the fruit and ice, Edith's eyes began soaking in all the little details she had never found to be important, like the copper kettle still occupying the back burner on the stove, the wooden cross aging over the sink, and the electric wall clock that buzzed a little on its hook near the dining table. It still buzzed a little. It was good to be home.

Papa came in from the fields and all the younger siblings gathered with great excitement. There was plenty of family news to catch up on. Betsy had a job cleaning the high school and now she and Little Carlos had their own place. Her brother Albert had gotten a good job driving truck, delivering rice from the provinces to the city. He was now living in an apartment in Tacloban. "He's got a girlfriend, too," Angie piped up, happy to have some news the others hadn't already told.

The two youngest siblings didn't remember her, not even José, four, to whom she had read bedtime stories every night before she left. "Who said, 'the sky is falling, the sky is falling?'" Edith asked, looking directly at José. There was an instant spark of recognition. "Chicken Little!" he whooped and glommed onto her leg. Yes, Edith was home again.

"Tell us about the baby," Angie begged. "Are you getting married? Can I be in the wedding?"

"Hmmmm, well, now, you see," Edith hemmed and hawed, giving herself more time to think. The room was all ears. "No, I'm not getting married, Angie, it didn't work out. I decided not to choose him. When I got to know him better I realized he was not right for me, or for our family. I know it was kind of late to figure all this out but better late than never," Edith faked the news with a song in her voice. Nobody needed to know the whole story.

"Was he a monster?" Angie wanted to know.

"Yep, he was a monster," Edith agreed, "but he sure was a handsome one." She left it at that.

It didn't take Edith long to know that coming home was the best decision she'd made in quite some time. She quickly fell into the groove of her family's daily life and as her belly grew, so did the family's level of anticipation and excitement about the baby's imminent arrival.

"Mama," Edith cried out one evening just after supper. "I think it's time. You better call Ana." Ana Lopez was still in the midwifery business and was quite proud of her scoresheet of delivering more than half the town's babies over the years. She was especially proud to deliver babies for the now grownup women she had delivered years earlier. And she still had the habit of making predictions about the future of each and every newborn.

"Edith," Ana said when she arrived breathlessly a short time later, "I hope this baby of yours isn't going to be quite as slithery as you were. The way you flew out of your mama's womb and tried to wriggle out of my grasp. I told your mama that you were going to be full of surprises. From what I hear, you did not disappoint!"

Edith wanted to smile at Ana's memory, but instead of a smile, she let out one long, last, wretched "Arrrrrg." Moments later, Ana settled a baby girl on Edith's chest. "What will you name this beautiful child?" Ana wanted to know.

"I'm going to name her Luna."

"Luna. Such a beautiful name, Edith. She is destined to light up your darkest days. You wait and see," Ana predicted.

Chapter 18

Reversal of Fortune

Luna was the apple of her lolo's eye, perhaps it was because grandfatherhood was so much easier and a lot more fun than parenthood. Every minute Carlos wasn't working, he'd carry his infant granddaughter through his garden singing: "Oats, peas, beans and barley grow / Oats, peas, beans and barley grow / Can you or I or anyone know / How oats, peas, beans and barley grow?"

Oats, peas, beans soon became their secret code for going to the garden.

By the time Luna was almost two she had become a slow and fussy eater. The rice couldn't touch the mango and the mango couldn't touch the egg. Carlos solved that little problem by starting his "Oats, Peas, Beans and Barley" song as he put his coffee mug into the sink. That was the clue he was going to the garden. "Me. Me. Me," she'd cry out, stuffing everything into her mouth and raising her arms to be lifted. He'd pluck his granddaughter from her highchair and off they'd go into the garden to see what new life had occurred since the day before. Carlos took great delight in teaching Luna all the things he learned about the earth the hard way while tending his patch with loving care and she became an avid student of his horticulture lessons.

"Here's how to plant the sweet potatoes," he'd say, handing Luna the smallest trowel. She'd scrape the earth alongside him as he dug his own trowel deeper into the earth.

Edith loved to watch the two from the bedroom window as she was getting ready for work. Her part time job at the library allowed her to continue supporting the family. She couldn't imagine herself in a better life than this. Contrary to what she once believed, she found that "living her mother's life" suited her. She could live like this forever.

But forever never lasts that long. This morning seemed routine as usual. Breakfast dishes had been cleared. Luna had been lifted from her highchair. Lolo had taken Luna by the hand and they had gone off into the garden. The last time Edith looked out the window all was well.

"Mama! Mama!" she heard her toddler crying from the bottom of the stairs. "Mama! Come fast!"

Edith flew down the stairs. The child tugged on Edith's skirt leading to the garden. "Lolo! Lolo!" Luna was crying. Edith found her father, white as a sheet, sitting on the ground with his back against the mango tree holding his chest.

"I'm alright. I'm fine. Just out of breath," he said on seeing the fear on both of their faces. "Really, I'm fine," he added, convincing no one, not even himself. Edith helped him to his feet and he was grateful for her shoulder as they made their way to the front room. Carlos was just happy to be in the house and out of the sun but Edith paced the room. Back and forth, back and forth she trekked thinking of a plan and wishing her mother was home.

"Papa, you've got to be checked out," she was saying.

"I'm all right. I just need to rest a bit."

"No, Papa, you need to be checked. Have you seen your doctor lately?"

Carlos had closed his eyes pretending to nap.

"Papa!" Edith said loudly, startling him. "Where's your doctor's number? I need to call him."

Carlos gave up and pointed to the drawer in the kitchen where papers were kept.

By the time Liezel returned, a plan had been made. Papa would go to town this very afternoon and get checked. Their neighbor, Daniel, was coming over with a car and would drive them. Because Liezel was now beside herself with anxiety, it was decided she'd stay home with Luna and the other young ones and Edith would be her father's advocate.

Carlos and Edith had two different versions of how well the doctor visit went. Carlos was happy. His state-run health care insurance kicked in which meant he didn't have to pay a peso. "Free health care," he beamed as they left the office.

"You know you have to go to the hospital tomorrow and get some tests, right, Papa? Dr. Mendez was concerned when he listened to your heart," she said.

"Yes, and that'll be free, too," he continued in a happy mood. "I'm glad to be checked out and I'm sure I'm alright. I feel good."

Dr. Mendez was not as optimistic as Carlos' interpretation of how the visit went. Edith was concerned.

"It was free!" Carlos boasted to Liezel as he explained the visit.

"Papa needs more tests," Edith added, "and he has to go to the hospital for them. They are scheduled for tomorrow," she informed her mother. "Daniel volunteered again to drive us. Do you want to go with him," she added, "or should I?"

"You're so much better at this," Liezel admitted.

"And the tests are free, too," Carlos chimed in, not at all concerned about results.

The results of Carlos' free state health care tests threw the family into a maelstrom. He needed a bypass, and bypass surgery certainly wasn't free. PhilHealth might cover half of it, if they were lucky. Even at half, nearly $4,000, it was well out of the family's reach. And as if that news wasn't bad enough, the hospitals in the provinces were not equipped for bypass surgery. It had to be done in Manila and Manila was out of the question.

It seemed that Carlos' days would soon run out. Liezel could not keep the tears from running down her cheeks. Luna couldn't understand why Lolo wouldn't garden. The family set about doing everything for Carlos and he felt like a total failure.

"Do you remember, Papa," Edith reminisced one evening, "that first day when you took me to school. I was five and although I pretended to be brave, I was as scared as a kid could be. I probably would have chickened out if you hadn't taken my hand in your big, strong, all-powerful mitt. With my small hand all wrapped up in yours, I became as brave and strong as you. I'll never forget that feeling."

Carlos nodded. It was just as momentous a day for him. No member of the Santos family had ever been as determined as she to get an education, and he remembered that moment distinctly and how proud of her he felt.

"Well," she said, "I'm about to return the favor."

Her decision to return the favor was not made on the spur of the moment. She had been mulling it all day. She would be trading her and Luna's financial security, the one she had secreted away, the one Mr. Wang had made possible, for the chance her father would survive a heart operation, one that would occur in Manila.

"What are you talking about?" Mama said. "There's no way Papa can take a twenty-two-hour bus trip to Manila. He hasn't the strength and we haven't the mon ..." she began. Edith quickly and quietly interrupted, "Mama, trust me. There's a way. I have savings." Before Liezel could start bombarding her with questions and doubts, Edith laid out her plan to the family. When those in the room heard her explain it, they rushed to embrace her. Edith had given them hope. Her safety net for Luna had become a life saver for Papa. In that moment these words crossed her mind: *God help me.*

It wasn't until later that evening, when Papa, the children and

Luna were sound asleep, that Edith found her mother in the kitchen, crying softly and praying aloud. "God help us, please God help us. Edith's heart is in the right place, but her senses are missing. What is she thinking? Oh God, oh dear God."

"Mama, we need to talk," Edith said quietly, startling Liezel right out of her conversation with God. Edith had planned never to tell anyone about her rape, but once she began, she left no detail unsaid. The telling was surprisingly cathartic for Edith. For Liezel it was incredibly saddening. Then it became incredibly guilt-inducing. "Oh, Edith, you paid such a high price for that money, and it belongs to you and Luna for your future success," Mama said through tears.

"The future never comes, Mama, we only have today," Edith said, looking deep into her mother's eyes. "And today I want to keep my papa alive. The money means nothing if he is no longer in our lives. It's settled. Papa is going to Manila and I'm going to take him. I have plane tickets already bought. Please, let's never speak of this again. It's our secret, one I never wanted to share with you, but am happy I did. This family is my world."

No other words were spoken, but their long tearful embrace said everything about their special mother-daughter bond.

Within the week all the arrangements had been made. Edith had been to the bank and her $3,000 check was now on a debit card. Carlos clutched a small duffle as he told the family not to worry, he'd be back in a week. The atmosphere in the room was cautiously jubilant as his well-wishers gathered for the send-off. No tears were shed until Luna ran to Carlos' leg and giving it a desperate squeeze, said, "I take care of our Os, Ps, Bees, Lolo, like you show me." At that moment everyone lost it and Edith hurriedly ushered her father out the door for their ride to the airport, not wanting her daughter to see her tears.

The operation was a great success. Doctors said Carlos would be as good as new, and in a few days, he'd be discharged directly to rehab. Even with PhilHealth paying most of the cost of it, rehab was definitely out of the question; recovery would have to happen at home. When Carlos' nurses learned he'd be going directly home they took Edith aside and gave her copious notes on how she should assist his recovery from home. As she watched their kind faces and listened to their spirited advice, she reminded herself of her teenage dream, the one she had dared to tell a perfect stranger on that bus to Manila nearly five years ago. "I want to be a nurse," she had said confidently to Michael Peters and, what had amazed her at the time, is that he seemed to believe she would make it happen. Just saying this secret out loud made the dream seem plausible. She had devoted a page in her notebook about her dream to become a nurse, but that was then.

Papa would be released in two days, on Monday. Her father was in good spirits on Saturday and insisted she take the day to go visit her former roommates. She hadn't called or written Lucy and Analyn since she left Manila. A short bus ride later she was knocking at the door of her old apartment. The young woman who opened it to her said Analyn no longer lived there but Lucy did. "Lucy," she called, "someone to see you."

The two realized what a mistake it had been in not keeping in touch. They fell into each other's arms and hugged and rocked in the happiness of finding something that had been long lost. There was a lot of sharing to do: pictures of Luna, news of her father's surgery, Lucy's new job, Analyn's marriage, Jun's rise to vice president of the Wang family business. Finally, they settled down to where they could explain all these highlights with more detail and less drama. At last Edith asked the one question that had been on her mind ever since she spent all her savings on her father's survival. "Have you heard anything more from Lyka?"

"Lyka!" sang Lucy, joyfully remembering another long lost friend. "No, as a matter of fact," she continued with a bewildering look on her brow, "just that one letter. You were here when it came. The one that said she had arrived in Lebanon, loved her new job, and was making so much more money there than here in

Chin's garment factory.

"I suppose she got busy with her new position," she continued. "She's probably still there or she would have contacted us again. We were pretty close in those days. Kinda like you and me."

"Hmmm," pondered Edith.

"Why do you ask? I didn't think you ever met Lyka."

"Just curious," replied Edith.

Chapter 19

Too Good to Be True

Edith had never been so anxious in her life. She had to get her papa home safely. This was no simple task. Not only did he need a wheelchair from the hospital to Lucy's car but from the car to the airport and the airport to the plane. There was a lot to maneuver in this process and he was as weak as a sick puppy. She tried not to worry about all the 'what ifs' that could go wrong. As Papa leaned his head onto her shoulder during the flight, she thumbed through the stack of notes the nurses had given her for his at-home care. Like it or not, she'd be his nurse. *I should have been more careful in what I wished for,* she caught herself thinking. So far though, the notes were very clear. *I can do this.*

When the plane landed in Tacloban the whole family and several neighbors were at the gate and Edith immediately stopped worrying; the burden was suddenly shared.

"Did you look after Lolo's garden while we were gone?" was the first thing Edith said to Luna on her return as the toddler ran into her arms. "Did you water his sweet potatoes? You know, you're going to be in charge of them for a while until Lolo gets strong again."

"Yes, I water them every day with Lolo's water can," she answered, throwing her shoulders back with pride. "And I sing

Lolo's song, too."

I was only gone for only ten days, Edith mused. *She was so babyish when I left and now this: so sure of herself. I didn't see that coming. It's like watching green beans pop out of the ground. So much happens in just one day."*

Fortunately, Edith's library job was only part time. She could administer to her papa as her notes dictated and leave some of the simpler duties to her mother while she was gone. It was obvious her mother had neither the resolve nor the courage of a nurse. Liezel worried constantly about Carlos, thinking he'd break if she even dared to fluff his pillow. She only understood one way to mend a broken heart, and that was to make more soup.

Carlos was shuffling around the house in just a few days. Liezel told everyone who stopped by that it was her soup that made the difference. Edith smiled every time she heard her mother take the credit.

Carlos was out in his garden within a few weeks. He spoke to his plants. "What are you doing?" he scolded them. "I was counting on you to pull your own weight while I was gone. Instead, look at you, still in bud when you should be in flower. And you, Sweet Potato, did you forget that you are the pride of Palo? Do I have to stand here every minute to get you to perform?" He sighed, turned away, and went in for a nap.

It was true. The garden, which supported them financially, was languishing and Carlos didn't have the strength to fix all the problems he saw happening. Luna filled her water can and dutifully sprinkled the first few plants before she tired of the job. She'd rather sing the O's song and sit on Lolo's knee while he talked to his garden. Her being in the garden with him was his only consolation. The family was falling behind, way behind. It was becoming clear that something had to be done.

At first, all ten of the Santos siblings (twelve, if you count Luna and Little Carlos) agreed to arrange their schedules so they could work Papa's garden and get it back to being the pride of

Palo. Since Betsy's job started at 4 p.m., she'd come mornings dragging a cranky, unwilling Little Carlos with her. Edith changed her part-time schedule so she could work mornings with Betsy. Albert was on the road all week so he could only come weekends, which he did for a while. Of the other seven, some were in high school and could only work early before school started and the littlest ones would work after school but they couldn't tell an edible sprout from a mean-spirited weed and the edibles became more and more scarce under their guesses.

It became apparent that Papa was the only one who could make this patch of stubborn plants behave like they were 'Proven Winners.'

"They only grow for you, Papa," Betsy dared to notice. "The plants don't seem to like us so much, but your plants want to jump right out of the ground to perform for you. These past few months I've seen what we grow with all of us working day and night. Our veggies are skinny and frail and drab. Yours were always plump and hearty, juicy and colorful. How did we not know you are the best farmer in Palo? Even when the people at market would ask specifically if this yam or those beans or these mangoes were 'grown by Carlos' and make us swear we were telling the truth, I still didn't realize that you are the best!"

Carlos laughed. "You should have asked. I would have told you." Then, as his smile faded he said, "And I have the best family in all of Leyte. Seriously."

The family managed to keep this crazy schedule up for another half year. Albert finally said he needed weekends free or his girlfriend would leave him, Betsy said Little Carlos was off a predictable schedule and was getting out of hand. Angie's grades were slipping. It just wasn't working.

Edith felt the pressure. Sure, Papa was alive and getting stronger every day, but what good was it if they all starved to death. She needed a better job.

While one door was closing on her, another one was opening.

Edith noticed a flier that had just been posted on the bulletin board in her library: Do you like to travel? Does an expense-paid trip to a foreign country intrigue you? Are you interested in working overseas at a high-paying job? If you answered yes to any of these questions, you owe it to yourself to learn more about a fantastic opportunity that awaits you. No qualifications necessary, anyone can apply.

The flier went on to say that a Mr. Arno was coming down from Manila to give talks throughout the Visayas about high paying jobs for women overseas. He'd be in Palo on Wednesday in the library community room and everyone was welcome to attend, especially women.

"Lyka!" A bell went off in Edith's head. "That must be the kind of job she took." Edith was trying to recall the details of Lyka's letter to her roommates. She remembered Lyka writing that she was making exceptional money, living in a beautiful home in Beirut, and loving the family who had employed her. Then there was that talkative woman, Sue, on the plane who bragged that her niece had a great job in Syria, "making lots of money and loving her job as an au pair where she gets to travel quite a bit."

The idea of travel had intrigued Edith since she was five. That's when two backpacking college girls from Berkeley showed up at their door looking for directions. As if it were yesterday, she clearly recalled the impression they made on her. She wanted a backpack just like they had, and she wanted to travel to Berkeley when she grew up. The girls had told her that she would love it.

So far, all she had attained was the backpack.

"I might as well go and hear what he has to say," she thought as she re-read the notice. "An expense-paid trip overseas? A well-paying job? It's probably too good to be true, but if the money is as good as the flier promises, I need to learn more. I should at least know what's out there," she concluded, more determined than ever to hear the spiel.

That night she confided in her notebook that if she didn't have Luna to think about, she would be the first to jump at the chance to travel and make good money. She dreamily continued writing. *What an opportunity for those free enough to go on such an adventure. If only I had known about this before going to Manila. I could have gone overseas instead! And I'd be back by now and I'd be self-sufficient. I'll tell you what I'm going to do. I'm going to go to that meeting on Wednesday and learn about the opportunities. Perhaps there'll be a time in my future when I can explore the world beyond these islands.* She closed the notebook and slipped under her covers imagining other places beyond the Philippines.

"Mama," said Luna, "I don't like rice and beans anymore. I want something else."

"And what would you want if you could have anything?" Edith asked.

"Chicken!" said Luna joyfully, "I want chicken, like we used to have."

"I know, honey," Edith answered ruefully, trying to find a plausible explanation a two-year-old could understand. "When Papa gets healthy again and can sing his songs to his vegetables and fruits, the garden will be prosperous again. Then we will have lots of money for chicken, but now all we have is rice and beans. Eat your rice and beans."

"No!" defied Luna.

"Then you'll go hungry tonight, my love," her mother added and meant it, but Edith still felt guilty. It was true the variety of foods the family used to enjoy had been reduced to the basics. Everyone, except a two-year-old, could keep their complaints to themselves because there was no alternative. Their struggles were becoming dire.

Chapter 20

Alluring, Lying Sales Pitch

On Wednesday, Edith went to the meeting. About fifteen people had already found seats, mostly toward the back of the room. They were somber. *Why do I get this sense of hopelessness?* she mused as she scanned their faces before choosing a seat toward the front. *Maybe they're scared. But why? This opportunity could be the most exciting thing that has happened to us, ever.*

Just then Mr. Arno burst through the door with an aura that seemed bigger than God's. "Good afternoon, ladies!" he sang out, "and you, too, sir" to the only man in the room. "Come closer so you can see all the gorgeous photos I have to show you of my overseas opportunities. One of these gorgeous homes, in fact, might even become where your next adventure takes you." The group shuffled toward the front and started looking at the photos. They were, as he said, beautiful homes. Trust began building.

"Some of you are here for the adventure of travel," he was saying, knowing full well that most of them were not here for the adventure of travel, but out of desperation. "And some of you are here for the money, I mean, job opportunity." He scanned the group and guessed that he'd get a commitment out of most of the attendees, maybe all of them, except, perhaps, the chick with the attitude in the front row.

"You are about to make $200 a month," he went on. "You will live in a house like one of my photos, you will have Sundays free to explore your new city, your airfare will be paid for, all your meals are included. Some of you will even have a car at your disposal. In addition, you will learn a new trade in high-end domestic arts. When you return to the Philippines at the end of your contract you will be highly employable here."

The faces in the room began to brighten. "Any questions?" he was saying.

Edith spoke up. "Tell us about the contract."

"Of course. You'll be required to sign a two-year contract, and I can assure you, those two years will fly by. My agency pays your airfare, so there'll be no cost to you. Then, when you arrive in one of the beautiful Gulf States, an agency representative will pick you up at the airport and take you to your assignment. It will be a family who is eager to accept you. In fact, they have probably been waiting quite a while since we try to find good matches between you and the family that will employ you."

At this point Arno handed everyone the contract they would be signing. "This is your contract, take it home, read it carefully and talk this opportunity over with loved ones. I'm in Palo until tomorrow afternoon. If your decision is YES, sign your copy and return it to me tomorrow here in the library."

Edith started perusing her contract then noticed the others had only given it a quick glance before folding it carefully and tucking it into a pocket or purse. The thought that the others might be illiterate crossed her mind, startling her. She decided to speak up and ask a few more questions, hoping those in the room who might not be able to read would get a little more information before they left for home.

"Yes?" he said, recognizing the woman with the question.

"What if the assignment we get is not a good fit?" asked Edith. "What options do we have then?"

"No problem," he answered, his voice smooth as silk.

"Although rare, it sometimes occurs. In that case all you need to do is make an appointment with your overseas agent and describe the issue. If he cannot resolve the problem, he will find a different assignment so you can fulfill your contract and get all the wages that are due you."

"But what if we are truly unhappy, or we are just too home-sick and cannot perform well, perhaps have become depressed? What then? Can we break our contract without penalty?" she asked as the others sat up straight to pay closer attention.

"It's possible to break a contract if circumstances become dire," he said slowly, wondering if this woman might be a plant from one of those organizations that go around trying to label his business as a domestic slave trade. "After all, our overseas clients are reasonable people who understand humanity. They care very much about your happiness. They want you to feel that you are actually a member of their family, loved as one of their own. In fact, most of the people I send overseas extend their contract for another year, sometimes even longer. And that's an option for you as well. However, if you really need to return to the Philip-pines without fulfilling your commitment, there may be a loss of some of your wages and, of course, you will be responsible for getting yourself back to the Philippines."

"Speaking of wages, exactly how do we get paid?" Edith con-tinued her questioning.

"If you want to send money back to your family on a regular basis, you can ask to be paid monthly," he explained. "However, if you let your wages accumulate until your contract is up, you will be earning interest on your wages, and your final take-home will be well beyond your expectations, or," he said, shrugging off the question because of its irrelevance to him, "you can work out some other payment arrangement with your employer. It's up to you."

"How many of your clients break this contract?" Edith asked as the others shook their heads in the affirmative.

"I've been sending good Filipino employees to my overseas agency for five years now," he said, "and I can honestly tell you, no one has broken his or her contract. It just doesn't happen," he bragged.

By now the attendees had warmed up to Mr. Arno. He seemed upfront with all his answers and, besides, he was a Filipino like themselves. He wouldn't lie.

"Go home and talk it over with your families," Arno was saying in conclusion. "Think over all the things I've explained and decide with your loved ones if this overseas employment is for you. Remember, your salary will be $200 a month. Where can you make that much here in the Visayas? I'll be here tomorrow from noon to three for those who want to sign up. I'll explain getting a passport and all the other inconsequential details at the time of your signing. You don't want to miss such an opportunity!"

They all clapped, including Edith.

Notebook! Help! I'm really confused! she wrote that evening. *Mr. Arno makes a lot of sense. Two years do go by quickly. $200 a month! There's no way I can earn that much money here. And if I send my wages home on the monthly basis, my family will actually thrive. But what about Luna???? Can I leave her for two whole years? She'll be four when I return. What should I do? I better talk to Mama about it.*

Liezel and Edith sat up well past midnight weighing the pros and cons. There were so many cons and only one pro. One minute they were resolute to stay the course, the next minute they recognized there was only one solution to saving the homestead. They cried. They prayed. They hugged. They agreed. "It's only for two years," Edith said.

"I'll make sure Luna never forgets you," her mama assured.

Chapter 21

Flying into Turbulent Fate

Mr. Arno was quite surprised the following day when Edith was the first to show up with her signed contract. He had been concerned when Edith had asked such intelligent questions and was afraid she might have talked herself, and others, into not signing up. "Miss Santos," he said jovially, "you have made a wise decision. I'll make sure you get employed in one of the best homes and get a job you love doing," he said, knowing full well once a new recruit boarded the plane to Syria, he had absolutely no say in her fate. Had he a soul, he might have felt guilty about that false promise, but he was more interested in securing his commission than in telling the truth.

By 3 p.m., four more women had arrived, signed contracts in hand. "I just know you are all in for the experience of a lifetime," Mr. Arno enthused. "Congratulations for taking this step toward your future prosperity! Here's what happens next." Mr. Arno handed each recruit a paper with details about the trip to Syria. "Do you all have passports?" he asked. No one nodded. "Ah, no matter. I have passport applications you can fill out now, and my agency will expedite them. The Filipino government is anxious to encourage young women like yourselves to better your situations and return home with solid skills. You will have your passports in plenty of time for your flight a week from today."

"We're leaving in a week?" Edith exclaimed, startled. She had hoped she'd have more time to get packed and say her goodbyes. On the other hand, she had a growing sense of excitement about this new adventure.

"We're leaving in a week!" she repeated excitedly to her mother when she got home.

That week went by in a flash. Saying goodbye to Luna was one of the most difficult things Edith had ever done. "Mama, will you be back for my birthday?" Luna implored. "If you go away, who will read me stories? Who will brush my hair? Will you be back in twenty-eleven days?" Luna was trying to process what her mother's absence would mean. "Mama, I want to go with you. I don't want to miss you. Stay here, please don't go away," she begged as tears fell. Sensing she hadn't achieved her goal, Luna drew a heartbreaking conclusion. "Did I do something wrong, Mama? Don't you love me anymore?"

Before Edith could even begin to assemble the words her daughter needed to hear, Lolo hurried into the room and in the most enthusiastic and robust voice he had used in quite some time, he spun her around and said, "Luna, of course your mother loves you. In fact, she loves you so much that she is going to do something that will make your life better. We have our own job to do while she is away, Luna. We must tend our garden to make sure your mama sees the most gorgeous veggies when she returns. So, little one, let's not fret any more. We have work to do," he said enthusiastically as he transported the mollified Luna to the garden.

At the Manila Ninoy Aquino International Airport, Mr. Arno handed out the hot-off-the-press passports to the five Palo recruits. While waiting for the flight to Syria to board, Mr. Arno scanned the crowd anxiously. As soon as he spotted his fellow recruiters, he shepherded his five women to join the large group standing off to the side. "Ah, there you are!" he said to the three other recruiters surrounded by a homogenous group of young Filipina women. "Come, ladies," he said motioning to his five recruits. "Come meet your fellow adventurers."

Her four travel companions wandered off toward the group, but Edith was on her knees trying to retrieve her pen that had escaped from her backpack and rolled under the seat. The recruiters standing nearby couldn't see her.

"So, Pedro, how many did you get?" Mr. Arno was asking. Edith heard a man respond "Only four" before lowering his voice and continuing. "I would have won this week if the other six girls weren't such homely fatties," he whined, eliciting laughs from the other agents. "Well, it looks like I won the bonus!" another voice said, "I've brought twelve." Mr. Arno sounded impressed when he said, "How did you manage to get that many, Angelo? That's quite a few!"

"All it took was a bit of imagination and exaggeration," the recruiter said laughing. With that, the men moved away.

Edith was able to guess that the men were talking about their number of recruits and was surprised to learn recruiters earned bonuses for high numbers. She was even more surprised to discover that recruiters rejected 'homely fatties,' a fact that was apparent as she looked at her traveling companions, mostly all thin, good-looking women. *Syrians must be very fussy*, Edith thought to herself. *I can hardly wait to see the beautiful home and awesome position Mr. Arno has selected for me.* At the time, it never occurred to Edith that the good-old-boys' backslapping and hee-hawing spoke of the human heist they'd just pulled off.

When it was time to board, the recruiters gathered their recruits for last minute instructions, and to ensure that every last one of them entered the jetway. "We have made arrangements with the airline," Mr. Arno told his five. "This entire group will be sitting together in assigned seats at the back of the plane." Ostensibly, he was indicating this would be a great opportunity for the girls to meet and get to know each other. But the true motive behind this arrangement was to avoid any chance of other passengers telling negative stories about life in Syria.

Edith found herself assigned to a middle seat for the 5,300-mile plane trip to Damascus. At the window sat a girl about her age with strikingly long black hair and an infectious laugh. The aisle seat was occupied by a quiet woman in her 30s who looked as anxious and frightened as Edith had been on her first flight. "Hi, I'm Edith," she said to the worried woman during the pre-flight safety announcements.

"We might need life jackets? Is there really a chance we'll end up in the South China Sea? I can't swim. Oh my God, this is awful," the worried woman exclaimed with heightened fear.

"I didn't get your name," Edith said. "Ramona? Nice to meet you, Ramona. Don't worry, you'll be fine. Do you want to read this book I brought? It will take your mind off flying. Here," Edith said, handing over her favorite novel.

Then Edith turned her attention to her long-haired companion gazing excitedly out the window. "You have such beautiful hair," Edith said to get her attention. "I'm Edith from Palo and I just can't help wondering if it's weird always having to sit on your hair."

The girl broke out into raucous laughter. "Well, it does keep my butt warm on cold days," she choked out between laughs. This flippant response made Edith giggle. "I'm Jasmine from Palompon. Nice to meet you," Jasmine said and then continued, saying, "The only downside to my long hair is when I have to use the bathroom. Then I pull it all to the front where it keeps my belly warm. I really hate when I miscalculate."

For the next hour of the eleven-hour flight, Jasmine and Edith talked hair. Jasmine claimed never to have had a hair cut and that it takes an hour every day to brush and untangle her bed hair. She added she might cut it a bit when it reaches her knees, but that would be like cutting off an arm. "This hair sets me apart. It gets me lots of attention and I wouldn't be me without it," Jasmine admitted. "I know that sounds crazy, but that's just who I am."

"I kinda like who you are," Edith declared.

Besides loving her hair, Jasmine loved to talk. She said she couldn't wait to see where she'd be working. "My recruiter took a shine to me, I think, or maybe to my shiny hair. Ha ha! I don't know. Ha ha! Anyway, he took me aside and told me he had selected me to work for one of the best families in Damascus. There is an opening for a housekeeper there and I hear that's one of the top jobs you can get. It involves a lot of scheduling, supervising, and making sure the household runs smoothly. I'm really good at organizing and scheduling. I hope and pray I get that position." *Gosh, all Syrian positions must be wonderful*, Edith thought. At the time, it never occurred to her that it was a strange coincidence that Mr. Arno had also promised her an exceptional placement as a housekeeper.

Jasmine never stopped stunning Edith with stories of her childhood, her family, the boys she left behind. "You call this food?" Jasmine exclaimed when the stewardess handed a tray of plastic-wrapped dinner to her. "Sorry! Ever since I learned to cook, I have gotten really fussy about what I eat. I'm a pretty great cook, if I do say so myself," she bragged.

Edith was soon to learn that as the oldest child in the family, Jasmine began her cooking lessons tied to her mother's apron at the age of six. "Mama always said, 'A woman's job is in the kitchen,' and usually added that it's never too early to learn how to please a man," Jasmine said. "Mama died when I was twelve, and I became the family's 'woman in the kitchen.' My three brothers would scoff anytime I prepared something new. But trying new recipes became my favorite pleasure. I figured if I had to cook, I may as well enjoy it. I swear my brothers would have eaten dog poop for dinner if I didn't cook. They were at that hungry age," Jasmine relayed, laughing. "Now, this," she said, pointing at her tray, "this looks exactly like plastic-wrapped, processed dog poop. Tastes like it too," she said after taking a bite of the sausage. Edith remained mesmerized by her new friend.

Shortly after the trays had been collected, Jasmine turned to Edith with another story to share, but before she got started, she let out a burp loud enough to be heard five rows away. "Told ya," she said, "dog shit makes me sick" before hurrying off to the rest-room. Jasmine looked pale and had really bad breath when she returned. She looked at Edith and said, "Oh, splash."

"What are you talking about? Splash what?" Edith asked.

"Oh, it's just a silly word our family used to say when we didn't want to talk about something. Since we were babies, my mama always told us that 'shut up' is a bad word. So if one of us was about to spill a sibling's secret, if the other said "Oh, splash," it meant if you know what's good for you, you'll shut up. Or if the dinner table got too rowdy, a quick "Oh, splash" from my mama would instantly quiet us down. Old habits die hard. Guess that's why I blurted out "Oh, splash" to you when I sat back down. I did not want you to ask if I just vomit-bombed the rest-room. Which I just did, by the way. But don't tell anyone." Despite the bad breath, Jasmine's infectious laugh was catching and Edith found herself doubling over in giggles.

The hours flew by. Slowly but surely the chatter in the back of the plane died down as night fell and the recruits nodded off.

Some time later, Edith was nudged awake. Jasmine was talk-ing excitedly. "Wake up, Edith, wake up. We're getting ready to land. We made it! Woo-ee! I have the feeling I'm going to get the housekeeping job and live in an expensive beautiful home, and I hope you find yourself in a happy place too. I'm going to miss you. It would be awesome if we end up sort of close to each other and we can stay friends. Woo-ee! The next two years are going to fly by so fast."

Edith totally agreed. At the time, it never occurred to her that in less than twenty-four hours she'd be beginning the longest years of her life.

Part 2

Decisions & Consequences

"It's always impossible until it is done."
— Nelson Mandela

Chapter 22

Off to a Bad Start

"Grab your stuff and follow me," Mr. Habib barked as he gathered the new Filipina arrivals in the concourse of the Damascus airport. There he was joined by six other agents whose job it was to deliver the new recruits to their various assignments. "We need to take your passports to be processed," Mr. Habib ordered. When this task was completed, the passports were shoved into the pockets of the various agents. "Hey!" yelled Edith, getting in Mr. Habib's face, "that's mine! I need that back!"

Mr. Habib rudely told her to "shut the hell up, troublemaker" in Arabic, to the laughter of the other Syrian agents. Then he smiled at Edith and explained in English she'd get her passport back once she arrived at her new home.

Now that the passports were safely in his possession, Mr. Habib was barking again. "You!" he said pointing to Edith and two other Filipinas. "You ladies come with me," he said as he led them to the parking lot. "I'll be taking you directly to your new assignments," he said in a softened tone. Edith was surprised when she looked at the neighborhoods they were driving through and even more surprised when he dropped one of the girls off in front of an aging apartment building. "I'll be right back," he said to the remaining two girls, and in Arabic, he said to the driver,

"Keep an eye on them, especially the prettier one. She looks like she would like to escape already," eliciting chuckles from the younger man.

The next stop was a few blocks away. Mr. Habib elbowed a nervous girl into a boxy, charmless building even less appealing than the first.

Now they were enroute to a neighborhood just outside the Old City. The agent, glad to have his contract of delivering the domestic workers to his clients almost fulfilled, began telling Edith in English how lucky she was to be placed in one of the nicest neighborhoods in Damascus. As he drove down the narrow streets, horns honking, Edith gawked at buildings the likes of which she had never seen. They exuded antiquity, nothing at all like the landscape of the sprawling city of Manila and certainly not peaceful and pastoral like home. People everywhere. Bars everywhere. Shops everywhere. Nondescript buildings everywhere.

The car stopped. They had arrived. Edith was unhinged by her first impression. Nothing on this street looked anything like the photos of palatial homes Mr. Arno had shown at his seminar. *Where are the houses?* she wondered. *Just ugly old buildings. Does everyone live in old apartments?*

No trees lined the street. No front door flower pots filled with begonias welcomed passersby. A labyrinth of overhead wires said electricity had haphazardly come to this ancient place. Was this a neighborhood of residents who could afford hired help from overseas? It certainly didn't look it.

She followed him inside and up a set of chipped and well-worn marble stairs where many feet had gone before. Her suitcase hit each riser with a racket that echoed throughout the stairwell. He finally stopped in front of apartment 2A.

Mr. Habib banged loudly on the knocker. The door opened.

"This is yours," he said, pointing his thumb behind himself at Edith, while addressing the round woman dressed entirely in black except for a highly starched white peter-pan collar, which served to accentuate her pumpkin-shaped head.

"Is madam home?" he asked in Arabic.

Without saying a word, the woman slowly ran her exceptionally dark eyes up and down Edith's body, expressionless, exposing Edith to anxieties she thought she had overcome years ago. The woman nodded, opened the door wider and led the pair into a small room that looked like a study. She directed them to enter with merely a nod then disappeared into other parts of this spacious apartment.

While they waited for madam, Habib pulled a business card from his pocket and handed it to Edith. "I'm obligated to give you this information," he told her. "I don't expect to hear from you. Ever," he added. "This is the number of the agency. If there's trouble ..." he said, his voice trailing off. She took the card. It was in Arabic, of course.

"My passport," Edith said. "I want it now."

"We'll see what madam says about that. It's customary that your employer maintains it in safe keeping for you. It would be most difficult for you to return home to the Philippines if it should get lost."

Just then a very handsome Mohammad Saleeb, the master of the house, entered the room. He and the agent smiled warmly and spoke for a while in Arabic. Every once in a while, they both turned and looked at Edith. At times she felt as if she was being inspected, as one might inspect a puppy in a pound or mangos at the market. At last Mr. Saleeb handed the agent the remainder of the $3,000 he had paid for this domestic worker's two-year contract. With the transaction over, the agent handed Mr. Saleeb Edith's passport, then bowed several times before backing out of the apartment. The passport quickly slipped into Mr. Saleeb's pocket.

The two who remained were cautiously evaluating each other. First impressions mattered. Mr. Saleeb looked at Edith admiringly as if he had just bought something he had always wanted. Edith was skeptical, but since there was no going back at this point, she smiled optimistically and waited.

In that awkward moment before either could think of how to begin, Mrs. Saleeb entered the room. "Welcome," she said curtly, "you must be our new cleaning lady." *Cleaning lady?*

"Oh," Edith spoke up in disappointment. "I was told I was going to be the housekeeper."

"Let's get this clear from the beginning: you are never to cross me. Whatever gave you that idea? You're lucky to have any job here. And you won't if you ever question me again. Now, come, I'll show you around the house and explain your duties."

"Layla," Mohammad intervened, "give the girl a chance. Introductions first. Let's tell her about us, our family, our servants, and then give her a moment to get comfortable with us."

Layla didn't like to be challenged and shot Mohammad a quick look. Edith caught it but Layla surprised Edith by acquiescing to Mohammad's suggestion. "You're right, dear, where are my manners? I had a challenging day at work and didn't mean to bring my troubles home. So yes, Edith, let's get to know each other a bit."

Edith began to doubt her ability to size up people on her first impressions. The Layla that was now so welcoming was not the Layla who had entered the room a moment ago. The Layla-of-first-impressions had an aura that prickled Edith's neck hairs. The riveting almond eyes of this very attractive woman were fiery, resolute, and accentuated by bold, straight, perfectly shaped brows that poked at Edith's anxiety. The Layla-of-first-impressions said *you are a nothing.* Edith hoped the hostile welcome she'd received wasn't a harbinger of things to come. It was starting off badly.

She learned the Saleebs had three children, two boys, Ahmed, seventeen, Fadi, fourteen and a twelve-year-old girl, Nadia. There were two others who lived in the home as well: Abeena, the Ethiopian housekeeper who had answered the door, and Maya, the Filipina cook.

"I hope you'll be happy here," Mohammad added cheerfully.

"And why wouldn't she?" Layla challenged, then indicated that Edith should follow her to learn the layout. "Kitchen ... off limits to you unless you're cleaning it. Nadia's bedroom," she said, quickly opening and shutting its door so the messiness within was obscured. "Here's Ahmed's bedroom and that one is Fadi's." She pointed to Abeena's quarters and finally Maya's room. "Unfortunately, we are out of private spaces," she was saying as she directed Edith toward the front of the large apartment, "so we fixed up a bed on the sun porch off the living room for you. Follow me."

"But Mrs. Saleeb, there's no door. It's totally open to the living room!" she complained on seeing the space.

"Have you already forgotten who's in charge here?" Layla snarled. "Like it or not, this is your space. See? We put the bed at the end where there's this partial wall between the two areas. No one can see you there. Besides, it's only temporary. Maya's contract will be up soon, then you can have her room."

Edith couldn't stop herself from persisting. "I need some privacy," Edith whimpered. "At least let me stay with Maya."

Layla put her hand on Edith's shoulder, dug her fingernails in hard and sneered, "You're starting off on the wrong foot, my dear." She turned on her heel and disappeared from the sun porch.

Bitch, Edith thought to herself as a weary smile crossed her lips for she had never used that word before. She massaged her shoulder, realizing that Layla was one not to tangle with.

Edith looked around trying to determine how she could acclimate herself to these horrible surroundings. Before she could come to any conclusion, the hall door banged open and Nadia barged in throwing her backpack and a soda can on the foyer floor. Edith stepped into the opening that separated her quarters from the living room and seeing Nadia said, "Hi." Nadia looked at Edith curiously for a moment then realized the new help had arrived. "I see the pooper scooper has arrived," she called out to her mother in Arabic. "Her name is Edith," Layla yelled back, "and don't call her the pooper scooper. That's rude."

Edith didn't understand the words that were spoken but she had no trouble discerning the snide attitude. "How fast can I learn Arabic?" she asked herself. As the scent of onion and herbs wafted toward the living room, Edith realized she hadn't eaten anything but a dry pita since yesterday. She heard Layla say, "Maya, dinner at 6 p.m. tonight. Fadi has football practice, so keep a plate aside for him and don't overcook the rice like you did last night. I have my meeting, I'll be back at 5 p.m."

"Yes, Madam Saleeb," a small voice from the kitchen responded.

"You! You start tomorrow at 7 a.m. sharp," Layla called toward the sun porch as she passed it on her way out the door.

Dinner isn't until 6 p.m.? I don't think I can last that long, Edith worried. She listened for a few minutes and when all she could hear was the chop, chop, chop of a knife she knew Nadia had disappeared somewhere and Maya was alone in the kitchen. She ventured toward it.

"Hi, I'm Edith," she said in Filipino. Maya turned quickly to see who had spoken, smiled briefly then turned back to chopping. "I was told you are the cook," Edith said, trying to make conversation. Chop. Chop. Chop. "What part of the Philippines are you from?" Chop. Chop. Chop. "I'd feel so much better if I could learn a little bit about how this household is run. Can you give me any advice?"

Maya stopped chopping and shot a quick glance at the closed door across from the kitchen. "Oh," said Edith, then mouthed "the housekeeper?" Maya nodded. "What time is dinner? I'm starving," Edith whispered, as all that chopping had released interesting aromas and Edith was already salivating. "For you," Maya whispered back sadly, "dinner will be whenever the family has finished eating and whatever is left. You should pray that something is left. And hope they don't stay at the table long after, because that's when you get to eat," she concluded.

Maya looked again at the door across from the kitchen. Without another word, she handed Edith a bowl of mujadara, a blend of lentils and rice that was left over from lunch. "Go," Maya warned, "before she sees that I've given this to you." Edith disappeared into the sun porch, grateful.

What have I gotten myself into? she wrote in the notebook in between bites of mujadara. *Here's what I've figured out so far. Maya, the cook, is intimidated by the madam and perhaps by the housekeeper, Abeena, as well. Nadia is beautiful in face but ugly in nature. She could make my time here most unpleasant. I had better figure out how to manage our relationship. Mr. Saleeb seems nice enough though my best guess is he's henpecked. Then there's Layla, the gestapo. Abeena? She's the wildcard right now. Maya seems to fear her. I'll have to make my own opinion. There's two more to meet. The boys. I can't wait, ha ha.*

The front door opened. Edith quickly tucked her notebook in her backpack and put the empty bowl under it. "That must be Ahmed," she said to herself, judging by his deep voice. "Where's mother?" he asked Maya in the kitchen, grabbing a carrot as he surveyed the ingredients for tonight's dinner.

"You're home early," said Abeena, opening her door when she heard his voice. He was her favorite. He was only two years old, fifteen years ago, when Abeena became the housekeeper and his nanny. She signed a two-year contract, just as Edith had, but her reason "to be hired abroad" was to escape a husband in Africa who beat her. By the time her two-year contract was nearing expiration, Ahmed had come to love her like a mother and cried whenever she told him she would be leaving soon. "No, no, no Auntie Abeena," he'd sob. "Make Auntie Abeena stay, Mama" he'd beg while clinging to Layla's leg. Ahmed, usually a calm and loving child, was now throwing tantrums and wetting the bed. He wanted his Abeena. During this unsettling period Layla discovered something about herself: she didn't like children, she *really* didn't like children.

"Yes, honey," Layla told Ahmed during one of his episodes, "your Abeena can stay but only if you stop throwing tantrums and wetting the bed." Abeena was happy as well. She had heard from a relative at home that her husband was demanding she return at the end of her contract, that he was meaner than ever from all the alcohol he was drinking and that he somehow had gotten himself a gun. She feared for her life.

Abeena quickly became an integral member of the Saleeb family and for the next several years Ahmed and his nanny were inseparable. She taught him all her Ethiopian childhood games: Akukulu (hide and seek), Maksegno (Monday Tuesday, a game of hopscotch), and Tegre, (or mancala, like backgammon). As he became older, his only ambition was to beat his Auntie Abeena at Tegre and their games had become intense.

As she stepped into the doorway of the kitchen Edith was happily surprised to see the tenderness Ahmed was displaying toward Abeena. This raised her own hopes for a warm welcome, if not warm, at least cordial.

"Hi, I'm Edith Santos," she said, "I'm new on staff."

They turned. If looks could kill.

"Another one," sneered Ahmed in English so there'd be no mistaking his disdain for household help. Edith retreated.

Fadi was the only member Edith hadn't yet met and she wasn't looking forward to it. He arrived home before his parents; practice had been called because of rain. He dropped his backpack and gear on the foyer floor just as his sister had, but when he noticed Edith he smiled and said hello. "Oh," he said, "I forgot that our new girl was coming today. Welcome. I'm Fadi."

"And I'm Edith. Edith Santos," she replied, grateful for at least one warm welcome. "I'm staying on the sun porch for now. Your mother made up a bed for me there. I hope that won't disturb you."

"No, I never go out there. Nobody ever does. Have you seen

the whole apartment and met Abeena and Maya yet?"

"Yes, briefly," Edith replied, "your mother walked me through."

"Did she show you my bedroom?" he asked, horrified.

"No, I didn't go into anyone's room. Why? Is there a problem?"

"We're a very messy family," he said sheepishly. "Our last maid left a month ago and nothing has been cleaned or picked up around here since. At least my room isn't as bad as my sister's. I actually like a neat room but since nobody cares about anything around here I decided not to care either."

"Wow," said Edith, surprised by Fadi's frankness. "Can I see your room? That way you can tell me how you like things kept. Let's work together. I'll keep it clean. You keep it neat. Win–win."

"Really?" Fadi replied, thrilled someone actually cared. "Okay." He opened his door and fortunately entered the room ahead of her. He didn't notice that she was rolling her eyes and holding her nose. "Socks," she thought.

"One more thing," he said, "can we keep this arrangement just between you and me?"

"Sure," she answered, "and the reason would be …?"

He hated to admit it but since he already liked Edith he finally said, "My family isn't very nice to our help and if my mother thought I was talking to you about how things are done around here, well, it wouldn't be good for either of us."

"You have my word," Edith said.

Life here will be going from bad to worse, she scribbled in the notebook when she got back to the sun porch.

Chapter 23

It's in the Contract

The next morning at 7 a.m. sharp Edith, dressed in a black tee and black pants, was heading toward the hub of the house, the kitchen, when she heard her name snarled through Layla's teeth. "Edith, you're late."

Edith couldn't believe her ears. Late? At exactly 7 a.m. she was standing five feet from the kitchen entry and this was considered late? *Oh, God,* she prayed, *give me strength to persevere here.*

"Yes, Madam," she replied, "it won't happen again,"

"Begin in the bathrooms," Layla directed without acknowledging the apology. "I want them scrubbed on your hands and knees. No shortcuts. Start in the squatter. Abeena, check on Edith to make sure she understands how I like it done."

With a bucket, a mop, a toothbrush and a foul smelling product that Syrians clean with, Edith gagged as she filled her bucket and took the toothbrush to the moldy grout around the hole in the floor. And so began the first of the 730 days until she could leave this god-awful place.

Although Abeena corrected a number of Edith's deficiencies as Edith worked through the day, Layla was not at all pleased. "What did you do all day?" she nitpicked. "Two bathrooms and the kitchen? That's all you accomplished? Just look at this kitchen! The cupboards are still full of flour dust. You are the slowest cleaning lady we've ever had, perhaps the worst. I have a good mind to report you to Mr. Habib. He'd make sure you were sorry that you didn't perform as promised."

"But Madam," Edith retorted, "I spent a great deal of time getting the kitchen floor spotless. It was sticky with honey and rice kernels that had been ground into the grout. The door pulls were terribly gummy. The grease on the backsplash took an hour to remove. I wanted to make things perfect for you and your family. I don't do things half-assed as you will come to see when you know me better."

It took Layla a minute to build a hefty steam of indignation to the inferred accusation that she, Layla Saleeb, ran a dirty house. When she got her blood pressure high enough she walked to within an inch of Edith's face, took hold of her ponytail, and yanked it ever so firmly, tilting Edith's head back into a painful position. "You've been warned," Layla bristled. "Talk back again and I'll return you to the agent who sent you. He has a way with problem help. He is likely to move you to a less compatible situation," she threatened.

If only, Edith wished but she knew this was an idle threat. She had been in the household for twenty-four hours now and already figured that Layla, though mean as a hornet, was in reality a feckless bully.

One back-breaking day followed another and Edith no longer knew whether it was Wednesday or Thursday or Friday. Each passing day was as miserable as the one before it. With all Edith's scrubbing and sweeping and window washing, she couldn't see that her efforts had made any difference. That is, until Saturday when Fadi poked his head around the corner of the sun porch. "Edith," he said, startling her, as no one ever visited her so-called room. "You're making our house shine again. And my room is perfect. It suits me once again. Thanks for that."

His words lifted her spirits. Then she realized he should be in school. "You better scoot," she said, "or you'll be late for class."

"Today's Saturday," he laughed, thinking nobody ever forgets Saturdays.

"Saturday already!" she sang out, "Tomorrow's Sunday! My first day off! Tomorrow I get to go to Mass, maybe find a cafe for coffee, and just be outdoors for a while. Where's the closest Catholic church, Fadi?"

"I have no idea," he replied, "but I'll ask my mom. Maybe she'll let me take you there because I know all the streets and alleys of this neighborhood."

"Great idea. And I'd love for you to show me around."

Minutes later he returned with a long face. "I can't go. Neither can you. Mom's having a party here tomorrow. You have to work and I have to stay out of her way. I'm sorry, Edith."

"Not your fault," she told the disappointed boy. "Next week, then."

"Not next week either," Fadi sadly admitted. "Mother says I can't be seen in public with you, not *you* exactly, but the help. The help is not in the same category as people," he tried to explain but he was digging himself into a deeper hole and he knew it. Finally he said, "I can't explain it."

That was the last straw for Edith. She stomped toward the kitchen and in a voice loud enough for the whole household to hear, she called, "Mrs. Saleeb, I need to see you."

Layla appeared. Her silk robe with hibiscus flowers billowed behind her like handmaidens, her hair, freshly coiffed, was lifted with ivory combs, a scent of White Diamond perfumed her aura. Layla's appearance as queen intimidated Edith for the moment but she quickly remembered her deprivation.

"I don't work on Sundays," Edith said firmly, her heart pounding in her chest. "It's in my contract."

Layla smiled coyly and said, "Oh, I didn't know that. Why don't you show me exactly where it says, in your contract, that you have Sundays free so we can work this issue out."

Edith's knees wanted to buckle. Her throat tightened. Perspiration bubbled on her brow. The room grew foggy. Contract? She had no contract. Yes, she had signed a piece of paper that a salesman had so gloriously touted, but he had kept it. She had no copy. This was Edith's moment of truth. She had been duped. She had been sold into slavery. She might never leave this house again. Worse, she might never get home again.

The smile never left Layla's face as she turned and left the room.

"Damn it," Edith said, pounding the pillow. "What a fool I am. There is no 'contract.' It was all a get-rich-quick scheme and I was the chattel that made it all possible. Sundays off, letters home, $200 a month! Ha! I've been sold into slavery and I went willingly. Damn it, girl. You are so stupid." She yanked her notebook out of her backpack and wrote *stupid girl* as many times as it took to fill the whole page.

She was still berating herself when she heard her name called from grand central, the kitchen. It was evil-child, Nadia. "I don't like your name," the twelve-year-old told Edith, "so I'm changing it to something I like better. Sloth. I like Sloth better." She picked up her toy wand with its silver and purple beads and tapped Edith on the arm. "I hereby rename you Sloth. Get me some juice, Sloth, I'm thirsty. Bring it to my room."

"I can't. Your mother specifically said no food or drink in the bedrooms. So no."

"When mother finds out I saw you steal a bowl of raspberries that she just bought for her party tonight ..."

"Nadia! You can't tell lies like that. I'm here to make your life, *all* your lives, nicer, more comfortable. Why would you do that?" Edith replied, disgusted.

"Sloth, I want juice, now," evil-child repeated. Edith reached for a glass, a straw, the grape juice and took it into Little Layla's lair. *Blackmailed by a twelve-year-old,* Edith told the notebook. *And this is only Week One. Can it get any worse?*

Chapter 24

The Lying Letter Home

On the following Tuesday morning, the house was unusually quiet. "Where is everybody?" Edith asked Maya who was already chopping greens for the evening meal. "It's Tuesday," she replied, "nobody's home. It's Abeena's morning out. She goes to market precisely at 9 a.m. every Tuesday morning and brings home the week's groceries. She usually gets back around noon."

"It's just me and you this morning?" Edith asked, a look of escape filling her face. "How long will everyone be gone?"

"Don't even think about it," Maya quickly replied. "You aren't the first to think of escaping."

"What do you mean? There've been others?"

"Do you think I'm a quiet little mouse with no opinions? Do you think I'm content chopping and sauteing all day, preparing foods that I don't even like. No!" she continued, "I hate it here! But I'm not willing to let happen to me what happened to the girl you replaced. I saw it all."

"What happened?" Edith questioned, more concerned than ever for her own well-being in this household.

Edith listened as Maya told the story. The girl's name was Teressa and she was becoming more and more despondent working for the Saleebs. One beautiful sunny Tuesday, like today, soon after Abeena had left the house, Teressa decided to escape. She left with nothing. She just stepped out the door, down the stairs and out onto the street. This was her first time out and she didn't know which direction to go. She walked north for a few blocks and that didn't look promising, then she turned south and passed the apartment again.

Agi, the grumpy old man in the next apartment who had nothing better to do, was the building's busybody. He happened to be looking out his window and saw Teressa wandering the street. Everybody knows the help never goes out and he felt it his duty to report what looked quite suspicious. So he called Abeena. Abeena knew Teressa was trying to escape and called the police who quickly captured the poor girl, roughed her up and held her until Abeena could retrieve the runaway.

Abeena then tied Teressa to a kitchen chair and berated her verbally until Mrs. Saleeb returned home from work. Layla untied Teressa from the chair and pushed her into the bedroom.

"I could hear the sounds of the leather strap ripping the clothes and skin off Teressa. Her wails sent chills up my spine. I thought for sure she'd be dead. But she wasn't. Her wrist was broken and the parts of her skin that weren't torn, were black and blue. Please, Edith, don't leave the house."

Please, God, send me a sign of hope, Edith wrote, having decided not to try anything stupid, at least not yet.

At 2:30 p.m. Fadi burst through the door. "Guess what everybody?" he announced excitedly. "On Tuesdays, from now on, we get out at 2 p.m. instead of 3 p.m., teacher conferences or something.

"Where is everybody!" he called again, when no one responded.

"That's great!" said Edith from behind her wall. Fadi walked through the living room to her quarters and dropped his backpack on her bed. "I guess it's just you and me to celebrate the good news," he said happily.

"You're lucky to be going to school, Fadi. In the Philippines, not everybody gets to go. I wanted to go to school so bad that I made my parents enroll me. We were so poor they wanted us kids to work in the fields alongside them, growing and harvesting vegetables to sell at the market because that was how we survived. But I told my Papa I needed to learn everything there was to learn and I finally convinced him and Mama that I should go to school. Not only that, Fadi, because I'm such a nuisance I pestered my parents to let all of us go to school and there are ten of us! Even now José and Tomás, the youngest ones, are in school. Know that you are lucky. Not everyone has opportunities as great as yours."

Fadi loved listening to Edith. He liked the way her voice went up and down in a soothing cadence as she told her stories. It held him spellbound; and he seemed to be taking her messages to heart.

"By the way, Fadi, what do your papa and mama do for work?" Edith asked casually so Fadi would be comfortable telling things to the help that should never be told.

"Baba's a banker," he answered, "and Mama works as a counselor in a government building."

"Counselor? That's interesting. Whom does she counsel?"

"Women who are in abusive relationships. I think it's called the human dignity department or something like that," he explained.

"What a perfect job for her," Edith said, hoping Fadi didn't catch her sarcasm.

"Yeah, she likes to help others. By the way, my birthday's coming up," he said, changing the subject. "Next month I'll be fifteen."

"Mine, too!" she exclaimed, surprised that she hadn't remembered. "Two weeks from today I'll be old."

"You're not old!" Fadi assured. "What day? We'll have a party."

"I doubt it," she replied. "It's the tenth."

They both heard the key go into the lock. Fadi grabbed his

backpack and was gone before the tumbler had a chance to move.

Edith's birthday coincided with her first month anniversary of working for this family. This was all good news to the Saleebs for they could kill two birds with one stone. It was time for the letter and the check.

Savvy practitioners of duping poor, mostly illiterate Filipinas into becoming "domestic workers" called for at least one letter back to their Filipino families with a juicy fat check in it. This ploy's intended purpose was to make the family back home feel confident that their daughter had made a good decision in serving abroad and was now gainfully and happily employed. Also, the family would feel assured that payments like this would be forthcoming on a monthly basis. Even when the following month's check would never arrive, families would surmise it was slow in the mail, or two payments would be coming the following month. By the third month families were frantically trying to find out what had gone wrong but the agent who had set them up was long gone.

On Edith's twenty-third birthday Layla had Maya make a chocolate cake bejeweled in jimmies and sprinkles. After the family had eaten their luscious dinner of lamb shish kabobs and rice, Layla called Edith to join them at the dining table.

"Our celebrant gets the place of honor," she said as she summoned Edith to sit at the table in front of a cake ablaze with lighted candles. Then she posed Nadia and Fadi to Edith's left and Ahmed standing at Edith's right. Layla and Mohammad stood behind her with their hands on her shoulders. Abeena held the camera.

"Everyone smile!" commanded Layla. "Abeena, is Edith smiling?" she asked over Edith's head.

Edith smiled a smile that didn't feel true but no one noticed and no one cared. The next day, Layla, sweet as pie, called Edith to the kitchen to write a letter home, one that would include her first month's wages of $200, the birthday picture and a cheerful note, all to mollify the family back home. As she put the check under Edith's nose, she handed her a ballpoint pen and said, "Write what I'm going to dictate." Edith knew enough not to argue, so she wrote what she was told.

Dear Mama, Papa, Luna and family,

I'm excited and proud to be able to send you this check. The family I work for sends you their best and wants you to know that they already feel I am part of their family. Here's a picture of the birthday party they had for me on Tuesday. That's me, of course, about to blow out the candles. My parents-away-from-home, Layla and Mohammad, are behind me in this photo. On the left is Nadia, twelve, who is very friendly and pretty, you all would love her. Next to her is Fadi. He's fourteen. His goal is to meet my Filipino family some day and the tall one is Ahmed. He's seventeen and handsome like his father. I am very happy here. Time is going fast and soon I'll be home. To Luna: kisses, kisses, kisses.

Love you so much,
Edith

"Can I add a personal message?" Edith asked, "I'm not illiterate, you know."

"Do you want this check or not?" Layla hissed, ending the conversation. But inside, Edith was seething. *That was not the letter I would have written at all,* she fumed. *I bet all letters 'home' are dictated like this. Lyka's letter to her roommates was probably full of shit as well. A 'friendly' Nadia, a 'handsome' Ahmed, 'my parents away from home'. What crap. I wish I could have written about my subhuman, nasty enslavers. I hope I had a convincing smile for the stupid photo during my birthday 'party' and my parents believe the letter's lies. Last thing I want is to worry them. At least I got to stuff myself with sugar-loaded cake, after being denied real dinner. Oh lord, I am so screwed.*

Weeks droned on. On Tuesdays when no one but Maya was home, Edith would go into the master bedroom and look in the mirror. "No wonder I have to keep pulling up my pants," she told the mirror. "How much weight have I lost?" She looked in the closet for a scale. "Ten pounds!" she shrieked as she pulled a scale out from under silk robes. She looked again into Layla's dressing mirror and gasped. "I can see my cheekbones!" she said, feeling her face. "I could get sick and die here and my family would never find out. I have to escape. Dear God, please help me find an escape," she said as she pulled the sheets from Layla's bed to do the laundry.

Every day seemed the same as the one before. Edith's knees were red and sore from being on the floor of this sticky house. The skin on her hands was dry and flaky from being in that damned bucket all day. One subtle change had occurred in the household, and Edith noticed because it impacted her. Ahmed no longer came home in time for dinner. He told his parents he was taking an accelerated course to better his chances to get into a university. They were very supportive and, quite frankly, proud of his ambition since he hadn't shown much interest in higher education until now. As a result of this simple change, Maya had to make a plate for Ahmed and keep it warm until he finally got home. This meant Edith didn't get her share of the leftovers until Ahmed was well-fed. She was starving by the time her scraps were available.

Maya was no longer morose. She chopped with enthusiasm and even sang tunes while she scurried around the kitchen. Two weeks and her contract would be up. She and Mrs. Saleeb had already discussed the formalities of her final day and how she would get to the airport. The happier Maya became, the more morose Edith grew. It was torture knowing she still had twenty-two more months in this hell.

One day while collecting the dirty laundry in Fadi's room, she noticed a few architectural sketches he had drawn in a book that laid open on his night stand. The drawings were incomplete but they weren't bad for a fourteen-year-old. It made Edith long for those days in Manila when she was learning fashion and drawing her fashion design ideas in her sketchbook. She thought about how much she loved sketching and was getting good at it, getting promoted for her work and ideas. Once she had learned to sew, she knew the sky would be her limit, until everything all fell apart. Regrets filled her with grief. It would have been so different if only, if only. "Stop it right this minute, Edith Santos!" she screamed at Fadi's walls. "There'll be no pity party in this room today." She grabbed the dirty clothes and left, slamming the door behind her.

She knew she should never write in her notebook when she was starving, but Ahmed still had not come home. She needed to hear herself think so she pulled the notebook out. She drummed her fingers on her table for a few minutes before she let the words get a life of their own. Surprised by her subconscious courage, the word 'escape' wanted to be recognized. *Escape. Escape. I've got to get out of here somehow. But how? I can't let what happened to Teressa happen to me. If only I knew this city, knew which way to go when my chance comes. How? How?* she wondered, still drumming. Finally she wrote down one word: *Fadi.*

A few days passed before she had a chance to privately chat with Fadi.

"I saw your architectural sketches when I did your laundry," she began. "You're quite good. Did you know that when I worked in the garment business in Manila I got pretty good at fashion design sketches?" she said. He liked that they had something in common. "The building on the last page of your sketchbook, what building is that? Where is it?" she asked.

"That's just down the street from here," he answered, happy for her interest. "You can see it if you stick your head out the window of this room. Come over here, look," he said, opening the window wide enough for both of them to stick their heads out.

"Wow," she said, "your sketch catches its essence. What else have you drawn?"

"Let me get my book," he said, leaping off the end of her bed.

"My school," he said on his return, "the Great Mosque," he added turning the page, "and Al Azem Palace."

"I wish I could get their locations in my head so I can appreciate your beautiful city," she said.

"I know!" he said excitedly. "I can draw a map of the city and put markers on my map to let you know where they are located."

"Great!" she replied. "You can show me where you go to school, where the mosque is that you go to, even the marketplace. Where are we in relation to the airport?" she quizzed.

"Okay," he said, "I know everything in Damascus. I'll draw the whole city for you!"

"And because I'm Filipina," she cleverly added, "show me where the embassy is."

"I can do that!" he said excitedly, "but we better keep this a secret because my mother does not want me to be friendly with the help if you know what I mean."

"I *do* know," replied Edith, "and you better not let Nadia know what you're doing either. She could spoil the whole project for you."

Chapter 25

Oh, Splash

Edith grew more and more depressed the closer Maya's last day approached. Despite Layla's law that Edith was forbidden to enter the kitchen except for cleaning it up after meals, she and the cook usually had a few minutes each day to get to know each other. By the end of two months, Edith had a lot of respect for this hard-working, seldom-complaining woman. She also had a very good idea about how her remaining time in this household would go. And she wasn't looking forward to it at all.

On the day before Maya's departure, Edith pushed open the kitchen door a bit and saw Maya in the kitchen prepping vegetables for the Saleebs' dinner. "I'm really going to miss you," Edith whispered, on her way to the laundry room. When Maya looked up, Edith was shocked to see Maya had been crying. "What happened?" Edith mouthed.

"I'll tell you at clean-up," Maya whispered, wiping tears away with her free hand.

For the next hour, Edith fretted and worried about Maya. Just this morning, Maya was exuberant and bubbly, even for her. She kept saying how excited she was to be going home. What had happened? Edith wondered if the Saleebs had decided Maya couldn't leave. She worried that perhaps Maya had learned some devastating news about her Filipino family. Edith's mind was running through every horrible scenario she could imagine. In spite of an hour's worth of wondering, Edith never could have guessed the real reason Maya was so distraught. She was to find out soon.

"What are you talking about?" Edith said in a shocked, angry and loud whisper when Maya told her after dinner that for the past two years, the Saleebs had been withdrawing $80 for room and board from her $200 monthly paycheck.

"That can't be true!" Edith exclaimed in a horrified whisper. "You mean to tell me that we are only getting paid $120 a month??? That room and board are just snatched out of our paychecks??? Why didn't anyone tell us this? What the hell!"

"Yes, what the hell!" Maya agreed. "I'm going home with $2,880 after two years of cooking three meals a day, every day, for this ungrateful family of users and abusers." Dropping her voice to a very low and menacing whisper, she added, "Had I ever guessed how this would end, I swear I would have slowly poisoned the lot of them. With pleasure." Maya paused for a moment before whispering again, "I'm sorry, I didn't mean that. I am just so devastated."

"Oh, Maya, of course you are. And so am I," Edith said.

The next morning, Edith watched as the despondent Maya left the house for the first time in years ushered out by the elbow by Habib. No one in the family came to say thanks, or even goodbye, except for Fadi who was getting ready for school. "You've been a great cook," he told her with sincerity. "I'm really going to miss you."

Not even twenty-four hours passed before mealtimes in the Saheeb household became a disaster three times a day. The kids were left on their own the next morning for breakfast. In their wake, they left crusted cereal bowls, two fry pans of burned bacon, a quart of milk left out to spoil, and spilled orange juice caking up on the floor next to a shattered glass. "Those little slobs,"

Edith said to herself when she saw the mess.

"We're eating out tonight," Layla announced when Moham-mad returned home from work. "Come on, let's go children, it's time to go eat." Edith was amazed to note this was the first time all three had immediately obeyed her. As the family hurried through the door, Edith had the feeling they wouldn't be bringing doggie bags home for her. "I'll be damned if I'm going to bed hungry again tonight," Edith thought, as she marched into the for-bidden territory of the kitchen and began to rummage through the refrigerator. She was just about to dip a fork into a forgotten bowl of rice when she found Abeena staring disapprovingly from the doorway. "That is against house rules, Edith," the grim-faced old lady said sternly. "Screw you," Edith said in Filipino and contin-ued to fill her belly.

The next day was floor-scrubbing day, her least favorite chore. Not just because the kids were so adept at dropping and slopping, but also because this duty required her to cross paths with Abeena more often than usual. For her part, Abeena was a lot more snarly than usual. This day, however, Edith had a chance to eavesdrop on a phone conversation Abeena was having.

"Look here, Mr. Habib, you must find us a cook immediately! The children are underfed and getting cranky and the madam and master are pissed that eating out every night is getting too expen-sive. This is your job, Habib. As far as I can tell, your *only* job. Get us a very good cook. Immediately! You have until tomorrow morning, or madam says we'll be looking for another agent to handle our affairs. Good day!" Abeena fairly shouted before slamming down the receiver.

Geez, I hope I like the new cook. There's got to be something *I like about being here*, Edith moaned.

The next morning Edith was muttering to herself in the kitch-en after the children left for school. *What the hell? Do they al-ways have food fights for breakfast?* she wondered as she scrubbed dried-up egg yolk off the kitchen cabinet. "Those little slobs," she said under her breath.

The next voice she heard sounded exactly like Mr. Habib. Edith was not at all surprised that the imperious Abeena's threats produced such instant results. "I have brought your new cook," he announced grandly to Abeena. "Is madam home?"

"Madam was expecting you at 9 a.m. and it's now 10 a.m. Madam has left for her hair appointment," Abeena said inhospitably. "Bring the girl in. I'll be letting you know if madam doesn't approve of your choice when she returns."

The thoroughly cowed Mr. Habib grabbed the new cook by the elbow and pushed her into the foyer. Edith pulled her ear away from the ajar kitchen door and decided to sneak a peek at the newcomer. *She looks kind of familiar, but who is she? Where have I seen her before?* Edith thought. Just then introductions were being made and Edith heard a nervous, yet still infectious, laugh from the young woman. *Oh my God, it's Jasmine! The new cook is Jasmine! Oh my God, I am so happy!* Edith wanted to rush out and hug her friend but instantly thought what a mistake that would be. Layla would never keep this cook if she found out Edith and Jasmine were friends. Co-conspirators, even.

"I'll show you around the house now," Edith heard Abeena say. Edith quickly turned back to washing the dishes at the sink and just as the kitchen door opened, Edith dramatically said "Oh! Splash!" before turning around.

Abeena was looking quizzically at Edith. Jasmine was also looking at Edith. Although she was in surprised shock, she still managed a totally dead-pan expression on her face. *Oh thank God*, Edith thought, *Jasmine gets the message.*

"Oops, didn't mean to startle you. I just splashed dirty water all over my apron. I'm sorry! I didn't know we had company," Edith said calmly, avoiding Jasmine's eyes.

"This isn't company, it's the new cook, Jasmine. Jasmine, this is Edith, our cleaning lady."

"Yes, I'm the cleaning lady," Edith said to Jasmine. "I sure hope you are not a sloppy cook because it's my job to clean up the kitchen after meals," Edith said sharply, knowing that Abeena had an uncanny nose for smelling deception and could perhaps, even detect electric excitement in the air.

The conversation was over as far as Abeena was concerned, and she beckoned Jasmine to follow her, but not before Edith winked at Jasmine and not before Jasmine smiled and sadly touched her hair that had been cut hideously short.

Chapter 26

Hair in the Soup

"I understand you've met the new cook," Layla said on her way out to a meeting. "I expect you to obey my rule about making friends with the help."

Edith inwardly groaned. "Oh, don't worry about that. She seems a little stuck-up. But while you're here, I want to know when I can move into Maya's old room."

"Oh, I've decided to let the new cook, what's-her-name, have that room. She is getting settled in already."

"But you told me ..." Edith began.

"You can't seem to remember your place here. My house, my decisions," Layla snapped. "You better learn to keep your sassiness to yourself. Today I want you to clean every window in this house by the time I get home for dinner. I'm running late for my meeting. Remember what I said, missy," Layla warned as the front door slammed behind her.

Edith was seething. She had been dreaming about moving into Maya's room and anticipating the joy she'd feel having a door to shut out this obnoxious family. As she began to clean the windows in the living room, she couldn't help but look with jealousy at the closed door of Maya's old room.

It was nearly four in the afternoon by the time Edith and her squeegee got to cleaning the small window in the kitchen. A few minutes later, Jasmine walked in to begin dinner preparations. "Oh!" the two said at once with huge happy smiles. They both started to whisper to each other. "We have to be careful," Edith cautioned. "Layla warned me not to get friendly with you," Edith continued in a low whisper. "She warned me too," Jasmine mouthed back.

"The way I see it, the only way we can be friends, is if we act like enemies," Edith murmured. "By the way, I'm sorry about your hair. But you still look awesome. I'm so glad you are here." Edith's eyes were brimming with tears of joy. "I didn't think I was going to be able to stand another twenty months in this house."

"I'm not sure I can either. That housekeeper reminds me of the Wicked Witch of the East. Would you believe they stuck me in a broom closet? At least in the other house I had an actual bedroom with a window," Jasmine lamented.

Edith was instantly happy that she didn't get the room she had been wishing for. "About the housekeeper," she warned, "Abeena is Layla's spy. Do not trust her."

Just then, Edith heard the squeaky floorboard in the dining room and raised her voice. "Try not to splash that sauce on my clean window. You seem a little sloppy. I'm just saying, I don't want to spend my entire evenings cleaning up after you," she said, winking at Jasmine.

"If you don't stop harassing me," Jasmine snarled loudly, "I just won't cook enough for there to be any leftovers for y…"

At that moment. Abeena marched into the kitchen, interpreting what she heard as a cat fight and she was pleased to hear them snapping at each other. "Dinner is promptly at 6 p.m. in this household, Jasmine. The mistress and master are expecting a delicious meal, served on time."

"I doubt that cook could feed a dog properly," Edith muttered before grabbing her squeegee and leaving the kitchen.

Edith's stomach was the happiest it had been in months after dinner that night. Ahmed had come home in time to eat with the family and Jasmine had heaped Edith's plate with delicious, satisfying food, still warm.

"Edith, come here," Layla ordered from her reclining chair in the living room a short time later. "I understand that you are having an issue with the new cook, what's-her-name, the one with the bad haircut. I don't tolerate that kind of animosity in this house. You will learn to get along with her, or else."

Edith raised her eyebrows. *What could the 'or else' be?* she wondered. "Or else," Layla continued, "you may find yourself in another family. Jasmine is said to be an exceptional cook. You, on the other hand," she sighed, "can't even do simple cleaning jobs right. Look here," she said pointing at the high window near the cathedral ceiling. "It's streaky."

"Yes, ma'am. I'm very sorry about that. I'll do much better next time," Edith promised, wishing she could retort with what she really wanted to say: *Guess there was still some shit on my rag after cleaning your squatter. Pretty sure it was your shit, Layla.* Inwardly she smiled.

It was three days before Edith and Jasmine had another chance to talk. It seemed like Layla was always finding stupid little tasks for Edith to do while Jasmine was putting the food away after meals. It also seemed like Nadia was interning to be her mother's extra spy, popping in and out of the kitchen when the friends were working there together. "I have so much I want to tell you," Jasmine lamented one evening in the kitchen, "but we're never left alone."

"Don't worry, we can talk on Tuesday. It's Abeena's day to go to market. I'm dying to hear your story and can't wait to share mine."

"What are you two whispering about?" Nadia had slipped into the kitchen while their backs were turned.

"You're interrupting me. That's rude," Jasmine quickly reprimanded the snooping twelve-year-old. Dropping her voice to a threatening whisper, Jasmine turned once again to face Edith and hissed, "As I was saying, Edith, don't you ever tell me I'm deliberately scorching the fry pans. Learn to scrub a little harder." Disappointed, Nadia huffed out of the kitchen.

"Wow! That was quick thinking! Maybe we should learn to speak in Pig Latin," Edith said with a muffled laugh. "Except that little pig can probably speak it," Jasmine replied, on the verge of one of her infectious laughs.

At promptly 9 a.m. on Tuesday, Abeena was heading out to market, but not before reminding Edith that Layla wanted her to dust and clean all the china cabinets. Edith and Jasmine didn't say a word until they saw Abeena out the window lumbering down the road toward the market.

"First things first," Edith said, "what happened to your hair?"

"I sort of have to begin at the beginning. It's all one long horror story," Jasmine said. "When I arrived at the Khaleb household, I was assigned as a nanny. Not quite the housekeeper job I'd been promised. The household included Mr. Khaleb, a fifty-ish older woman, a thirty-something sexy-looking woman, a very young gay guy named Miguel who was the cook and a three-month-old baby. Turns out the old lady and the sexy lady were both Mr. Khaleb's wives. The Filipino gay guy? It didn't take long to figure out the gay guy was sort of an unwilling third wife in the household."

"I had no idea polygamy was allowed in Syria," Edith said. "Guess it really is a man's world here, unless you're a gay man."

Jasmine nodded, then explained that polygamy is indeed legal, but only for those who get permission from the government. "Turns out that Mr. Khaleb is a government bigwig, in some high-ranking judicial job. Guess he gave himself permission. But, good lord, he was a piece of work. If you pissed him off, he was as nasty as a dose of syphilis. I quickly figured out that Wife #1 was quite jealous of Wife #2 who had produced an heir for the master, something Wife #1 could never accomplish. So the two wives squabbled all the time and Mr. Khaleb took sides, depending on his mood. The week I arrived, he locked Wife #1 in her room for three days after maliciously beating her because she called Wife #2 a lazy slut. I'm pretty sure it wasn't the first time she'd been punished like that. After that incident, #1 rarely left her room, so I didn't have much to do with her.

"It was Wife #2 who I came to fear and hate. She berated me constantly, said I was an awful nanny and that I was stupid, lazy and incompetent. I began to realize she might be jealous of me, because Mr. Khaleb would never back her up when she complained to him about all my failings. She might also have been jealous of Miguel who was forced into Khaleb's bed several times a week. Worst of all, she didn't even seem to like her baby. I overheard her talking to the infant one day, saying really awful things to him. Blaming the baby for her out-of-shape figure. Saying she wished he had never been born. That 'even your baba doesn't love you.' Stuff like that.

"One day I was walking past the nursery door just in time to see the baby fall, truthfully I should say drop, out of her arms. There she was just standing there, staring down at the baby lying on the floor. Not even bending to pick him up as the baby screamed. When I saw the pool of blood, I rushed in, picked the infant up and called for an ambulance. The poor thing had hit the edge of an opened dresser drawer and had a severe laceration on his forehead and deep cuts on his arm. She told her husband she had just lotioned herself up and the baby slipped out of her arms. I saw what I saw. Worse yet, she knew that I knew."

Jasmine paused to take a breath. "And I thought *I* was in an awful household!" Edith said sadly.

"It gets worse," Jasmine continued. "It's about Miguel who became the only ally I had. Nah, more than an ally, he became my friend. He was a kind, sweet person and an awesome cook. I sometimes helped him with a new recipe or two, so we had time to get to know each other. Although we laughed and joked around a lot, I always felt he was deeply troubled.

"One day when he was particularly down, I asked him if he was okay, if something was bothering him. His floodgates burst open. He started telling me how abusive Mr. Khaleb was to him and got into sexual details that I wish I had never heard. It was frightening, disgusting, abhorrent. I felt so bad for him. Then he told me he felt like a prisoner here. A Filipino like me, he, too, had signed a two-year contract which had expired over a year ago. But either the family liked his cooking so much, or Mr. Khaleb liked the cook so much that when Miguel's contract was up, they decided to keep him on. Although he begged the Khalebs to release him, he finally realized he was never going home again. I'd never seen him so despondent, and I had no idea how to console my friend.

"At 4 p.m. I was wondering why Miguel wasn't already busy in the kitchen. Just then I heard the police siren right outside the apartment window. I wish I hadn't gone to see what had happened. It will stay with me forever. It was Miguel, in a pool of blood. He had jumped from the balcony.

"I thought for sure the Khalebs or Syria or somebody would send Miguel's body home for burial, but no, they couldn't be bothered. He was buried in a pauper's field on the outskirts of town. Nobody would ever have known about Miguel's death if the organization that's trying to shed some light on abuses in the Syrian domestic slave trade market hadn't made inquiries that forced an investigation. And I certainly would never have known what happened to Miguel except that Khaleb happened to bring home an English version of the local newspaper that ran a story about 'the accidental death.' I overheard the family gloating that their names had not been published. So I kept my eye on the whereabouts of that paper and when it hit the trash bin, I plucked it out. According to the article, the Philippine embassy decided to start an investigation when they learned Miguel had been working without a contract. They wanted to find out if it was voluntary or forced. I saved the paper to take it home. I will find Miguel's family if we ever get back and tell them I knew him."

Edith noticed Jasmine's eyes well up at the memory. "I'm so sorry, Jasmine," Edith said, hugging her friend. "So, so sorry."

Jasmine pulled herself together. She had to finish her tale before their time ran out.

"Now I'm finally getting to the answer to your question. After Miguel died, you would have thought the people in that house believed they were going to starve to death. Such whining. It turned out that the first wife who mostly stayed in her room had seen me cooking occasionally alongside Miguel. Before the very next meal, I was reassigned as cook. Well, not exactly. It was in addition to being the nanny. I was working fourteen-hour days, not to mention being awakened for the late-night bottle feedings. I am the first to admit: being overworked and sleep-deprived made me a bit snappy. I was especially testy with Wife #2, as she reclined with a magazine in hand while I cradled the baby with one arm and chopped lettuce with the other.

"One night after I had served Mr. Khaleb and the wives dinner, I heard a god-awful shriek from the dining room. "Oh my God! Look what is in my food!" It was Wife #2, with a horrid look on her face.

"I rushed from the kitchen in time to see her pull a two-foot-long piece of black hair out of her stew. My hair, of course. There could be no question that it was mine; the others were either bald, permed or bleached.

"All eyes turned to me. 'Please excuse me,' Wife #2 said to the others as she rose from the table, took me by the shoulder and pushed me into the kitchen out of sight of the family. 'This is disgusting,' she said as we passed through the kitchen door. 'And it won't happen again.' That's when she picked up the kitchen shears, grabbed my hair and held it tight against the nape of my neck." Tears well in Jasmine's eyes. "My first haircut," she said, catching the tears on the back of her hand that were trying to escape from her eyes. Then the evil woman said, smirking, 'There! Problem solved.'

"Edith, you've seen me cooking in the kitchen. I always wear a hair net when handling food, as I had been that day. I'm quite sure that that baby-loathing, vindictive airhead had gotten a hold of my hair brush and plunged my long strand into her stew."

"Whoa! Then what happened?" Edith wanted to know.

"Khaleb walked into the kitchen for his coffee. 'What the hell!' he roared when he saw my black hair strewn all over the floor. Then he saw #2 with the shears in her hand and, I swear, he looked ready to kill her. 'Are you crazy?' he yelled, 'that girl had the most beautiful hair I've ever seen. I loved looking at it. When she moved about the house, the sun catching strands...' he sighed and slowly shook his head. 'It looked so good on you,' he said to me with genuine sincerity. 'I am so sorry she did this to you... what's your name again?' he asked.

"How long had I been in his house, Edith?" Jasmine fumed, "Two months? And he didn't even know my name!

"And that's the story of what happened to my hair," she added, unconsciously touching her mangled mess.

"Compared to Khaleb's house of horrors, this place must seem like Disneyland," Edith kidded. "I am so glad you are out of that house, and most of all that you wound up here! By the way, how did you manage that? I've heard it's not that easy to change home placements. Did you contact that slimeball, Habib? Did he actually help you out?"

"I kind of knew it was going to be futile to try and get any help from Mr. Habib. He just thinks of us as property. He shoves us around like we're just dogs on a leash. No, surprisingly, I got out of there thanks to Wife #2. Turns out she is what the Americans call a bimbo, a jealous one at that.

"One day Miguel told me that nearly every night at dinner, #2 complained to her husband about something I had done wrong.

Miguel said most of her complaints were made-up lies and that he thought she was sabotaging me because she was jealous of me. This idea made me laugh out loud. As if I'd ever be hot for someone like that old man. Turns out Miguel was right. Without Mr. Khaleb's knowing, #2 called Mr. Habib and away I went!"

"So, a happy ending to a sad situation. Again, I'm so sorry you had to experience all that," Edith said. "I nominate you for the best horror stories so far."

"I hope to God we get out of here when our contracts are up," Edith said. Jasmine's stories were so captivating that neither realized how late it was getting until Edith jumped up saying, "I better get those china cabinets cleaned, or I'll be facing another *or else.*"

"And I better get cooking."

Chapter 27

Whispers of War

Ahmed came home long after the dinner hour at least three nights a week. His parents didn't question him about what he was studying and why the course or courses he was taking had such sporadic hours. Edith, though, paid a lot of attention to his schedule for her dinner depended on it. One hungry evening as she waited to hear his key in the door she heard, instead, a motorbike come to a stop beneath her window and she heard Ahmed talking to someone.

"At last!" Edith said, looking at the clock on her table. It read 10:00 p.m.

But Ahmed didn't come right in. She strained to listen to the conversation he was having with someone. It wasn't a girl. She moved closer to the window, curious now to hear what was keeping him. It was difficult to hear because they kept their voices low as if they didn't want to be overheard. She caught the word 'meeting' several times. She thought she heard the word 'cocktail.'

"So that's it," she said to herself. "He's not going to school. He's meeting friends and they're out drinking three, four nights a week. Soon she heard the putt-putt of the motorbike taking off and shortly after that, Ahmed's key in the door.

His father was in the small study and on hearing Ahmed in the foyer called him into the room. It was Edith's lucky night for eavesdropping.

"How's the studying going?" Mohammad asked cheerfully.

"Not as hard as I thought it would be," Ahmed replied. "Economics is going okay but statistics is tripping me up. I think I'll have to get extra help."

"I'm really proud of you, son," Mohammad said, "Maybe you'll go into banking like your old man. I'd really like that. I wasn't sure you wanted to pursue higher studies so I can't tell you how much this pleases me. Keep at the books. It's not that easy getting placed into university."

"That reminds me, Dad, I could use some extra money. I need to find a good tutor, buy more books, and there are other incidentals."

"Sure. How much do you think you'll need?"

Ahmed pretended he was counting up the costs of tutoring, books, and incidentals and finally said, "A few hundred would be a great start."

Interesting, Edith thought. *If Mohammad only knew!*

A few nights later while waiting to eat something, anything, she heard the motorbike stop under her window again. This time she turned her light off and tiptoed around the end of her bed. She didn't dare cross the opening that separated her from the living room lest she be caught crouching and then questioned. Again, she strained to hear. Again, it was the same two voices. Ahmed and another male. This time she heard the other voice say, "Good work, do you think you can get even more money out of him?"

"I don't know," Ahmed answered. "He likes to know exactly where his money is going. He's a banker, remember. I'll have to wait a while."

"Okay," the other voice said, "But do anything you can to get your hands on more. Every bit helps. Rob the kids' piggy banks if you have to. They'll blame the help, they always do. The meeting's at 7 p.m. on Thursday."

"I'll be there," was the end of the conversation.

They're up to something, Edith surmised.

On her next opportunity to talk to Jasmine, Edith relayed her guesses about what Ahmed could be getting into. "He might be one to keep an ear and eye on," Edith said. "Maybe you'll notice him doing something odd or overhear something at dinner some night." Jasmine was all in on the idea. It sounded like something exciting was about to happen and she could certainly use some excitement.

Jasmine's opportunity to eavesdrop on the family happened sooner than she'd hoped. Even Ahmed showed up on Friday in time for dinner. The family was celebrating Nadia's thirteenth birthday. It would have been too extreme if Ahmed skipped it. He even participated in the event by presenting Nadia with thirteen of her favorite candy bars while making wisecracks about the terrible teens. Fadi gave Nadia an exceptional portrait he had drawn of her that made her shriek with delight. When Jasmine peeked through the kitchen door, she noticed Mr. Saleeb speaking to his wife in a low voice while the kids were in an uproar. The conversation was serious and he looked worried. Jasmine couldn't hear everything, but she clearly heard him say, "It's true. Aleppo has been bombed. I'm afraid trouble is coming to Damascus."

Nadia, who had the uncanny ability to tune into two events at once, shushed her teasing brothers with a wave of her hand and asked, "What kind of trouble, Baba?"

Mr. Saleeb was like a deer in headlights who had to think fast. "Oh, it's nothing. Besides, princesses like you never have to think about trouble," he said soothingly, then smoothly changed the subject. "Hey, it's almost time for the birthday cake, don't you think? Jasmine!" he called out. "The birthday girl can't wait to see her cake!"

Nadia was not to be deterred. "What happened in Aleppo, Baba? You remember my friend, Cala? The one who moved to Aleppo last year? Did something bad happen in Aleppo? I hope

Cala is alright."

"Jasmine!" Layla called out again.

Jasmine quickly moved away from the door and deliberately ran a knife over the icing on the cake, messing up a floret. "The cake is on its way. I just have to fix a little icing," Jasmine said just as Layla strode into the kitchen with an impatient face. "Sorry, Mrs. Saleeb, in my haste, I accidentally ruined this flower. I so want Nadia's cake to be perfect," she apologized as she redesigned the floret. "I just need a few more minutes. So sorry."

When she heard Layla explain the delay to the family, Jasmine hurried back to the crack in the door to hear Mr. Saleeb say to Nadia, "Okay, I agree it's unfair not to tell you what I've been hearing around town. You're all teenagers now and I think you're old enough to know some grown-up things. You know, of course, that our president Bashar al-Assad has been ruling Syria for the past eleven years, and before him, his father ruled for twenty-nine years until his death in 2000. Because of him, your mother has a good-paying government job, and as a banker, I benefit from his financial decisions. However, here we are in 2011 and there are some Syrians who don't like what they're calling 'al-Assad's authoritarian practices.' These groups have been banding together to hold anti-regime, pro-democracy protests around the country. Rightfully, the government has been quick to respond, using police, military and paramilitary forces to suppress these demonstrations. I've been hearing talk that the anti-regime forces have been trying to establish opposition militias of their own. One such militant group is said to have set off bombs in parts of Aleppo."

Mr. Saleeb wondered if he'd said too much. "Well, no doubt al-Assad will quickly squash any such resistance before it goes any further. But this is not happy birthday talk. Where is that cake?"

On cue, Jasmine presented the sprinkle-covered cake to Nadia. It was an instant distraction from Mr. Saleeb's somber conversation, but a totally temporary one as Fadi spoke up as soon as the last of the icing was licked from his lips.

"But Baba," he said, "are you saying that Syrians are bombing other Syrians? I thought bombs only came from enemies outside the country. Why would Syrians fight each other?"

"They foolishly want change," Mr. Saleeb said. "The kind of change they want will change our family's wealth and standing in the community. We can't have that. And we won't have that if we all stick together."

Jasmine was astonished by what she'd been hearing. The thought of bombings was alarming, but she was more alarmed by Ahmed's reaction. He was not participating at all. Rather he looked fidgety and unwilling to meet his father's eyes. He kept his mouth full of cake, hoping to avoid attention.

"You're nearly eighteen, Ahmed," his father's voice penetrated Ahmed's self-absorption. "What's the talk around school about the resistance? What are your friends saying about these uprisings?"

"Well, ah, no, not much. I mean, I don't pay much attention to politics. I stay focused on my studies and don't socialize much. This is all news to me."

Liar, Jasmine thought to herself. *Edith was right: Ahmed's up to something and it looks suspicious.*

Chapter 28

The Urn

Not long after Nadia's birthday, the household vibe went up a notch. Edith and Jasmine wondered what was happening and soon found out.

"Get up!" Abeena barked, looming tall over Edith's bed. Edith's eyes popped open in terror. Abeena had never stepped into Edith's corner of the house before. "What? What's the matter?" Edith cried out, startled.

"Get up, you foolish girl," Abeena demanded. "We have important guests coming tomorrow and this place has to be spit-shined." Edith looked at the clock on her night table. 6 a.m.

"I don't start my chores until 7 a.m.," Edith protested.

"I said get up. Take your mattress and night table out of here and put them in Jasmine's room. We need the sun porch for entertaining."

"Have you been in Jasmine's room?" Edith sassed back. "I couldn't squeeze my body in there, let alone my mattress and night table."

"Shall I call in Madam?" Abeena threatened.

"No," Edith relented, remembering Teressa's whipping. "Give me a minute to get dressed."

As Edith passed the kitchen door to collect her bucket, rags and dusters, she saw that Jasmine, too, had been awakened early. She shot Jasmine a what-the-hell-is-happening look and Jasmine returned a shrug.

By 8 a.m. the last of the family had left for work or school. Abeena was in high anxiety as it had been a while since she last arranged a party for international guests at the house. Everything had to be perfect. She would be a stern taskmaster over the help today.

"Why is Edith moving her stuff into my room?" Jasmine demanded of Abeena when she saw the mattress being shoved into her already cramped space. "Are you calling Habib to come and get me?"

"Don't I wish," Abeena replied, "but no. We have international guests coming to the house tomorrow night and everything has to be perfect. We need the porch. I'm afraid you'll have to put up with each other for two nights. If either of you grouse about it, I *will* call Mr. Habib."

Edith caught the end of Abeena's threat and winked at Jasmine as she passed, arms full of cleaning supplies.

"Baseboards, windows, bookcases," Abeena directed, standing in the doorway of the drawing room. On closer inspection of the room she added, "That bookshelf hasn't been touched in years! I can see the dust from here."

Edith hadn't even noticed the bookcase before. Books were lying upside down and sideways, most were leather bound, and there were a few pieces of thick crystal with inscriptions in Arabic and dates on them that looked decades old. Then behind it all was a vase with a lid. From the shoulders of the vase a beautiful painting of purple wisteria draped toward the base. The wisteria was accented with dots of gold. She hadn't noticed it before as the dust had dulled its colors.

"Be careful with that!" Abeena demanded, as Edith slid the vase out from behind the dusty crystal.

"What is this thing?" Edith asked.

"That's Madam's grandfather."

"What?" shrilled Edith, beginning to realize the vase was actually an urn.

"Madam's grandfather was appointed poet laureate of Syria in the 1930's. That's him in there. Those books are volumes of his work. Madam treasures all of it. In fact, rearrange these mementos so our guests will see they are definitely visiting the home of a prominent family."

Edith wondered how often Layla's grandpa had turned over in his urn watching this household of horrible people, as she gave his resting place a final buff.

As the day and the household jobs wore on, Abeena was surprised the help was not begrudging the long list of chores. She never suspected that putting the two in the same sleeping room, small as it might be, was the first best thing that had happened to them since they arrived in Damascus.

The second best thing happened shortly thereafter.

"You, Jasmine, come with me," called Abeena. "You need to come to the market with me. I can't carry everything I need for the dinner party tomorrow. You'll have to help. And don't think you can get away," she added as she pulled out her cellphone. "I have the police number right here in my hand. They know me. I know them. One call from me and you will be in jail."

Then she turned to Edith and said, "I'm locking you in," at which Jasmine looked at Edith and said snidely, "Better hope there's no fire."

"Come along, Jasmine," Abeena ordered and Edith heard the bolt turning on the other side of the door.

It was a fourteen-hour day for both women with no breaks for meals. At least Jasmine could nibble as she chopped while Edith went hungry. "Don't worry," whispered Jasmine as she unpacked the groceries from their trip to the market. "I've made you a sandwich." She held the pocket of her apron open and Edith could see a big fat sandwich tucked there. "For you. For later."

"What kind?" said Edith, salivating.

"Prosciutto!"

That was enough to hold Edith until she was told she could retire for the evening. And when she and Jasmine closed the broom closet door behind them, they argued loudly for the benefit of Abeena who surely had her ear to the wall. They quarreled about where to stash Edith's mattress, who had to sleep with her face to the brooms, who had just farted. When Abeena was satisfied the girls were not plotting to spoil the party or even escape, she banged on the wall and shouted, "Quiet in there."

The girls giggled quietly with their hands to their mouths. Their ploy to show discontent with each other had worked. Now they could whisper and try to figure out how to escape their miseries.

Jasmine was quite excited to tell Edith about her morning at the market. It was the first time in months she had gotten out of the house. Now she knew where the market was and the streets surrounding it. She said she memorized all the surroundings and could get there again with her eyes closed if need be.

"It's called Al-Hamidiyah Souq," she told Edith. "It's huge! You can find anything there. I've never seen anything so vibrant." She went to describe the clothes emporiums, the craft vendors and jewelry shops, the grocery stands, the food stalls and "oh, my!" she exclaimed, "there's even ice cream vendors."

Edith, too, had something to report although it was nowhere near as exciting as Jasmine's adventure to the souq. Edith told how she had befriended Fadi and that he was a fairly good artist. She said she had asked him to show her around his city via his drawings and he was delighted to have a project that finally interested someone in this house. "He should be a cartographer!" Edith whispered. "Each week he adds more streets. He even puts in the important buildings. I know I could identify the buildings he has drawn if I ever get to see them. He's really a sweetie," she added. "I hope he doesn't get into trouble when *they* find out he helped us escape."

"Escape?" laughed Jasmine. "Do you *really* think we're going to escape this hell hole?"

"I *know* we're going to escape. It says so in my notebook."

"Don't bullshit me, Edith. I'm not up to it," Jasmine said dreamily as her breathing slowed and sleep was closing in.

"Dream it, my friend. We're out of here one of these days. I don't know when, I don't know how, but we're out of here."

"Whatever you say," were Jasmine's last words as she drifted off.

The next morning at 6 a.m. Abeena banged on the broom closet door. "Up!" she demanded. "I want this house to look like it was featured in a magazine and the food to be the best our guests have ever tasted. Hurry!"

Jasmine was sent to the kitchen. The apartment was humming with excitement. Today there would be guests for dinner from Dubai. "Some Croatians," Layla told the children as they slurped up their fava bean salad of yogurt, tahini, chickpeas and pita bread. "A banker and his wife from Zagreb who now live in Dubai will be here to meet with your father. It's important we present our whole family as people of international importance. That means you must be on your best behavior."

"That's crazy," Nadia said, "what's a Croatian banker doing in Dubai? And what's that have to do with Baba?"

Hurriedly Layla tried to explain. "There's a new national bank that just opened in Dubai, Emirates National Bank, and it's making a big impact in the banking world. Our guests are from HSBC which has a presence in Dubai. Our bank, well I mean your father's bank, has significant dealings with HSBC. Oh, Nadia, don't ask so many questions. Just be charming."

"I don't speak Croatian and my English is not all that good," whined Nadia. "I'll be afraid to talk."

"Just try your best," Layla went on, now preoccupied with making sure she had everything in her briefcase that she would need for work. "I'll be home at 1 p.m.

"Edith, do up the master bedroom today. Top to bottom. Jasmine, here are the recipes I want you to follow. Oh, and set up the drink cart on the sun porch. Make sure all the good liquors are on it. Bye Nadia, bye Fadi," she said, giving each a kiss on the head. "I know," she said to Ahmed, "you've outgrown my kisses. Bye, love," and she was gone.

Edith assembled her tools for the day's cleaning and headed toward the master. She looked at the king bed longingly. She would love to climb into it and sleep there until her contract was up. She sighed and set down her bucket. Although she had cleaned this room every week, she hadn't taken the time to really look at it and the objects that made it so unique. For one, there was a beautiful tapestry tacked to the ceiling's corners and drawn up in the center where a chandelier hung, creating the feeling of being under a beautiful tent in the desert. The headboard was solid walnut, carved to depict rays of the morning sun. At the foot of the bed two bedposts, each three feet high and four inches square, stood sentinel. A highly polished, silky smooth walnut post cap topped each of these stanchions. Edith put her hand on one of the post caps and let the satiny wood talk to the palm of her hand. She told herself the wood was hugging her hand and she gave into the hug, only then realizing how much she needed one.

The moment passed quickly and she became Edith the Cleaning Lady once again. She began dusting the furniture then moved on to the heavily framed artwork that occupied the walls. As she stretched to reach the top of one of the frames it moved a bit, becoming crooked, and when she moved it back into position she noticed it caught on something from behind.

"Look at that!" she said as a metal door with a key slot appeared. "A safe!" she whistled. "I wouldn't be surprised if my passport is in there."

It took Edith two more hours to finish the room. When she finally stood back to see that everything was in order, she noticed one of Mr. Saleeb's black socks on the floor just under the edge of the bed. Tired, she grabbed the bed's post cap for balance so she wouldn't have to get down on her knees to retrieve the sock. But instead of the bedpost being as sturdy as it looked, the post cap turned and she almost fell on her face. "Shit," she said, angry at herself for breaking the bedpost. "Maybe I can get it back on." She started an attempt but when she turned it just a bit it fell to the floor.

"Shit. Shit," she repeated, picking up the post cap and inspecting it. "Hmm," she noted on further inspection, "it looks like it just screws in."

As she lined up the post cap to fit it into its bedpost, she noticed the hole seemed even deeper than it needed to be. On closer inspection she noticed a wire in that hole. She plucked the wire out and found a small key attached. "Hmm," she purred again, considering the key. "Is this the key to that safe? Could be!" Then fear of Abeena overcame her and she quickly stuffed the wired key back into the hole and screwed the post cap back into its original position. *Happy day!* she wrote in her notebook when she had her ten-minute break. *All things are possible.*

Edith and Jasmine were handed new black shirts and skirts and highly starched white aprons for the evening's event. They looked like Abeena only prettier. They both were to serve the canapes before dinner then Edith was to disappear while Jasmine continued on as waitress.

The guests, the Glamuzinas, were extremely congenial. They marveled at the richness and antiquity of the apartment, they avoided all talk of business and engaged the children in conversations. Soon Nadia and Fadi were competing to show the guests their favorite things. Nadia stood up and pirouetted in front of Mrs. Glamuzina, saying she had chosen all the elements of her outfit so she could look international. "Charming," said Victoria Glamuzina, "you certainly could be on any world stage with your choice of these fashion components. Absolutely stunning."

Nadia beamed. "I want to be a fashion designer," she bragged in fairly decent English as she swirled around the room.

Fadi excused himself then returned with his sketch pad in hand. "This is what I like to do," he said as he sat himself between the Glamuzinas and turned the page to his drawings of Damascus. Edith panicked. She almost dropped the tray of stuffed mushrooms she was about to place in front of the guests.

Steve Glamuzina looked carefully at the drawings and said they were well beyond a boy of his years. He asked Fadi if he wanted to be an artist.

"Yes," Fadi enthusiastically replied. His parents looked at each other as if saying 'since when?'

"Looks like you should be a cartographer," Mr. Glamuzina continued.

"What's that?" Fadi replied.

"An artist who draws maps, all kinds of maps. They could be geological or landform maps, historical maps, political boundary maps and road maps, like your city map," he explained. "What was your inspiration for this map?" he asked.

"Well, I wanted to show ..." then he caught himself. He was not supposed to talk to the help. Ever. So he quickly revised his story. "I wanted to show my class how to get around the city. It was an assignment. We each had to pick a topic and represent it through art. I drew Damascus because I know where everything is here. Mine was the best. My teacher said I should pursue my art."

"And so you should, young man," Mr. Glamuzina wholeheartedly agreed.

Ahmed sat quietly as usual. "Will you go into banking like your father?" Steve asked, turning his attention to the young man.

"I think so," Ahmed mumbled. "I'm not sure."

"Of course, you're sure," his father interjected.

"You've been spending many nights in the library studying for the exams that will get you into a university program, hopefully finance," his father said looking admiringly at his oldest son.

Ahmed was saved from further questioning by Abeena's announcement for dinner.

With just the nod of her head, she had summoned the help from the living room to the kitchen, officially ending the cocktail hour. "Your job is done," she said to Edith, "go to your room and stay there until the guests are gone. You, Jasmine, start plating. Remember, you are the help, be as invisible as possible as you serve. Serve the ladies first, then Mr. Glamuzina, the master, and finally the children. Now hurry."

The guests were so conversant and the family so engaged that no one noticed the invisible Jasmine as she brought full plates in and empty plates out while taking in every word.

"You know, Mohammad," Steve was saying, "Victoria and I worried about coming on this trip. Even in Dubai we heard talk of a war going on here in Syria. We weren't sure it was safe to travel here."

"It's perfectly safe here," Mohammad assured. "It's the rebels up north who are trying Assad's patience," he continued. "It's mostly kids throwing rocks and a few Molotov cocktails. Sure, it's a problem, rebellion always is. But Assad's taking care of it. His army will put a quick stop to it."

"I hear the worst of the fighting is in Aleppo, that the government is spraying gas on the citizens," Steve persisted.

"Nonsense," Mohammad quickly replied.

"How far is Aleppo from Damascus?" Steve continued to probe.

"At least 220 miles, maybe more," Mohammad answered, trying to sound casual. "I assure you the rebellion won't get this far south."

"You're sure of that?" Steve said, needing one more affirmation to be convinced.

"Positive," Mohammad said firmly.

"Hear that, Victoria? We're perfectly safe," he said to his wife. "So tomorrow before we leave for the airport, we should visit the famous souq. It's around here, isn't it?" he asked Layla.

"You are so close you could walk there," Layla replied, mentioning a few of her favorite shops.

The two younger children sat quietly getting an earful of war talk, becoming frightened. Not Ahmed. He kept his eyes to his plate pretending none of this concerned him.

Eventually good-byes were said; promises were made to bring Layla along to Dubai for the next round of meetings; compliments were paid to each of the children and finally it was over.

Abeena was exhausted. "I'm going to bed," she said. "Tomorrow morning I don't want to see any evidence of a party here, do you understand?" The girls understood perfectly. Then Abeena noticed the soup tureen. "And don't touch the soup tureen. It's a family heirloom, a most prized family treasure, and I don't trust you to put it away. I'll take care of that myself in the morning."

The children had already disappeared into their rooms. Layla and Mohammad sat in the living room sipping one last nightcap before walking toward their bedroom past the kitchen, without saying a word, not even a thank you.

Although everyone seemed to be out of earshot, the girls did not dare say a word to one another lest the walls had ears. They each had news but it would have to wait.

"You'll never guess my news!" Edith whispered as soon as they shut themselves into 'The Broom,' as they now called their sleeping quarters. She related the secrets of the master bedroom. "I bet our passports are in that safe," she added, "and it needs a key to open it. Wait for it!" she added, barely containing herself, "I think I found the key! It's in the bedpost at the foot of the bed! Oh, they think they are so clever, those Saleebs."

"Did you look in the safe?" Jasmine wanted to know.

"No, I chickened out. Any minute Abeena or somebody could have walked in." Jasmine looked disappointed, but Edith promised she'd "take a peek next Tuesday when the gestapo goes to market."

"You won't like *my* news," Jasmine began. "Tonight's guests said that in Dubai the talk is all about war here in Syria. They almost canceled their visit but Mr. Saleeb had assured them war wasn't coming to Damascus. The guests said they had heard the Syrian government was gassing citizens in Aleppo."

"Where's Aleppo?" Edith asked.

"A couple hours from here. Not all that far," she relayed. "One more thing," Jasmine added, "I kept my eye on Ahmed's response to all the talk of war. His reaction was not like the other children who looked scared and very concerned. He looked like he was trying to disappear. He kept his head low to the plate, eating without looking up. I'm pretty good at reading people. He might know more about the war than any of us. Maybe he knows it's coming here, too. Maybe he's one of the rebels."

"Phew," Edith blew a long sigh. "We have to get out of here Jasmine. But how? Do you ever pray?" she asked.

"No," Jasmine admitted.

"It's time to start," Edith said as she folded her hands and started a petition. "Repeat after me," Edith said and Jasmine was more than willing. "Please God, please get us out of here, we pray."

Chapter 29

A Lucky Break

By morning everything was back in its place except, of course, the soup tureen. "Edith," Abeena commanded, "fetch the step ladder from Jasmine's room. I need to put the tureen up there," and she pointed to the top shelf.

"That's pretty high, are you sure you want to climb that high? I'm much ..." she was going to say "thinner" but decided to say "younger."

"No, I don't trust you. I've done this a dozen times. Just get on with your chores."

"Okay," Edith said, and then added, "can Jasmine help me put my mattress back on the sun porch?"

Abeena waved Edith away with one hand as she set up the ladder with the other.

Edith and Jasmine were still trudging the flopping mattress through the house when a combination of ladder crashing, tureen breaking and Abeena screaming occurred concurrently. They dropped the mattress and ran. "Help me! Help me!" Abeena cried. "My knee, my knee!" Edith tiptoed through the shards of porcelain while Jasmine attempted to remove Abeena's leg from between the ladder's rungs. "Don't! Don't touch it!" Abeena cried even louder.

"We have to untangle you," Jasmine said, "I'm being as careful as I can." The girls put their hands to their mouths and looked at each other when they saw the damage. Abeena's leg was pointed in an unnatural direction from her body.

"What should we do?" Jasmine cried.

It looked like Abeena was going into shock. "We have to call Layla," Edith said. "Abeena, where's your phone?"

"Help me! Help me!" shrieked Abeena.

"Abeena, quick, where's your phone?"

"In my pocket," the woman struggled to say.

"I'm going to roll you over a little to reach your phone." Abeena let out a blood-curdling scream as the phone was extracted from her pocket.

"Your passcode!" Edith demanded, holding Abeena's cheeks in her hands to help her focus on the question. "What's your passcode?"

For a moment Abeena didn't know her passcode. "Think," cried Edith. "We need to get you some help. What's your passcode?"

"4321"

"Madam Saleeb," Edith said into the phone. "There's been an accident. Abeena has fallen off the ladder while trying to put your soup tureen on the high shelf."

"Oh my God," Layla responded, "can it be repaired?"

"I doubt it but that's not the emergency. Abeena is hurt. Badly. Her leg is twisted. I think something's broken. Can you come right home?"

Within the hour the medics had carted Abeena off to the hospital. Layla went with her and as the bolt clicked from the outside, Layla was calling through the door, "I'm going with Abeena, Mr. Saleeb is on his way home now. Tell him I've gone to the hospital."

"Damn," said Jasmine. "I thought we could be alone."

"Fat chance," concurred Edith.

Abeena's broken tibia and torn ACL created a long-term problem for the Saleebs. Their taskmaster would be incapacitated for weeks after surgery, maybe even months. How were they going to control the help without her oversight? Layla suggested to Mohammad they send Abeena back to Ethiopia and get someone new. Ahmed overheard his mother's comment and for the first time ever, vehemently objected to her edicts.

"I heard that! How can you be so cruel, Mama!" he said, storming out of his room to confront her. "Abeena's been like a mother to me. Sometimes more of a mother than you. Who hugged me when I didn't make the football team? Who took me for stitches when I sliced my finger fixing my bicycle? Who took me for ice cream? No, Mama, you will not send Abeena away. She's mine. I love her."

"That cut deep," Layla said when Ahmed's diatribe finally ended. "I'm so sorry that's how you feel. I didn't realize I have not been here for you all while you were growing up and that Abeena was. I thought you were an easy-going child without a care in the world."

"I don't think you even know who I am, what I'm all about," Ahmed said soulfully.

"I suppose there are a lot of things I don't know about you. But I'll change that. I'll spend more time with you. And I won't send Abeena away."

"I love you, Mother, I really do," Ahmed replied, giving her a hug. "We're good. We don't need to spend more time together." He had just dodged a bullet because he certainly didn't want his mother more involved in his life. She wouldn't like it, or accept it.

Layla turned her attention back to Mohammad and the problem at hand. "How are we going to manage this crisis?"

"Let's not make this a crisis," he said. "We'll help Abeena get to the living room each morning. It's a convenient place from which to run the household and she can keep an eye on the help more easily. Ahmed," he added, pulling his son into the conversation, "will you help Abeena navigate to the recliner on her crutches? She trusts you and would do anything for you. In the meantime, Jasmine will have to go to the market on Tuesdays. But how can we make sure she doesn't bolt?" he wondered aloud.

"She couldn't get far even if she tried," Layla said. "We have her passport. I'll read her the riot act. I'll tell her that her passport will never be returned if she tries anything. I'll tell her the police are always noticing Filipinas who are out and about alone, handcuffing them until their owners can be notified. I'll remind her that she has no rights as an overseas worker here in Syria and that life in jail is more than an idle threat. And I'll finish by saying if she tries anything foolish, she will work without a salary until we toss her out onto the street."

"That should do it," Mohammad agreed. "She'd be a fool to attempt an escape. Call the help in. Let's get this over with."

Although Edith and Jasmine listened to the Saleeb's plan without showing emotion, inside they were both jumping for joy and couldn't wait for a stolen moment when they could discuss Jasmin's new routine of Tuesday trips to the market.

"Yes, Madam," they responded in unison with solemn faces, "we understand. You can trust us."

The first week after the fall was the best. Abeena was so terrified she'd pull her knee and her shin apart again that she refused to try her crutches. She insisted she needed to stay in bed.

"No," said Layla, "You have to keep moving or all your muscles will atrophy." With that, Layla spelled out the plan. "Ahmed is going to help you get used to your crutches. He'll help you get to the living area each morning before he leaves for school. Once you're in the living room it will be easy to keep an eye on things and control our workers."

Abeena unwillingly agreed. The accident had depleted her piss and vinegar. She wasn't her old self and the help was quick to notice.

"I don't know how long Abeena will lack the courage to stand up without assistance," Edith said to Jasmine, without the need to whisper. They knew Abeena was literally stuck in her bed for now. "Before Ahmed gets her up on crutches, snooping around, we need to see if the key fits that safe. Getting caught could be the death of us. So here's what we're going to do." She told Jasmine her plan.

"Noooooo!" wailed Jasmine. "I am *not* going to give that woman a shower. It's bad enough looking at her with her clothes on. I can't do that, Edith. I've never seen anyone naked before! Except," she added, a sly smile crossing her lips, "for Eduardo."

"There you go! You're halfway there! Besides, it's essential that Abeena is under our control for once. She's not going anywhere naked. A nice, long shower is the answer."

"*You* give the shower, Edith. *I'll* check the safe."

"Nope. It's only fair. On Tuesdays you get to use your get-out-of-jail card for a few hours while I shrivel up in here."

"I guess," Jasmine capitulated, and to show her disdain for the idea, she puckered up and threw Edith a kissy face.

Chapter 30

Chewy Ice Cream

The next Tuesday morning, Jasmine woke up so excited she could hardly stand it. Today was the day she was getting out to go to the market. Alone. It took only minutes to dress since she really had no choice but to put on her work uniform. She hurried to the kitchen to make breakfast and was humming to herself when the grumpy-faced Layla came in for her coffee. "Jasmine," she began, "don't forget what I said about the consequences of any escape attempt when you go to the souq today."

"I wouldn't dream of it," Jasmine quickly responded. "But I am looking forward to seeing all the foods the market offers. When I went to market with Abeena last week, we were shopping for your guests' dinner party and I didn't have a chance to see it all. I've made the shopping list for the week, but I'm hoping to discover other foods that I can use to make something different and delicious for the family." Jasmine was immediately informed that the food budget must not be exceeded. "I carefully review the shopping list every week and I also know how much Abeena spends on the groceries. I expect you to stay within budget, as she does," Layla commanded. "According to Abeena, shopping will take you three hours, max. At precisely noon, Abeena will be at the front door to unlock it for you. Be there on time."

At 9 a.m. Jasmine was on the other side of the apartment door and resisted literally skipping down the street toward the market. When she arrived, she was astounded at the size of Damascus's largest and most popular market. She and Abeena had only visited a tiny corner of it, she realized, so she spent her first twenty minutes just exploring its vastness and window shopping at the hundreds of display cases. The overwhelming smell was a jarring combination of freshly-slaughtered lambs and goats, and glassy-eyed fish. The stench took some getting used to. Some stands offered goat heads and lamb carcasses, while others were overflowing with fruits and vegetables she had never seen before. If she took any interest in a particular display, the vendor would rush over and enthusiastically promote his food as "freshest and best price in the market."

She was on the lookout for the ice cream stand she'd seen the week before. Catching sight of it, she stood there gazing longingly at the vast array of flavors. *If only I had a little extra money, I'd treat myself,* she thought ruefully. Remembering Layla's penny-pinching orders not to exceed the food allowance budget, Jasmine reluctantly turned her back on the creamy confections, took out her grocery list and began to shop. She was halfway through her list, buying two pounds of this and a pound of that. She approached the prosciutto stand and asked the vendor for three pounds of the family's favorite ham. Abruptly, she changed her mind. "Make that just two pounds," she said. She had suddenly realized Layla would never know the difference, but that she would end up with a bit of spending money. Ice cream was now in her near future. Jasmine finished buying the rest of the items on the list, and by just slightly shorting the amount of everything else she purchased, she had more than enough for ice cream. She also realized that she had completed the shopping list in just over two hours. *Aha!* she said to herself. *Abeena's been snagging an extra hour out all this time!*

Soon she was standing in front of a tempting array of ice

cream, some of which she'd never heard of. "I haven't decided yet," she told the vendor more than once. On his third attempt to take her order, the vendor quickly and impatiently turned to a man standing nearby who ordered a coffee. The man had overheard Jasmine's indecision and offered his advice. "I recommend that one," the man said, pointing to a pinkish ice cream in the case. "It's very good. Has a mango flavor and bits of fruit. Never tasted anything that good back home."

Jasmine turned to the man and said, "I'll try it! Thanks!" and summoned the vendor who rolled his eyes as if snarling "finally!" "I guess Syrians never heard of good customer service," she said quietly before breaking into a short, but cathartic laugh. It was infectious enough to make the man laugh along with her.

Jasmine was astonished at how good it felt just to laugh out loud and to have a normal everyday conversation with someone. Especially someone who spoke English so well. "You better eat that before it drips on your clothes," he said. "You're right," she said, taking a big lick, knowing a fresh stain on her uniform was the first thing Abeena would notice. "I better sit down and finish this. Wanna join me and finish your coffee?"

"I'm curious. What kind of ice cream do they make 'back home' and where is back home, anyway?" she asked as they sat at one of the three tables outside the stand.

He told her back home was Phoenix, Arizona where he was born and raised. "An American!" Jasmine exclaimed. "Never met one before. You're not what I pictured, but you seem okay. Did you decide that Syria might be fun to visit, or what?" Jasmine said, making the man laugh again.

"My name is Joe Voltz," he said, "and I work for a newspaper. I'm on assignment here," he said, reaching into his pocket and handing over a business card. "This is my first trip outside of the U.S. and to tell you the truth, Syria would not be my first or even fortieth destination choice. It's so different and strange. Heck, they even sell ice cream made from the hardened sap of a chia tree. It's called booza, a chewy ice cream studded with pista-chios. I've been googling," he admitted.

Jasmine stopped licking and exclaimed, "Chewy ice cream! Sure sounds weird."

"I was going to recommend you try that," Joe said, "just to see the expression on your face, but since I wasn't adventurous enough to try it myself, I couldn't recommend it to you."

"Well, for someone who came all the way to Syria to eat ice cream in a market, I'd say you were pretty adventurous," Jasmine said.

Joe laughed, saying, "Well, yes, I was expecting this trip to be an adventure, but so far, I'm a little disappointed and a tiny bit bored. That is, until I discovered this market. It's quite exciting. Actually, I'm supposed to be at my computer writing an article, but there's not much news to report. Maybe I should write a story about this market and about the interesting people one might meet here! It might even include you, but I didn't get your name."

"I'm Jasmine," she replied.

"Well, Jasmine, I've told you part of my story. What's your story? You don't look Syrian. Where's 'back home' for you?" Jasmine hesitated. Although she had felt comfortable with the casualness of their conversation, she began to worry that perhaps this Joe person was sent by Layla to spy on her. She decided not to directly answer. "My parents are Filipino and I'm from here and there," she hedged. "I came to Syria to find a good job." She desperately needed to change the subject. "So, Joe, what story are you supposed to be writing? I'm sure you weren't sent all this way to write about goat heads," she teased.

"I'm here to cover the civil disturbance between the govern-ment and the anti-regime rebels. But nothing's going on here. I may have to travel to Aleppo because I hear that's where the ac-tion is right now."

Just then Jasmine caught a glance at the oversize clock hang-ing on the wall. "Oh my lord," she said, jumping up and grabbing her groceries. "I've got to run. And fast. It was fun talking to you," she said over her shoulder as she darted away in panic.

He shouted after her, "When will you be here again?"

Jasmine hesitated, but just for a second. "Next Tuesday, same time," she hollered back before disappearing into the crowd. *Wait 'til I tell Edith about this. We now have a source for war information,* she thought as she ran like hell.

Chapter 31

Shower Power

Without a minute to spare, Jasmine knocked breathlessly on the apartment door. Abeena, now on crutches, was waiting near the door to unlock it. She wobbled a bit as she followed Jasmine into the kitchen where she examined the purchases. Satisfied that the grocery list had been completed, she hobbled back toward the recliner at a snail's pace. Jasmine said to Abeena's back, "I even have a little bit of money left. Where should I put it?"

In short bursts over the next few hours, Jasmine relayed her market experience to Edith. Edith was astonished when she learned about Jasmine's serendipitous meeting with an American reporter and was even more excited to hear Jasmine could have a second chance next Tuesday to hear more about the war. "That seals it," Edith whispered. "This confirms what we've been hearing about a civil war. If, or perhaps when, Damascus becomes a target and war breaks out here, that is our escape window of opportunity. Be ready to pick this Joe's brain," she said, before adding, "Are you sure he's trustworthy? Maybe he was just trying to pick you up. What does this Joe Voltz look like? How old is he?" Edith wanted to know.

"Gosh, I never even gave it a thought he might be trying to pick me up. I was only worried that he'd been sent by Layla or

Abeena to spy on me. Sometimes I'm quite oblivious, unconscious even. But, really, I didn't get any pick-up vibes from him. He's just a nice guy, maybe around thirty, tall, slender and a little bored in Damascus. I guess he was good-looking, but I was so delighted to have someone to talk to, someone who could make me laugh, that I really didn't pay much attention to his looks. I think he is who he says he is. So, yes, I'd say he is trustworthy," Jasmine answered.

Just then Edith heard the front door open and in voice loud enough to be overhead said, "Jasmine, you've got to stop being so obnoxious. It's making me mad." This was for the benefit of Nadia who had burst into the kitchen to hoping to witness an uproar. "Oh, that was close," Jasmine said after Nadia realized the fireworks were over and left.

"Where did this money on the counter come from?" Layla wanted to know when she arrived home from work. "It was left over from my trip to the market," Jasmine said. Layla's eyebrows shot up in surprise and she actually smiled. "Well done," she said, looking as if coughing out a compliment was killing her. "What's for dinner?"

Throughout the rest of that week, Edith was consumed with planning and plotting the logistics of their escape. She had memorized the maps Fadi had already shown her. He was still working on a couple of others. But most of all, she was eager to see if the key fit.

"Ready or not," Edith said to Jasmine, "today is shower day. Please don't tell Abeena she stinks."

"But she does!" Jasmine said, wishing to get out of the task. "This is going to be so gross! Okay," she finally relented. "I'll just tell her she has a strong body odor that needs tending to."

"Be nice, Jasmine," Edith said thoughtfully. "Even though Abeena thinks she's the boss of us, she's in the same boat we are in. She's just another slave in this house. Her story is different, that's all. And she really does need a shower. I don't see any of *them* offering any kindnesses," she added, nodding toward the rest of the house.

The next morning Abeena was reluctantly convinced that she needed to be washed and soon was sitting on a shower bench, getting drenched by Jasmine who was wishing she had a nose plug. As soon as she heard the water running, Edith snuck into the master bedroom. "One more favor, God, please let this key fit," she prayed as she unscrewed the bedpost finial and retrieved the key. To her utter ecstasy, the safe opened easily. Inside were several Syrian passports and beneath those were Abeena's, Jasmine's and hers. Then she noticed a fat bank pouch and discovered a huge amount of money inside. "Thank you, lord," Edith said with sincere gratitude. She closed the safe and returned the key to its hiding place.

She knocked on the bathroom door. "Jasmine, next time put the cap back on the honey jar," Edith said to the door. "It took me twenty minutes to clean that sticky mess off the counter and now we're out of honey," she whined. Edith immediately heard the water turn off.

"Let's get you dried off, Abeena," she heard Jasmine say. "Now you smell nice and fresh."

Chapter 32
The Safe Cracker

The shower had exhausted Abeena and she fell immediately asleep, snoring without a care in the world.

"Our passports are in there and so is a whole lot of money," Edith whispered, not taking a chance their warden would awake. "Shall we assume that's where the Saleebs are safekeeping the wages they owe us?" she said hopefully.

"Yes! Let's assume!" Jasmine added, clapping her hands. "How much is in there? Let's take it all!"

"You'd make a terrible thief!" Edith giggled. "They'd discover it was gone and blame us right away. Besides, we're good Christian women," she added with a puff of dignity. "We'll only take what's ours."

Edith retrieved her notebook which had a calendar on the inside back cover. "Let's see. I've been here for thirteen months. The first month I sent a letter home with $200. That means I'm owed for twelve months. Of course, they'll deduct $80 for monthly room and board, just like what happened to Maya." She scribbled some numbers on the notebook's last page. "As of today, I've only earned $1,440," she lamented. "Let's see what they owe you," she continued.

"I've only been in this house eleven months," Jasmine replied.

"Did you get paid in your previous situation?" Edith asked.

"Nope. They never gave me a cent, except for the first month, same as you.

"You, too?" Edith said surprised. "Writing a letter must be the scheme to make loved ones back home think all goes well for us in Syria." Edith went back to her numbers. "I think the Saleebs will want to make up for your 'pain and suffering' in the nanny job. I think they'd be happy to pay you the same as me, fourteen months and counting."

"I'll have to write them a thank-you note when we get home," Jasmine wisecracked, adding somberly, "if we ever do."

"Everyone will be back any minute," Edith warned, as she tossed the notebook under her mattress and grabbed a mop. Just as quickly, scents from Jasmine's knife slicing through a fragrant onion drifted into the hall. The scent woke Abeena. "I feel so much better," she called out to Jasmine. "Thank you for the shower. I know I needed it, but didn't know how to accomplish it."

"No problem," Jasmine replied, "I'll be happy to do it again for you," she gagged.

Keys rattled at the door as Ahmed let himself in. "How did your day go, Abeena?"

"I had a fine day," she replied. "But, except for a nice shower Jasmine gave me, I've been in this chair most of the day. Could you help me to my room, dear?"

Within the hour everyone had returned home and the house became a living entity once again. Aromas from Jasmine's culinary skills put everyone in a fine mood of anticipation. Mohammad was in the study reading his newspaper. Layla was thumbing through the latest edition of *Marie Claire*, the one with Loris Kraemerth on the cover, Fadi was gaming on his Playstation and Nadia, usually on the phone until dinner, was knocking on Ahmed's door.

"Go away," he said as she opened the door.

"Can I borrow your earbuds?" she asked.

"No, you can't borrow my buds."

"I need them," she bellowed "give them to me."

Everyone in the house looked up from what they were doing. A moment of silence was followed by Nadia yelling, "You better give them to me or..." and then she lowered her voice to a whisper, "I'll tell Mom and Dad."

Ahmed lowered his voice, too. "Tell them what, Nadia?" he said, trying to sound nonchalant when he actually felt cornered. "What are you talking about, Nadia?"

"I know what you're doing. I know you're hanging out with kids in the neighborhood who are planning to join the rebellion," she said, still whispering.

"I am not," he said, as calmly as he could. "Where did you get that idea?"

"Claudia."

"Claudia? You mean that stupid fat ass you hang around with? What would she know?"

"She says her brother picks you up on his motorbike and takes you to meetings with him, that's what she knows," Nadia shot back. "Now can I have your earbuds?"

"No," Ahmed reiterated.

"Motorbike!" Nadia yelled, sure there was an audience on the other side of his door.

"Okay. Okay," Ahmed said, shushing her up. "What Claudia told you is a big fat lie. I swear to you it's a lie. But if you are willing never to bring this up again, you can use my earbuds. Please bring them back when you're done."

"Thank you," said Nadia sweetly, "I knew Claudia had to be lying. She always is." She left the room with a satisfied grin. She now had Ahmed in her pocket.

"What's going on?" Layla asked as Nadia stuck the earbuds in her ears and walked toward her room.

"Nothing," Nadia replied, pointing to her ears indicating she could no longer hear what her mother was saying.

Everyone in the house sensed something was going on, but only Ahmed and Nadia knew what it was. There was tension that evening at dinner, even the lamb was tough.

"What was that all about?" Edith asked Jasmine a little later when they had a chance to sneak in a few words.

"It started over Nadia wanting Ahmed's earbuds and he did not want to give them to her. She threatened him with something and he was quick to hand them over. There was one word that seemed out of place in all this," Jasmine continued. "We all heard it. Nadia yelled out 'motorbike.' I'm sure it made no sense to Layla and Mohammad. But I thought you would find it interesting."

"Indeed I do," said Edith.

Ever since she tore her ACL and smashed her tibia, Abeena showed a little less animosity toward the help. She became a little less strident in her orders. She began to trust that Jasmine would return from her Tuesday trip to the market exactly on time and Edith would do as told, almost cheerfully, especially lately. So right after lunch, letting down her guard, she tucked the house key into her bosom, gave some afternoon orders and announced it was time for a nap.

Edith needed to make sure the 'nap' was not just a ruse to spy on them and decided to test her theory. One time she slammed a door loudly. "What's that?" Abeena awoke startled. "I tripped over the vacuum cleaner," Edith called back. Another time Jasmine left the tea kettle whistling. That, too, woke Abeena. "Sorry," called Jasmine.

"I can tell by the snores when she's asleep," Edith confided to Jasmine. "But it doesn't take much to wake her. Let's not get careless."

During the next few days of Abeena's naps, Edith and Jasmine began to plan their escape in earnest. First on their agenda was breaking into the safe, retrieving their passports and stealing the money they calculated they were owed, adding $10 with each passing day. Second, they needed to find a good hiding place. This conversation continued over several afternoons. Hiding places were in short supply in this house. They lamented the destruction of the heirloom soup tureen as that would have been perfect. Not on the sun porch, not in The Broom and certainly not under Edith's mattress. While Abeena snored, they stood in the living area looking around.

"Grandpa!" Edith suddenly exclaimed, pulling the vase off the bookshelf. "Grandpa, are you up for a caper?"

"That looks like an urn!" Jasmine said horrified. "There might be a body in there!"

"It's just Grandpa," Edith laughed, opening the lid to a cloud of ashes that rose to the occasion. "This is where we'll stash our cash," she coughed.

"We can't do that! That's so gross, it's so ... so disrespectful," Jasmine cried as she held her mouth to keep from puking.

"Grandpa's a good man, Jasmine, he wants us to get out of this horrible household. He's been tolerating Layla's nastiness for years and now he has a chance to get even. He's willing to help us," Edith said, putting the urn to her ear as if to confirm this as truth. "Or," she continued, "do you want to refuse his generosity and be a slave to Layla for a few more years? This is the best hiding place ever. It's our chance to escape."

"Will you actually enjoy sticking money up Grandpa's ashes?" Jasmine asked flippantly.

"No," Edith replied, now serious. "But I'm a survivor and this is necessary. Agreed?"

"Agreed," Jasmine relented.

Chapter 33

The Black Eye

Jasmine could hardly wait for Tuesday to come. It had been a pretty disgusting week: first, having to unfold Abeena's folds to clean her up and then having bits of Grandpa fly up her nose.

I wonder if that American will show up, Jasmine mused as she headed out to market when Tuesday finally arrived. *He makes me laugh and I could use a good one.*

Her second shopping trip was much more efficient than the first and she finished easily by 11 a.m. With the extra money she had retained by skimping on the grocery quantities, she stopped and bought Edith a candy bar that she immediately concealed in her bra.

"There you are!" Joe boomed when he spotted her nearing the ice cream stand. "I was hoping you'd be here," he said as they approached the ice cream display case together. "Are you feeling adventurous today?" he asked.

Jasmine immediately wondered if Edith was right about Joe trying to pick her up. "Well, um," she answered, not knowing what to say. Before she could spit out any words, Joe suggested, "Let's both try that booza ice cream for an adventure. If it's chewy like they say, we'll just both have to do some serious chewing," he said smiling.

Jasmine relaxed. "Let's go for it," she said enthusiastically.

She was already having fun. A short time later, they were seated at a table, both chewing their ice cream in earnest.

"How did your week go?" Jasmine asked after a serious swallow.

"Well today isn't the first time this week I've had something to sink my teeth into," he quipped, laughing at his own joke. "I just got back from Aleppo. The war there is quite real and I saw plenty of burnt-out stores, offices, even houses. A Molotov cocktail started a huge fire in some government office just a few blocks from my hotel. Although al-Assad's forces quickly retaliated, I heard there have been hundreds of casualties among the citizens there. It's really quite scary there. You just never know when or where the next bomb will hit. I was happy to get out of there yesterday. But there are rumors that the rebel forces are growing larger and more aggressive. I heard talk that Damascus may be the next target.

"But enough war talk. I'm curious as to why you have a candy bar popping out of your blouse like that."

Jasmine was chagrined, realizing how easily the candy bar had escaped her boob hiding place. "Um, it's just a surprise for a friend," she said quickly, adding, "I was afraid I'd sit on it and spoil it if I hid it in my pocket."

"Well, it's going to melt where it is now," Joe said with a laugh. "Do you give surprise candy bars to all your friends?" Joe wanted to know, intrigued by the mystery surrounding this woman. He immediately followed up with, "I'm so curious about you. You told me you moved here for a good job. What do you do? How long have you been here in Syria?"

Jasmine knew this barrage of serious questions would be difficult to evade. "It seems like I've been here forever," she answered honestly. "More than a year."

"Just a year? Why does that feel like forever?" Joe inquired. "They always say time flies when you're having fun. Sounds like you're not having fun here."

"Well, I'm a little bit homesick," she told him, wishing she could just blurt out that she was basically imprisoned here. "I'm hoping to get back to the Philippines soon." *At least that much is true,* she thought.

She changed the subject. "I can't believe how long this ice cream lasts. Most ice cream melts much quicker. It must be the gum in it. Eating this ice cream is truly an adventure. And it's actually quite delicious. By the way, last week you told me you found out what was in booza by googling it. How does that work?"

Joe was surprised at her question. "I just used the internet on my cellphone and asked Google 'what's in booza ice cream?' You don't sound very familiar with Google."

"Oh, I've heard of it, of course, have just never used it. Do you have to have a cellphone to use it?"

Joe was flabbergasted. He had just assumed that in 2011 everyone, everywhere googled everything. "Do you have a cellphone?" he asked. "If you do, I can show you how to google."

"No, never had one. I grew up in a large family that struggled sometimes just to have food on the table. Besides, the family I work for now doesn't allow workers to have one," Jasmine said with instant regret. *I've said way too much*, she thought ruefully. Joe didn't question her remarks because he had become quite interested in showing Jasmine how the internet works.

"I'll show you how cool Google is," Joe said, pulling his cell out of his satchel. "Hey Google," he said into the phone, "what's the highest mountain in the world?" Within seconds, 'Mount Everest' appeared on the screen. Suddenly Jasmine became very animated and excited. "Joe, can you ask how much a plane ticket from Damascus to Manila is?"

"Easy one," Joe said, telling her a few seconds later, "the lowest fare I see is $1,023 per person, one way, economy class."

Jasmine's face fell, along with her spirit. *What if their money wasn't in the safe the next time they opened it? Then there would be no chance she and Edith could ever escape.*

"Yeah, it's a chunk of change," Joe remarked. He had been studying her expression as she talked about herself. He had seen her withdraw from being a carefree young girl excited about ice cream to a troubled woman with secrets she wasn't sharing.

Jasmine knew she was dangerously close to telling him everything about her horrible life in Syria. She had met up with him to learn more about the civil war, not to end up whining and wailing about the trickery that led to her current misery. She had succeeded in finding out more about the war, and she also succeeded in resisting the urge to tell him she was enslaved.

When she finally was able to speak, all Jasmine could say was, "Oh dear. Looks like I better get over being homesick. My friend Edith wants to go back to the Philippines, too, and we were planning to leave Syria together. This is really upsetting. I had no idea it would cost that much."

"Let me check something else," Joe said, picking up his phone. Moments later he looked up at Jasmine and said, "When I leave Syria, I have to buy an exit visa and it looks like you'll have to also. The cost is $82."

Jasmine looked crestfallen. "Getting here was easy; getting out looks very difficult, and expensive. Who knew?" Jasmine wanted to hide the depths of her disappointment from Joe.

"I understand being homesick. I'm getting a bit homesick myself," Joe said, becoming more intrigued the more Jasmine talked. "I'll be back in good old Phoenix at the end of next week. I look forward to having some normal American ice cream," he said.

"But on a more serious note, if you really want to go home, you will find a way. There's always a way. Nothing's going to stop a woman like you," Joe said, making Jasmine's smile return.

"Oh, oh, I have to get back to work," Jasmine said abruptly, noticing the time. "This was fun. In fact, the most fun I've had all week," she added, recalling the folds in Abeena's skin.

"Yeah, I've got to get my Aleppo story emailed today," Joe

said. "Deadlines, you know. I'm coming back here before I go home to pick up some special spices for my mom and some friends back home. I won't be tempted to hide them in my shirt, though," he said laughing. "I'll try to make it next Tuesday at 11 a.m. if you think you'll be here again."

"I'll be here," she said.

As Joe watched her scurry out of eyesight, he sat thinking about Jasmine for a while. She intrigued him with all the things she *hadn't* said. The reporter in him was curious. He wished he knew what her story *really* was. He was determined to find out next Tuesday.

But he didn't have to wait that long. With his phone still in his hand, he googled, "Why are Filipina girls moving to Syria?" The answer astounded him. *Could Jasmine be a domestic slave?*

Edith expected Jasmine to return bubbling over with excitement like the week before. What she saw was a look of despair on Jasmine's face.

"Abeena," Edith said kindly to the woman with big ears. "Can I help you into your room? It's nearly your nap time."

As soon as the snoring rose to full intensity, Edith hurried to the kitchen where Jasmine was unloading the groceries.

"What happened?" she asked.

Jasmine could only say, "Do you know what the internet is?"

"Yes," Edith replied, "but I've never used it. Wa used it in his garment factory and he was about to teach me so I could use it for pattern ideas," she sighed. "Of course, that never happened. Why do you ask?"

"Joe showed me Google on his phone. It was incredible. He could look up anything. I asked him to look up plane fares from here to Manila. $1,023! What if the money in the safe is gone? We're never getting out of here," Jasmine said, tears welling in her eyes. "Not only that," Jasmine said, now in a full bloom of tears, "we can't leave Syria without an exit visa and that costs another $82. How the hell are we going to get an exit visa, let alone a plane ticket?"

"We'll get it," Edith assured her uneasily, wrapping her arms around her sobbing friend.

"There's more: war is coming here. Joe heard rumors that rebel groups are forming in Damascus."

"Jesus, Mary and Joseph!" cried Edith. "We might have a rebel living with us. Ahmed. This is scary stuff." For the next hour they discussed their options, revised their plans and mostly, just worried.

Jasmine heard the clop-clop-clop of the crutches first and quickly pulled away from Edith, snarling, "I lugged these heavy bags all the way from market, the least you could have done is help me put them away."

"For God's sake, Edith, that was not very nice of you!" Abeena said harshly, coming up from behind her. "Those bags *are* heavy. Maybe by next Tuesday I'll be able to go to the souq with you, Jasmine. I'm doing a lot better on these sticks," she added, lifting one crutch off the floor.

Jasmine quickly darted out to the kitchen to keep from bursting into laughter at the thought of Abeena navigating the cobbles on the way to market.

With the news of war, the plan to escape, the thought of stealing money and passports, and the constant harassment by either Abeena or Layla, Jasmine was getting as jittery as a cat on hot bricks. Edith was concerned. "It's going to be alright," or "just keep your cool," or "I've got this," she would whisper in passing.

On Friday Nadia came home from school in a snit. She threw her backpack on the foyer floor and a bottle of soda with a loose cap spilled over the tiles that Edith had just washed. "Nadia, would you get the mop out for me?" Edith asked pleasantly.

"Get it yourself, Sloth."

"Nadia, please," Edith asked once more.

"Nadia!" Jasmine bellowed from the kitchen, "stop being a little snot. Get the mop!"

She had barely finished her scold when a claw dug into her shoulder and swung her around. It was Layla, still holding the novel she'd been reading when the bickering started. Before Jasmine could react, Layla swatted Jasmine across the face so hard that her nose began to bleed immediately.

"Don't you EVER talk to anyone in my house like that. You are a servant. Servants are nothing. You have no opinions, no rights, no freedoms."

"You treat us like vermin!" Jasmine retorted. That remark was followed by a second swat across the face, this time with the hardback book.

Chapter 34
The Reporter

"I almost don't care if we never get out of here," Jasmine confessed to Edith that afternoon. "A bomb could go off in the living room and kill me, and that would be fine. This is an awful mess I've gotten myself into. I'm so naive and stupid. Look at me, this black eye is looking worse every day. I'm a freakin' ugly mess. I'm ready to give up. I think my friend Miguel had the right idea."

Edith was shocked listening to Jasmine's despair. "Come to your senses, Jasmine. I'm depending on you to help get us out of here. I really need you. I can't do this alone. Just keep in mind how much better you will feel when you land in Manila any day now."

Edith was relieved to see that her words had a mollifying effect on Jasmine who took a very deep breath and said, "I sure hope you're right."

"Of course I am. Now here's the next part of the plan," Edith said, filling her in on what they still needed to do.

Three days later, Jasmine's black eye was looking only slightly less horrible. It was Tuesday, market day, and she was embarrassed to be seen looking so beat up. "What if Joe asks me about this eye?" she whined to Edith. "I feel hideous."

"Tell him you fell onto a toilet plunger! Or slipped off a ski lift. I don't care. Make something up," Edith retorted with fire. "Our plan depends on you getting more information from this guy. If you really want to get back home, you've got to do your part," Edith reprimanded. "Let's just pray that your reporter friend shows up today."

Joe was already at the market, haggling over spice prices with a grumpy vendor. Having time to kill before Jasmine hopefully showed up, Joe was on his second cup of coffee at the ice cream stand. He had spent several hours over the past week researching the Filipina slave trade, and what he learned had deeply disturbed him. He was hoping Jasmine wasn't a domestic slave here, but he suspected she was. When he caught sight of her heading his way, his suspicions doubled.

"Hi Jasmine, I'm happy to see you again," Joe said as Jasmine approached. "I wonder how the other guy looks," he added in an attempt to be funny.

"You talkin' about my black eye? Silly me, I walked right into an open cabinet door. Never saw it coming," she said with a laugh that felt very forced.

"Don't you hate when that happens!" Joe said lightly, resisting the urge to pry and changing the subject. "So, what ice cream should we try today?" he asked. "My treat. Let's go check out the case. If you see something that looks good, I'll google it and see what's in it. That way we won't be disappointed."

"Great idea," Jasmine said, feeling less self-conscious and more comfortable by the minute. They settled on a blueberry flavor. "You know, ice cream is better when you don't have to chew it," Joe remarked as they licked their cones.

Jasmine laughed and said, "Yeah, it's a good thing you were able to google booza last time. If you hadn't, we would have been really surprised! I'm fascinated that Google has so much information," adding off-handedly, "while you have your phone out, could you look up something for me?"

"Am happy to," he replied. "What do you want to know?"

"Ask where the Philippine Embassy is."

Joe struggled to keep his eyebrows from lifting. Her request just about confirmed his suspicion that Jasmine was a domestic slave. It wasn't the reporter in him that had to know, it was the human in him. "You're not just homesick, are you Jasmine? You're in trouble. Please tell me: how did you really get that black eye?"

The charade was over and Joe knew it as he watched Jasmine's eyes brim with tears. "There was no cabinet door. I didn't want you to know about the mess I'm in. I got out of line and the lady I work for hit me in the face with a book." Once those words were out, Jasmine's floodgates opened. Over the next half hour she told him her story, starting with the con she fell for in the Philippines. "My family is dirt poor. The lure of $200 a month was irresistible. I feel so stupid now."

She told Joe every alarming detail about the past fourteen months of her life, concluding with, "Yes I'm homesick. And I'm scared. I just don't think I'll ever get to leave here."

Joe had been listening carefully to Jasmine's story. He knew from his research that Jasmine was probably correct in thinking she would never be able to leave. But her questions about airplane costs and embassy location had given him a gut feeling. "You're trying to escape somehow, aren't you? Your friend, too," he stated.

At this point, Jasmine had no reservations telling Joe about her and Edith's escape plans. "I was devastated last week when you told me the cost of airline tickets. After working here fourteen months, neither of us has really been paid. 'You'll get your money when your contract is up,' is what we were told. I'm not going to make it another ten months," Jasmine said with despair as tears fell down her cheeks.

Joe felt so helpless. He'd just been told the path her friend Miguel had chosen to escape slavery. He was worried that Jasmine was beginning to think about the same way out. "Know what I think?" he asked her. "Someday, when you're playing with your grandkids, you'll look back on this time as just a bad chapter in your life. You and your friend will survive this. And not only that, you'll both go on and have beautiful lives. I'm sure of it."

"Ha! You sound just like Edith," Jasmine said, wiping away the last vestiges of tears.

Joe showed her his phone and asked, "Want me to write down the embassy address for you?"

"I've already memorized it, but thanks. No paper trail that way. I'm so glad we met when we did. I really needed this conversation with you today. You've been a big help, just listening," Jasmine said. "But I really must get going. Big plans to be made, yada, yada, yada," she said with the first smile she'd had today.

"I'll never forget you, Jasmine. If only I could help, I would." Little did he know that it wouldn't be long before he did just that.

Chapter 35

They're Bombing Damascus

Although the explosions sounded far away, people in the streets of Damascus stopped whatever they were doing and listened. Mothers pulled their children close, frightened faces appeared in building windows, shoppers in the souq stood collectively paralyzed. The mountains to the north where the explosions were happening were miles from the city, but that was no consolation. War was on the march.

The talk in the government building where Layla worked was encouraging. "One of my assistants has a cousin in al-Assad's army," Layla told her family. "According to the cousin, the president has plans to stop the rebellion before it gets to the city." Although Layla had come home early out of fear, she assured everyone that the news was good, that Damascus was safe.

Mohammad, too, came home early. His report from his business connections was much the same as Layla's. "Nobody needs to panic," he told the family. "Word from al-Assad is that the rebels will be annihilated in the mountains. He has assured us he's not going to let happen here in Damascus what has gotten out of hand in Aleppo."

"I hope they round up every one of those damn rebels and put them all before a firing squad," Layla fumed.

Listening to his family siding with al-Assad, Ahmed was no longer able to keep up his charade. "You've got it all wrong, family," he began, fire now lighting his eyes. Everyone tensed and turned to him in disbelief. "Assad's the problem. His government is totally corrupt. It's full of bribery and nepotism. And political freedom? Ha! That doesn't exist. This place is a snake pit of sectarian bias. Do you have any idea how bad unemployment is? People who are lucky enough to be employed make less than $170 a month. Assad has to go."

"You shut your mouth," his mother scolded vehemently. "You live a very privileged life, thanks to President al-Assad. How dare you side with those who want to bomb our beautiful city and destroy it. Your father and I have worked our tails off to prosper in difficult times. Under President al-Assad's leadership we were able to give you all the riches that life has to offer."

Ahmed had let the cat out of the bag and wished he could take his rant back. He had been so careful to conceal his opinion during the past few months. He knew his parents would be furious and obviously they were. "All I meant, Mother, is that there are two sides to every story. I see people begging for money and food on my way to school and it bothers me a lot. It just doesn't seem fair. I didn't mean to upset you. I'm so sorry I brought it up. Please forgive me."

"Of course, you're forgiven. But, Ahmed, you can't let your emotions cloud reality. It's not al-Assad that you are angry with, it's the state of discontent the world is in right now. I should have remembered that you're my bleeding heart. You would right every wrong in the world if you could. I'm sorry, too. I guess all this war talk is getting on my nerves."

Since the family was in discussion about the war and how it might impact them personally, Mohammad decided this was a good time to make a plan if retreat from the city became necessary. He called Abeena, Edith and Jasmine to join the family in the study.

"Although we don't think it's going to happen, there's been talk of war lately," he told them. "We all need to be safe and I'm making a plan to make sure we are. If, and I am saying *if* we need to get out of the city temporarily, we have a safe place to go in Tartus. It's on the coast, about a three-hour drive.

"If war comes to Damascus, I'll drive Mrs. Saleeb and the children there first and I'll come back the following day for you, Abeena, and you two," he added, nodding in Edith's direction. "It's not imminent," he went on, "so don't be frightened. I assure you all, we will be perfectly safe."

Not me. I won't be going to Tartus, Edith scribbled in the notebook before going to bed. *I'll either be on my way home, in jail or dead. Mark my words* and then she underlined *home* trying to imagine the details of her great escape. *Note to self,* she added, *tell Jasmine it's time for Abeena's next bath.*

The next morning with the water running and Jasmine singing the traditional Filipino children's song *When I was a small child with my dearest mother* while scrubbing Abeena's back a little too harshly, Edith was gingerly turning Mohammad's postcap to the left and, with the light touch of a seasoned burglar, was lifting the key from its hiding place. Cautiously she slid the picture aside and tentatively snuggled the key into the safe's tumbler. Click. It opened.

Gone! The pouch full of money was gone. She thrust her hand into the safe's dark abyss and rustled some documents before her hand felt the covers of passports. She pulled all the passports into the light. There were three. Hers. Jasmine's. Abeena's. "Why that liar!" she said out loud. "He knew for sure war was coming. He took everything he needed for his family. Asshole. He never did intend to come back for us. Poor Abeena, under the illusion that she had become a beloved member of this family."

She carefully put Abeena's passport into the back of the safe where she had found it and took hers and Jasmine's. With no time to waste she headed to Grandpa's urn. In her thieving excitement she popped the cover rambunctiously and a plume of Grandpa escaped into the room. "Sorry Grandpa," she said as she bent the passports to fit into the neck of the urn. "I hope you didn't need the parts that got away." Once through the tight neck, the passports fell easily to the bottom of the vase. Then, as Edith sucked bits of Grandpa into the vacuum cleaner, the joy of her thieving success evaporated. The money was gone and so was their passage home.

By 7:45 a.m. March 15, 2011, Nadia was in school having been dropped off by her father on his way to work. Ahmed was walking to school and Layla had just left the apartment and was probably still in the building when the explosions came. There were two, and the booms they created were so loud it was difficult to tell from which direction they had come. The house shuddered for a single instant once, then twice, as each of the car bombs carrying 1000 kg of explosives apiece detonated. Thirty seconds later sirens were blaring from all directions and finally emergency vehicles and police cars could be seen jamming the streets heading in the direction of the military intelligence building.

Layla was already on the phone as she burst through the door. She ran to her bedroom and frantically began stuffing her make-up and semi-precious jewelry into a travel case while simultaneously talking with Mohammad, "Pick up Nadia immediately. I'll throw mostly casual things in your valise. Maybe one suit and a couple of shirts. Are you wearing your Rolex? Good. I'll call upper secondary and tell them to send Ahmed home. We have to leave immediately. Immediately!"

Mohammad must have been agreeing because she was shouting a lot of yeses into the phone. By now the television had been turned on and cameras were showing bodies lying in the street and blood running into gutters. Layla started scrolling her phone for the school's number. She dialed it and impatiently waited.

When she heard a voice answer she started shouting instructions to send Ahmed home "immediately!" The voice kept talking over her. The recording was saying all students had been sent home due to explosions in the city. Layla threw her phone on the bed and kicked off her tangerine pumps, the ones that exactly matched the sweater set she was wearing, and began struggling to get into her Reeboks. "I'm going myself to find Ahmed," she told Abeena and the girls as the TV cameras panned the aftermath of the explosions.

She ran out of the apartment toward school. Had she had better mothering instincts and really listened to Ahmed's little speech on al-Assad a few nights earlier, she might have run toward the military buildings instead. Frantic shouts of "Ahmed! Ahmed!" could be heard as Layla passed beneath the apartment's balcony.

Abeena, Jasmine and Edith still stood in Layla's bedroom watching the story unfold. "Fifty-five dead bodies in the street," a reporter was saying, "and as many as four hundred have been wounded in the explosions."

By now small pop-pop-pops were happening throughout the neighborhood. While Jasmine and Abeena were immobilized by the scenes flickering on the TV screen, Edith was weighing her options. Mohammad would be home soon with Nadia. Ahmed could walk in the door any minute.

"This is it!" she said and knocked the unsuspecting Abeena off her crutches onto the floor. "Grab the crutches," Edith ordered Jasmine as she began rummaging through Abeena's pocket and pulled out her cellphone.

"Where's the house key, Abeena?" Edith demanded as Abeena struggled to lift herself to no avail.

"You think you'll get away?" Abeena wailed. "Others have thought so, too. The Saleebs know people in high places. You won't get away. You might as well be dead."

"Shut up, Abeena. Where's the key?" Then Edith remembered Abeena usually wore the key on the silver chain around her neck.

"Never mind," she added, as she ripped the chain and key from her neck.

"Here, catch," she said, tossing it to Jasmine. "Get the door unlocked while I grab our passports out of Grandpa." She reached into the urn, easily passing through Grandpa and lifted out their ashy passports. The urn slipped out of her hands and poor Grandpa soon spread like a dusty plume all over the carpet. "You, too, are finally free, lolo!" Edith cheered as she ran toward the unlocked door, then back in again to retrieve her backpack and notebook.

Out in the sunshine for the first time in nearly in months, Edith wished she had time to let it warm her skin but the pop-pop-pops going off throughout the city told her feet to start running.

"Baba, look!!" Nadia screamed as she spied Edith and Jasmine rounding the corner of their building.

Jasmine turned and caught a glimpse of the Mercedes. "They see us," she yelled.

"Faster!" Edith hollered as her lungs filled with smoke.

"That's our help, Baba! They're getting away! Catch them," Nadia yelled.

Mohammad laid on his horn hoping the string of cars ahead would let him through but it was no use. Nadia rolled down the window and shouted obscenities to the cars ahead and then opened the car door ready to chase. Mohammed grabbed his daughter by the strap of her backpack. "Get back in here! We do *not* chase cleaning ladies down the street like we're commoners. That's beneath us. That's what police are for."

"But Baba, they're ours. You paid good money for them. They'll get to the Philippine Embassy and then they'll be safe. We can't let that happen."

"You think I don't know people at the embassy, my sweet?" he calmly replied. "They can't leave the country without my permission. They'll pay dearly if we get them back and if not, I'll see to it that they spend the rest of their lives in a Syrian jail."

"Oh, Baba, you know how to do *everything!*" Nadia said, proudly. "I didn't like them anyhow, we'll get new ones," she declared, satisfied.

Mohammed rolled his eyes at his immature daughter and reminded her they were in a war zone and his first duty was protecting her, Mama and the boys.

With Edith's innate sense of direction and Fadi's map that she had committed to memory, she knew they had to run toward the southwest. They looked up as they ran and saw people standing at the edges of their living rooms that no longer had exterior walls, just staring into the wide open space in disbelief. Those walls were now rubble laying in the street several stories below their apartments.

Abeena's phone pinged; it was a text from Layla. Edith pushed 4321 and the message opened. *Has Ahmed come home? The devastation is even worse than what's on the TV.* Edith typed in *No. Be safe.* They continued running.

Police were everywhere and the girls were careful to dodge into alleyways or duck behind rubble to avoid them. At one point they had ducked into a doorway to avoid being seen by two policemen in the street. "Good morning ladies," said a third cop they hadn't noticed. "And what would you fine Filipina ladies be doing crouching in this doorway?"

"We're looking for Ahmed Saleeb," Edith said bravely. "He didn't come home from school this morning and his parents are desperate to find him, so desperate they've sent us out to help look for him."

"I doubt that. I know the Saleebs. Let me just call Mrs. Saleeb, she works in my building," he said as he pulled out his cellphone. He was still scrolling through his contacts when rubble fell from above, some landing on his boot.

"Holy crap," he shouted, cowering, "this building's about to cave!" He turned in panic and ran like this life depended on it. Edith and Jasmine also ran, but in the opposite direction.

They slipped down an alley that would keep them off the main thoroughfare. To make sure they were still going in the southwesterly direction, they stopped in front of a door that had been blown off its hinges, to think. "Look!" cried Jasmine, "there's something moving in that rubble! A cat maybe. Oh, my God! It's a baby!" she exclaimed on closer inspection. The legs of the bassinet which held the infant had crumbled under the pressure of the two-story fall but its foam mattress had provided a soft landing. The infant was crying. They looked up and saw the problem, the missing exterior wall of the building. The baby must have been in the room that broke apart. "We can't just leave her here, somebody must be frantically looking for her," Jasmine said as she picked through the rubble to scoop up the child.

"You're right," said Edith. The child's face, although smudged with concrete dust, reminded her of her Luna. "This might be the end of our escape but we have to do something," she added.

"Hello!" they called as they picked their way up the damaged stairs. "Hello! Hello! We found your baby!" On the second level they saw an opened door. Inside a young mother was sitting on the floor of a room with no wall, rocking a crying four-year-old while staring off into space as if in shock. When she saw her baby in the arms of Jasmine, a baby she had seen falling off the building, she came out of her trance and started crying hysterically, "Bella, Bella, my Bella!" was all she could say. "I thought you were dead, my little one. I thought you were dead." She took Bella from Jasmine's arms and started thanking Allah over and over. Finally realizing two Filipinas, probably migrant escapees, had saved her child, she said she didn't know how she could ever repay them.

"That's not necessary," Edith said, "we just happened to stop in front of your building to determine if we were going in the right direction. We're trying to get to the Western Villas district of Mezzeh."

"The Philippine Embassy?" the mother asked. Panic wiped the smiles from Edith and Jasmine's faces.

They were caught. Game over.

"It's a mile from here," the mother continued. "If you can get there, you'll be safe. In fact I'll see to it that you get there safely." With that, she picked up her phone and called someone. The conversation was lengthy and in Arabic.

"That was my brother," she explained. "I told him about my building and how I thought Bella was dead and how you found her. Malik said it would be his honor to drive you to your embassy." She described his blue Hyundai, said he had a mustache and a very round face, then added, "Malik says the street at the back of this building is still open to traffic. He'll meet you there in a few minutes. By the way," she continued, as they were about to pick their way back down the broken staircase, *"some of us Syrians will not hire foreign domestic workers. We know what's going on, it's a slave trade. Shame on us. I hope you will not always think poorly of Syrians. Godspeed."*

Malik was waiting. He didn't speak English or Filipino except for one phrase: thank you. He wildly waved Edith and Jasmine to his parked Hyundai and with the broadest of smiles repeatedly called out, "Thank you thank you Bella thank you."

"That must be our guy, mustache and all," Edith said. "Let's take the chance and trust this is a good decision." In ten minutes he was pointing to the door of the embassy still offering a profusion of thank yous. They blew Malik kisses, looked at each other and high-fived. They were going home.

Chapter 36
Eyewitness to War

On that same morning at 7:20 a.m., Joe Voltz had just emailed his last article about the war to Diane Smith, his editor in Phoenix. "Sorry, Diane, not much going on here to report. I'll fill you in tomorrow when I get back home," Joe prefaced his email.

Minutes later, all hell broke loose when the first of several car bombs exploded in the heart of downtown Damascus. *There's gonna be a story here for sure*, Joe thought as he grabbed his camera and raced out of the hotel. He ran a few blocks toward the sound of blaring sirens and was shocked to see the utter devastation. Rubble from buildings blocked the sidewalk and broken glass was everywhere. As much as he disliked doing so, he took photos of three lifeless bodies lying in the street and was horrified to see two of them were children. Police were busy setting up barricades and Joe was turned back from going any further. Just then, a few blocks away, there was another earth-shaking explosion. Joe ran in that direction, and came upon a scene more horrifying than the first. Entire walls had been blown out. He counted at least thirty people covered with blood from gaping wounds. Many of them were dead or dying. He could never have imagined such a scene. He felt both terrified and nauseous. Nevertheless, his reporter instincts were on high alert and he continued taking hundreds of photos and videos until he was told to leave the area or face arrest. He hurried back to the hotel and immediately fired off an email to Diane. "Stop the presses!" he wrote urgently, attaching huge files of photos and videos. "Civil war has come to Damascus."

"Holy shit!!" Diane's responding email began. "You really took some chances to get those incredible photos. This is a true 'breaking news' story and we have it first. Awesome job, Joe. I know you planned to leave tomorrow, but we need you to stay a bit longer. The real story is just beginning. Be careful and be safe."

Joe couldn't resist the urge to get more information about the bombings, but as he was headed toward the door in the lobby, his way was barred. "Sorry, no one's allowed to leave the hotel right now. The whole city is on lockdown for the next twenty-four hours," he was told by the apologetic doorman.

Back in his room, Joe was reliving the morning's events when suddenly he had a heart-stopping thought. What if Jasmine and her friend had decided to make their escape during the bombings? He recalled Jasmine saying they were waiting for a diversion. What better diversion than a civil war?

Ever since their last conversation at the market, Joe had been doing more research about the domestic slave trade in Syria. Jasmine had put a face on it that he couldn't forget. He had been replaying their conversations over and over in his head, and the question that he couldn't figure out was how this blatant human trafficking was still so pervasive in the 21st century. It wasn't happening only in Syria, he discovered, but in many Middle Eastern countries. He felt naive, thinking, *here I am, a thirty-two-year-old American and this is the first time I even heard about the slave trade in this part of the world. I'm ashamed of my ignorance.*

With that thought, Joe was drawn to his computer and began to write Jasmine's story. The words just poured out of him, at times making him smile and at other times, bringing tears to his eyes. He hadn't realized how emotionally upsetting Jasmine's story was until he'd put it in black and white. When he finished and reread his words, he was amazed that he, a reporter of wars and other fact-filled events, had been able to capture depths of feelings and emotions he didn't know he had.

Joe spent a restless night, haunted by the sights and sounds he had witnessed that day. Wailing women, terrified men and mutilated children populated his nightmares. Throughout the night, sporadic explosions continued, some distant, some frighteningly near. At 6 a.m. he awoke in a sweat, wondering if he could take another day of reporting on war and devastation.

With a few hours remaining before the city curfew was lifted, Joe reread the story he'd written about Jasmine and was suddenly inspired to email it to his editor. *Just maybe Diane will realize my potential as a feature writer, spinning human interest stories,* Joe thought, *rather than a reporter stuck writing about wars, car accidents and other human tragedies.* He hit Send then packed up his camera and tape recorder and went back out into the war zone.

He spent the rest of the day photographing the bomb scenes, interviewing eyewitnesses and terrified residents whose homes and places of business were in shambles. When he checked his email later that afternoon, he found a cryptic one-liner from Diane: *Why did you have to make me cry?*

He didn't know how to respond to that, so he spent the evening writing his report and collecting the best photos before emailing it all to Phoenix. He was just doing his job, totally unaware that Diane had submitted Jasmine's story for publication in the paper's late edition.

By the third day, al-Assad's militia had squashed the rebellion, at least temporarily, bragging that they'd killed sixty-three rebels and had arrested many more. Damascus was eerily quiet except for the sound of bulldozers scooping up rubble. Joe was more than ready to get back home and he emailed this request to Diane.

Her response was quick. "Joe, just want to thank you for the superb reporting you've done in Syria. If you could stay just a few more days, well, I think it would be worth your while. You wouldn't believe what's been happening here."

Geez, Diane and her cryptic messages, Joe thought, not even bothering to guess what could be happening in Phoenix.

Chapter 37
Gabby Gabs

As they waved Malik off, the girls' attention turned to a foreboding structure in front of them, one that seemed official, modern and, impenetrable. "Where's the entrance?" Jasmine asked, looking around. "There must be a door."

"There it is!" Edith said, "and look, it's protected by a gargoyle." Jasmine laughed at Edith's description when she saw the size of the burly guy, huge for a Filipino, guarding the entrance. "Our next challenge is getting past the gatekeeper," Edith added as they approached. But there was no problem. He asked what it was they were seeking and when they said "asylum" he smiled a knowing smile and let them pass.

"Hellooo," Edith sang through the large empty foyer, a foyer where one might have expected a receptionist. "Hellooo, anybody here?" Whatever image their minds conjured up as to what their embassy might be like, this was not it. It wasn't long before heels clicked on the terrazzo floor. They expected a secretary but instead it was a well-dressed man who accounced he was the chargé d'affaires. When he saw two girls who looked like asylum seekers, his shoulders slumped, "Are you documented?" he asked wearily

"What do you mean 'documented?'" Edith replied.

"Are you in Syria legally? Let me see your passports."

"Of course, we're here legally," Edith said proudly. "I'm a housekeeper and Jasmine's a cook."

He flipped through their passports and said, "Well at least you're here legally, most of you aren't. What's the problem?"

Pointing to the remnants of Jasmine's black, blue and now yellowing eye, Edith began their story of mistreatment, lack of wages, long hours, no days off and finally today's escape. He tried to listen with patience but theirs was the twelfth same story he had heard today, and it was only noon.

"Yes, yes, yes," he hurried them along. "We would love to repatriate you but unless you can produce your exit visas, I'm afraid you won't be able to leave."

"How do we get exit visas? Isn't that what this embassy is for? To help Filipino citizens get the paperwork they need to return home?"

"Well, yes and no," he hedged. "Syria works a little differently. You will need to get your employer to sign for your exit visa. Why don't you go back to him and request he sign for you?"

"What!" both girls exclaimed simultaneously in disbelief. "We just escaped that evil family. If they could find us, they'd beat us close to death. You've got to help us."

"Yes," he said dispassionately, "I suppose I do. We still have a few beds open in our dormitory. You will be safe here until you can figure out how to get your exit visas. By the way, do you have enough funds for your plane fare?"

"Funds!" Jasmine said losing it. "Funds! Except for the first month, we haven't been paid at all. We are slaves. Slaves! I tell you. Slaves don't have funds."

"Calm down," the charge quickly added, "you are *not* slaves, officially you are Offshore Filipina Workers. Most OFWs are placed in excellent positions here in Syria and are treated like the professionals they are. Your story of abuse is not the norm. Most OFWs are very well paid and send their salaries home to their families. In fact, the Philippine economy counts on the money our

OFWs send home. Remittance is in the millions. As a result, both countries reap the benefits of good people like you."

What he neglected to truthfully say is "too many OFWs are in situations just like yours. They are often raped or not paid or beaten or verbally abused or all of the above." He certainly didn't want Edith and Jasmine to know the reality they would probably be facing even here in the embassy: that they might be guests of this place for a very long time, perhaps years. He concluded his little spiel by saying, "President Aquino is aware of the war situation here in Syria and he's trying to arrange flights to bring our offshore workers home. We're currently awaiting word when that might happen. Have hope, ladies. Still," he added, "without exit visas, I don't know. Perhaps you know someone who could buy out your contract."

"How much would that cost?" Edith asked.

"Depends on how much your employer paid to hire you. $3,000, maybe more."

"We're doomed," said Jasmine.

"Let me show you the dormitory," the charge d'affaires added, upbeat now that this interview was coming to an end. "You'll be fed and housed and safe here for as long as it takes."

The dormitory was a series of metal beds around the perimeter of a large, well-lit basement room. A number of tables and chairs filled the center space. Most chairs were already occupied with dispirited women. They looked up hopefully when the newcomers entered but quickly fell back into boredom when they realized it was just two more 'of them.'

Whether out of sheer boredom or the novelty of new dorm mates, sixteen-year-old Gabriella popped off her chair and welcomed the newcomers. "Hi, I'm Gabby, that's short for Gabriella. I'll show you where you can call home," she said with a smile, and directed Edith and Jasmine to two of the few remaining vacant beds. "You're lucky," she added, "once these next two beds are filled, asylum seekers will be sent to halfway houses. Since we are already at the embassy, we'll be the first ones on the plane when it comes," she added happily.

"If it comes," a despondent voice muttered.

"It'll come, Marguerite," Gabby insisted, then in a hushed whisper added, "Marguerite's been here in the embassy twenty-three months according to her. She thinks we're all going to die here. I can't think like that. I *will* get home and boy! I'm never going to lie about my age to go on an overseas adventure again. I should have listened to my mother. Put your stuff down and come sit at my table," she added.

"What a little rascal," laughed Edith as they sat on the edge of their thin, non-cushy mattresses. "She's a bright spot in our day. Go join her. Give me a minute. I need to sit here a bit, think, jot some things down in my notebook."

How the hell am I going to get an exit visa? she wrote. *Think! Who do I know? Wait! I have Abeena's phone. I'll call that Joe guy!* "Jasmine, come here," she said excitedly. "You still have that reporter's business card? You do? I need it."

She grabbed the phone and hit the power button. Nothing. She hit it again. Nothing. The battery was dead. "Anyone have an Apple charger?" she asked the room. A few women rolled their eyes, some didn't even bother looking up and Marguerite said, "Aw, did the rich Filipina forget her charger?" Edith put the dead phone back in her pocket.

"Let's stop fooling ourselves," Jasmine said despondently. "We're never getting out of here. I believed in you and your plan, Edith. 'We'll steal back our passports,' you said, 'and take only the money from the pouch we are owed,' you said. Are you crazy, Edith?" she yelled and all heads turned toward their beds. "They stole our lives, Edith! And you only wanted the wages we were owed! I should never have listened to your crazy escape plan. I should have stayed with the Saleebs and fulfilled my contract. At least I was being fed in that hell. I wasn't going to starve to death like I might here."

"She's right you know," called a voice from the middle of the room. "At least her other hell had food."

"Shut up!" Edith snapped back.

She turned back to Jasmine and took hold of her shoulders. "Jasmine, shush. We're going to get through this. I *am* going to get us out of here. Don't fall apart on me now. I need you to be brave. Believe it or not, I'm not that brave without you. I'm counting on you for strength. Yes, you," she emphasized, "and God."

"What's God ever done for us, Edith? He wasn't there when Layla pushed my face in. He didn't seem to care that we were constantly abused."

"He's making us strong, that's what He's doing," she replied. "He got us this far, didn't He? This is His first move. There's more to come. Trust Him."

Tears were rolling down Jasmine's cheeks. "I'm scared, Edith. Those bombs I hear are scaring me. These pathetic women who are just staring at us now are scaring me."

"I know, sweetie. Hang in there a few more days. That's all it's going to take."

"Really? You promise?" she asked, doubtfully.

"I promise," Edith lied, "now let's get off these hard mattresses. The little rascal is waving us over."

Gabby was well-named. As a chatterbox, she was a good diversion. She was always upbeat even though she revealed very little of the reason she needed asylum. Edith learned she was from the western Visayas and although 150 miles from Leyte, it was close enough to home for Edith to feel a real connection with this sprite.

"How long have you been at the embassy?" Edith asked to start a conversation.

"Months," Gabby answered.

"Months! Wow! So you were fifteen when you arrived in Syria?" she pried.

"No," Gabby said.

"Fourteen? You were fourteen?"

Gabby nodded.

"The agency let you sign up at that age?" Edith continued to pry.

"No," Gabby answered.

"You lied on your application?"

"I told you I should have listened to my mother," Gabby answered, no longer cheerful. "I don't want to talk about it anymore."

Jasmine changed the subject by asking how things worked here at the embassy. Gabby said there's cold toast for breakfast and in the middle of the day a bowl of rice with floppy vegetables arrives. We're basically starving."

"Do you ever get any news from upstairs?" Jasmine asked, rolling her eyes toward the ceiling.

"We ask the assistants who bring us food if they know whether the plane to take us home has come. The answer is always no but they expect it soon," she answered. "Sometimes, when we hear explosions nearby, we ask how close the bombs are to the embassy but we're usually told those are fireworks, that al-Assad is just celebrating some event."

"Does anyone ever leave here?" was Edith's next question.

"Oh, sure, every once in a while a name is called and someone gets up from her table, leaves the room and doesn't come back, not even to pick up her belongings. She's just gone," Gabby informed.

"What does that mean?" Edith quizzed.

"It means someone has paid for her plane ticket home and managed to get her an exit visa," Marguerite butt in from another table. "Or it means her old employer bribed someone on the staff here and she was returned to the place from which she narrowly escaped, and now she's in a shitload of trouble." With that said

Marguerite went back to drawing on her table's top with a Sharpie one of the assistants had left behind.

"Be careful what you say around here," Gabby whispered, "Marguerite has ears like an elephant."

"I heard that," came the quick reply from the center of the room.

As the euphoria of having reached the embassy safely dissipated and the walls of the basement room closed in, boredom chipped away at their spirits. "I've got to move my body," Jasmine declared. "It wants to be doing something."

"You're right," added Edith. "We need to exercise," and they both got up off their chairs and did a few jumping jacks. All eyes turned to the motion in the room. "Can I join you guys?" Gabby asked, jumping up from her chair.

"Sure," said Edith happily, "anyone else? Let's get off our butts and come up with a workout routine. It's something to do. What? No takers?" Edith asked as all eyes returned to staring at the table tops.

Edith began to notice that whatever she and Jasmine were doing, Gabby was right there doing it also. If Edith was writing in her notebook, Gabby would ask for a sheet of her notebook paper so she could keep track of her day. If Edith was making up her bed in the morning, Gabby decided to start making hers as well. If Jasmine was finger combing her hair in the reflective glass covering the picture of Aquino, the Philippine president, that was hanging on the wall, then Gabby started fussing with her hair in the same reflective glass.

"Gabby's following us around," Edith remarked.

"Like a puppy," laughed Jasmine.

"I wonder why," Edith mused.

She soon found out. The following morning when she and Jasmine were making up their beds, Gabby entered their section.

"Can I tell you my secret, Edith?" she asked.

"Sure," Edith replied. "Can Jasmine hear it too?"

"First I want to only tell you. It's pretty bad."

Jasmine shrugged her shoulders. "It's okay. I can't take any more bad news. I was about to go for toast anyhow."

"What's up?" Edith asked, patting a place on her bed where Gabby could sit.

"It's really nothing," Gabby fibbed.

"It must be something," Edith urged, "you don't look like your happy self this morning."

"It's just that …" Gabby began, and then it overcame her. Everything she had been holding in since she arrived in Syria let loose. She crumpled onto Edith's lap as sobs convulsed her body. Surprised, Edith wrapped her arms around what was now a little girl, a child.

Edith petted Gabby's hair, waiting.

"I'm bad," the child finally said. "I'm so bad. Even if the plane came today to take us home, I wouldn't get on it. I can never go home to my mother. She loves me so much and now I've ruined it. She will get it out of me like she always does and when she finds out what I've done she will hate me," Gabby continued through jerking sobs. "I'm thinking I should run away from here. The police will catch me and throw me in jail, or worse send me back to my owner. I deserve to be punished. I can't go home, Edith, I just can't."

Edith thought *this is no time for placating her with consoling words. I have to find out what happened that was so horrid and I hope it's not what I think.*

It was. Little by little Gabby unburdened her heart. She had been 'bought' by a young couple. The madam was a model. Cameras flashed whenever she arrived at openings and charitable events. Gabby's owner, as she now referred to him, was extremely rich and probably the reason Ms. Model had agreed to marry him, "because," Gabby added, "he's as ugly as a toad." She added that he didn't have any friends and didn't seem to want any. The couple would quarrel every weekend because she wanted to go out and party and he wanted to stay home. She'd leave and he'd head to his liquor cabinet.

"For the first few weeks of my being their cleaning lady (which was an easy job because he was very neat), I was thinking I had made a smart move in coming to Syria," she related. "He was really nice to me and was always leaving little treats like M&Ms and other candies around the house which he said I could take any time. Then one day ..." she hesitated for a long minute, "then one day he said I had to take a little pill. He waited to make sure I swallowed it. Every day after that he made me take another.

"Madam had a modeling job so she left early most mornings. He worked from home most mornings or at least that's what he told his wife he was doing.

"His 'work from home' was me." Gabby began having trouble getting her words out.

"I understand," Edith said, hugging her tightly. "You don't have to say more."

"As soon as she left the house, he'd grab my arm and push me onto their king-size bed and hump and hump until he was done," she said through a tumult of tears. "Then he'd take a shower and get dressed for the office. 'Have a great day,' he'd say as he locked the apartment door from the outside.

"I should have told him no. I *did* tell him no but I guess I wasn't forceful enough. I told him that I had lied on my application and that I was only fourteen and he said 'only fourteen? Lucky me, a virgin.' I should have told his wife, maybe she would have put an end to it. I did everything wrong. Eventually he didn't have to grab my arm and forcibly push me onto his bed. I just walked in and laid on my back. I pretended I was dead. And now I might as well be." Gabby had exhausted her tumultuous sobs and was now merely whimpering in Edith's arms, taking exhaustive breaths once in a while.

Why me, God? Edith prayed. *Why did you put this child in my*

*arms? I'm the worst person you could find to console this child.
I'm full of mistakes myself. You got to help me here.*

Eventually Gabby wiped her tears and runny nose on her arm
and lifted herself away from Edith. "I'll go," she said, "I really
shouldn't have."

Edith held Gabby's wrist preventing her from getting up.
"The crazy thing about being raped is that *we* rape victims somehow think it's our fault. Don't you dare believe it, Gabby. It is
never our fault," is how Edith began her own story, one that became words of consolation to this victimized child.

Chapter 38

Dirty Little Secret

Meanwhile, Joe was biding his time in Syria. He'd been keeping himself busy surveying the damage in other parts of the city and interviewing anyone who would talk to him, including eyewitnesses, clean-up crews, policemen and even several members of al-Assad's military. Everyone he talked to wore the same expression of shock, outrage and anger. As focused as he tried to be, his thoughts kept returning to Jasmine. Had she and her friend tried to make their escape? Was their residence one that had been bombed? Had the police captured the runaways? Were they sitting in a jail cell right now? These questions plagued him. He had to do something.

The only place he could think of to get some answers was the Philippine Embassy. Jasmine had asked for the embassy address for a reason. It made sense that's where they would have headed. *Unless they couldn't escape or unless they're dead*, he thought morosely as he once again googled the embassy's address.

It didn't take Joe long to walk to the embassy, housed in an imposing large building on Hamzeh bin Al Mutaleb Street. He wasn't quite sure what he would say when he got inside, but he hadn't needed to worry about that. He was stopped at the entrance by a burly, armed guard holding a clipboard. "Name?" the guard asked brusquely. "Joe Voltz." "I don't find a Joe Voltz on my list. You must make an appointment."

"Oh boy, this is getting complicated," Joe said to himself as he walked back to the hotel. When he called to make the necessary appointment, he was told it would be three weeks out. That wasn't going to work for Joe and he decided he would try to sweet-talk the English-speaking young woman on the other end of the line. To his amazement, she happened to "find" an appointment slot for the next day.

He returned at the appointed time. Once again, the burly guard asked brusquely, "Name?" This time he was on the list and was allowed inside, where he was escorted to the Philippine Embassy's offices. "I'm looking for two Filipina women who told me they were coming here. Can you help me?" Joe asked the woman in the outer office as politely as possible. "Names?" the desk clerk, Mrs. Morano, barked.

"Um, Jasmine and Edith," Joe said, knowing how inane that sounded as soon as the words left his mouth.

"I need last names. And what's your business with these women?" the clerk barked more ferociously. Joe was deflated, not at all prepared with any kind of answers, but also not expecting to be treated so unprofessionally. "They are new friends of mine, so I don't know last names, but I do know I want to make sure they are doing okay, if they need anything," he said weakly.

"Sorry, I can't possibly help you. We have over forty Filipina women staying here, waiting for exit visas" she said. "Needle in the haystack finding your Jasmine or your Edith."

When Joe next asked, "Is there someone else I can talk to about this?" the imperious barker went into attack mode. "Listen you, I already said you're out of luck. You have to leave now or I'll call security."

Exasperated, Joe instantly knew he didn't want to get tangled up with cantankerous security in this foreign embassy but he kept his cool and thanked the woman for her time. His exasperation turned to fury once he was back in his room. He started an internet search. After several hours, he realized how corrupt this government truly was. He decided he needed to play that game.

He called to make another appointment at the embassy and was relieved when the same young English-speaking girl answered his call. "Hi, this is Joe Voltz again," he began. "I really appreciate that you were able to get me an appointment at the last minute yesterday. Is there any chance you can squeeze me in for another appointment tomorrow. To thank you I'd like to bring a gift of appreciation." She was happy to oblige and set another appointment for Joe for the following morning.

At 4 a.m. the next morning, Joe was awakened by his phone ringing. He was surprised to see Diane Smith's name on the caller ID. He thought this call must be important. Diane would rather text than spend extra money calling internationally. He groggily answered.

"Oh, Joe!" she exclaimed, hearing the sleep in his voice. "I totally forgot about the time difference. It's probably the middle of the night there. Sorry. I should have waited, but I couldn't."

"What's going on?" Joe asked, now alert and wide awake.

"Remember when I texted you that you wouldn't believe what's been happening here in Phoenix?" she asked with an unusual amount of excitement.

Joe hadn't given it any thought at all and so he teased, "So, has it been snowing? Is the desert growing grass? Have aliens landed?" He was primed to continue guessing, but was quickly interrupted.

"Joe, what I have to say is more exciting than any of those. You know the Jasmine story you sent me a few days ago? Well, I went ahead and published it. Front page of the second section. The headline reads "SYRIA'S DIRTY LITTLE SECRET: SLAVES IN THEIR HOUSEHOLDS" with your byline."

"No kidding!" Joe was at a loss for words.

"That's not the best part!" Diane exclaimed with so much excitement that her voice had risen several pitches higher. "You won't believe what happened next!"

"Aw, c'mon, spill it, Diane! Such suspense at 4 a.m. is torture."

"The girls in your story are about to go home," she said exuberantly. "Your story has touched the hearts of Phoenicians, and not just their hearts but their pocketbooks too. So far, we've received nearly $4,300 in donations from people who want to help get your girls back to the Philippines. Money keeps pouring in. Lots of letters and phone calls expressing shock about the slave trade and gratitude for your excellent story. The paper has never seen anything like it."

Joe was momentarily stunned but the wheels in his head were rapidly spinning the money into his plans to bribe embassy officials to fast-track the necessary visas. $4,300 would more than cover that and the plane fares. He felt like jumping for joy, until he realized he wasn't even sure the girls had made it to the embassy.

He told Diane about his unsuccessful embassy visits and his plans today to try and buy his way in. "The donations are a dream come true, Diane, but won't do any good if the girls aren't there," he said. "It's possible they never made their escape, or, worse, are in jail, or even worse, wounded by war. I will find out something today. Keep your fingers crossed."

This news was disheartening, but Diane was not to be deterred. "Here's what I can do for you now. Whatever the total donation amount, I'll add those dollars to your expense account which I notice is nearly depleted. That way, you can pull whatever cash you need from an ATM. You got some persuasive talking to do today at the embassy. And now you have the money to do it right. Let me know how it goes," Diane insisted.

"Oh, by the way," she continued, "while I've always known you were an excellent reporter, I never knew until this week that you had such talent for feature writing. I have to tell you: when I read your article about these girls, I was brought to tears. And that was a first for me. I'd like to reassign you as a feature writer, if you'd like that. You certainly know how to touch people."

"Diane Smith, you're the best. I can't think of anything I'd enjoy more," Joe said, totally surprised at how wonderfully the morning had gone so far.

Chapter 39

Palms Get Greased

"You don't give up easily, do you?" the guard at the embassy said when Joe arrived with a box of chocolates in his hand and a wad of cash in his pocket. The guard was less gruff than previous visits and was almost pleasant as he directed Joe to the reception-ist's location where the young woman's eyes sparkled when she was handed the candy. "Anytime you need an appointment, Mr. Voltz, I'll get you one. Anytime at all," she said, hiding the box in her desk drawer.

"I'm not familiar with embassy protocols," Joe said with a pleading I-hope-you-can-help-me look. "I spoke with Mrs. Morano yesterday but she didn't seem able to help me. Who should I see about finding out if two of my Filipina friends are here?"

"Ah, yes, Mrs. Morano, the gatekeeper. She can be a little dif-ficult. You need to go through her to get to the charge d'affaires, Mr. Flores. He's the big shot here. Good luck."

Joe had no sooner walked into Mrs. Morano's office when she looked up and barked, "You, again?'

Before she could spout that he was still out of luck, Joe polite-ly said, "Yes, I'm back. I realize I was woefully unprepared yes-terday, and was sorry that I had wasted any of your time. I'd like to make it up to you," he said, opening his hand to a $50 bill, ex-tended in her direction. "I want to see Mr. Flores this morning. If you could make that happen, well …."

He was amazed to watch Mrs. Morano transform from a cranky pit bull into a woman whose puppy dog eyes were captivated by the cash.

"Yes, I can arrange that, Mr. Voltz," she said most graciously, picking up her phone with one hand and snatching the $50 with the other. "You're in luck. He can see you now," she said. "His office is two doors down the hall."

Mr. Flores was a smooth, slick bureaucrat who looked up from his crossword puzzle when Joe knocked and walked in. "How may I help you, Mr. Voltz? Mrs. Morano said you had important business to discuss. I'm glad I have time to meet with you," said the man behind a desk who clearly looked like he had all the time in the world.

"It's nice to meet you, Mr. Flores. I'm here because I want to visit two of my friends who are seeking asylum here. See if they need anything. They would have come here within the past few days," Joe said, changing the approach he had used unsuccessfully with Mrs. Morano yesterday. "Their names are Edith and Jasmine."

"Oh, yeah, I remember Edith and her depressed friend, Jasmine. They're in the women's dormitory downstairs. But I'm afraid we only allow visitors between 2 and 4 p.m. on Thursdays, if you wanna come back," Flores said, dismissing Joe.

"What would it take to make an exception for me?" Joe asked politely, laying his hand on the desktop while fingering two $100 bills cradled there. Mr. Flores no longer looked bored. Nearly a month's salary was dangling in front of him. "Well, Mr. Voltz, it's a slow day here. I think that would call for an exception," he acquiesced as he slipped the bills out of Joe's hand.

"That would be wonderful. Thank you," Joe said sincerely. "Oh, one more thing, while I'm here. How does the exit visa process work?"

Mr. Flores was in a much improved mood. He explained to Joe all the ways visas are granted, including that usually the Syrian family must agree to release the workers from their contracts. "As a rule, sometimes it takes quite a while," Mr. Flores admitted.

"Are there exceptions to this rule?" Joe asked softly as he pulled another $100 bill from his pocket.

Mr. Flores didn't hesitate for even a moment. He answered just as softly, "I believe I can expedite the process for you, Mr. Voltz. Come with me, I'll take you to see the young ladies now."

Chapter 40
Well-Placed Bribes

After her meltdown a few days ago, Jasmine couldn't get her groove back. Seeing that she was slipping into a dark place, Edith tried to pull her out of her slump but it seemed futile. By now Edith was running a workout class and although Jasmine had to be coaxed to get up off her chair, she'd only go through the motions; her heart wasn't in it. "Come on, Jas," Edith would say, "show a little enthusiasm." Gabby, on the other hand, showed enough enthusiasm to coax two other women to join the class. Except for Jasmine, the others who exercised seem to have a more positive outlook for the day.

It was mid-afternoon, the dullest and longest part of the day for the self-imprisoned asylum seekers. Edith pulled the notebook out of her backpack and tore out another sheet for Gabby who was jotting her musings. Jasmine was slouched in the chair with her head on the table. It seemed like just another long day.

"Jasmine," a voice called loudly from the hall, "come with me please." Jasmine's head bolted from its lethargic position and Edith saw the panic in her eyes. "Edith," the voice added, "you come, too." They looked at each other momentarily with a mixture of fear and hope. Edith put her notebook away and slung the backpack over her shoulder as they both stood, straightened their shirts, smoothed their hair and started toward the door. Edith gave a quick look at Gabby and saw big tears running down her cheeks. "It'll be okay," Edith mouthed and gave a thumbs up as she and Jasmine headed toward the door to either their salvation or their doom.

When Jasmine entered the small room on the main floor of the embassy, she focused on Mr. Flores, merely glancing at the other man in the room who was smiling at her. Seconds later, it hit her. It was the reporter, Joe. "The souq!" she cried out unrestrained and bolted toward him. He had no idea whether she was going to knock him over or hug him so he lifted his arms just enough from his sides to catch a hug if that's what it turned out to be. And it did. She grabbed him around the waist and cried, "What in God's name are you doing here?" He had no idea this was the kind of reception he would be receiving so he stood there for a minute with her arms around his torso, dumbstruck.

"Edith! Edith!" Jasmine bellowed. "This is Joe Voltz! The guy I met in the market! Oh, I'm sorry, I didn't mean to, oh dear," she blubbered, releasing her squeeze.

He stood there for a moment enjoying his reception. *If she's this enthusiastic about my being here, wait 'til she hears the news I bring*, he thought.

He looked over Jasmine's head and said to Edith, "You must be Edith, the accessory in crime."

"I am," she replied, liking this Joe person immediately.

Satisfied that Edith and Jasmine were in good hands, Mr. Flores went back to his office, citing he had "a lot of work to do."

It took all three several minutes to recover from the initial reunion. Joe didn't waste any time getting to the point of explaining the circumstances that brought him here.

"Call it ESP, call it sheer curiosity," Joe began, "but I knew from our first meeting in the souq, that either you were in danger, Jasmine, or that I would be, if I followed my instinct to learn more about you. But I had to know. I started putting a picture together from the snippets of details you so reluctantly revealed and did some googling," he explained. "I hate to say this, ladies, but you've been bamboozled." He noticed the girls' bewildered look. "Deceived, lied to, tricked, conned," he clarified.

"Then it really is all a dirty scheme?" Edith asked, surprised that she was so easily duped. "Stupid me. I should have known better but all I could think about was how $200 a month would give my daughter Luna a better life. That creepy Mr. Arno made it sound so glamorous. I was hooked."

"The same Mr. Arno came to my town," Jasmine jumped into the conversation. "He talked glowingly about the adventure of going to foreign places like Dubai, Lebanon, Syria. I saw it as the opportunity of a lifetime: adventure, excitement and $200 a month! And a free plane ride! I'd never been on a plane before."

Edith was crushed. "Do you think the Philippine government knows we offshore workers are more often than not treated like slaves?" Edith asked, then pondered, "I wonder why it doesn't step in and stop allowing it."

Joe had already explored that answer. "The Philippine government goes along with the concept because when all goes well, you overseas workers send your monthly wages back home to your families and that bolsters the economy of the Philippines. That's what keeps the poorest of poor Filipinos off government assistance. It's called remittance."

"I find it hard to believe that my government knows that many of us Filipino citizens are being raped or beaten or verbally abused or locked in homes without rights overseas, and it just turns a blind eye. Why?" Jasmine fumed, disgusted.

Joe rubbed his thumb and middle finger together. "It's all about the moola," he said. "Recruits like you sign up thinking 'hey, I can do this. It's only for twenty-four months,' and before the ink is even dry on the contract you signed, one you didn't understand and will never see again, you're on a plane going to Syria or Lebanon or who-knows-where in the Middle East and BAM!

You are a slave, owned and operated by an unscrupulous employer. It's sickening!"

"Yep, that's *exactly* how it began," Edith declared.

"Well, I'm here to tell you there's a happy ending," Joe said, grinning ear to ear. "You're both going home, maybe as soon as tomorrow!"

Jasmine and Edith were momentarily stunned into silence, but quickly their excited questions were flying at Joe. "How? Why? What? Are you just teasing us?" they were asking in rapid fire while hugging each other and dancing. "How is this possible? What did you do, Joe?" Jasmine quizzed, suddenly convinced he had come to their rescue.

"I wrote your story, Jasmine, and sent it to my editor in Phoenix. She was so touched by it that she published it in the daily paper. The people of Arizona had no idea about the modern day slave trade and my readers were as appalled as I was. When I put your face to my story, our readers wanted to get involved. My editor, Diane, opened a *Free Jasmine* page on our website and money began pouring in. More than enough to get you two home."

As grateful tears streamed down her face, Edith said, "Aunt Agnes was right. Prayers do get answered. You're our hero, Joe. Thank you, thank you, thank you. And thank you, people of Phoenix!"

Jasmine was beside herself with relief. "All because you talked me into chewy ice cream!" she blurted out before her infectious laughter had them all laughing.

"Oh, but wait," said Edith, as a problem crossed her mind. "It's not just plane fare, we need exit visas."

"No problem," said Joe, "I think I've convinced Mr. Flores to solve that sticky piece of business. He assures me the Syrian government will expedite your visas without contacting your employer."

Then Edith nudged Jasmine, and Joe noticed a look of concern had crossed her brow. Jasmine began nodding her head knowing what Edith was thinking.

"Joe," Edith said hesitantly, "we have an ever-so-slight problem. We've taken a girl, a child really, under our wing. Her name is Gabby. She was only fourteen when she arrived in Syria and she has been sexually assaulted continually until recently when she managed to escape. She's here in the embassy. Unfortunately, she is undocumented."

"Good God, girls! Are you thinking what I *know* you are thinking?"

Both girls put on puppy dog eyes and gave Joe a look. He knew he was doomed.

"Her name is Gabriella Sanchez. She's sixteen. She's from Pototan in the western Visayas."

"Gabriella Sanchez," he wrote in a pad he pulled from his pocket, shaking his head slowly.

As he was writing, Mr. Flores poked his head in the doorway. "Everything all right here?" he asked. Joe assured him it was and that he was just leaving. With good-byes said, he and Mr. Flores started down the long hall. The girls could hear Joe asking about a girl named Gabby. "Yes, yes, we are protecting Gabriella," Mr. Flores was saying.

"What would it take for you to help me get Gabby home?" they heard.

"More than you probably have," was the response as his voice faded into the length of the corridor.

Edith and Jasmine had one more hurdle to face. They knew they'd be barraged by questions from the desolate group of women on the floor below.

"We can't tell them we're going home, that the good people of Arizona are our angels," said Edith. They stood for a minute thinking.

"Here's what we'll tell them," Edith finally said, "and it's only a little white lie. We'll say we had a friend in our old neighbor-hood who hoped we had made it to the embassy, and he had come to check that we had. He gave us good news that President Aquino is sending planes to take every offshore Filipina worker out of Damascus now that war has broken out. It's just a matter of days before the plane arrives, is what we'll tell the others.

"One more thing," Edith added. "Don't tell Gabby she'll be going home with us."

"Why not?" asked Jasmine, surprised.

"Because Gabby ... is gabby."

"Well?" Gabby blurted out before Edith and Jasmine even reached the dormitory doorway. A roomful of faces looked up in curiosity and hope as the girls returned to the room. "We just heard some great news," Edith said. "It comes from Jasmine's friend, someone who learned of our escape and wondered if we had made it safely to the embassy."

"And? And? " Gabby urged. "What did you find out?"

"According to a BBC news report, President Aquino has or-dered a Philippine Airlines plane to come and get his OFWs out of Syria. That's us, ladies. We're going home."

A chorus of "whens?" erupted as the desolate ladies came to life. "Is it free?" someone called out. "What about exit visas?" someone else chimed in. "What about me?" Gabby pouted. "I don't have a passport. Without it I won't be able to get an exit visa. My passport was taken away in Dubai on my way here. I have no documentation."

"Let's not get ahead of ourselves," Edith told the room. "If President Aquino is sending a plane, he must have made a deal with the Syrians. According to the BBC, he says he's going to fly everyone home who wants to come home. That's all I know."

They had heard this all before but now that it came from the BBC it seemed real. The dynamics in the room changed as if a switch had been pulled. The women perked up and started communicating with each other. They talked of their hometowns, some wondering if their spouses had gone off with another woman, others wondered if elderly parents were still okay or even alive, some pondered aloud if their kids would remember them or think ill of them for abandoning them. A few praised Jesus and some just wept. Edith looked around the hopeful room and realized how powerful a little white lie can be.

Chapter 41

Flight to Freedom

"Do you still have my business card?" Joe asked Jasmine as the four stepped out of the cab in front of the Philippine Airline terminal. Jasmine pulled the now wrinkled business card from her pocket with delight. "That'll never make it home! Here," he said, pulling a fresh one from his wallet, flipping it over and writing his home address on the back.

Edith and Gabby gave each other a surprised look as they recognized the little conspiracy of hearts that was playing out before their eyes. It was apparent Joe Voltz was interested, but he was also Joe Cool and quickly stepped back to include the trio. He'd leave the next move up to Jasmine. "Here are your tickets and your exit visas," he said. "And there's just enough money left to get all three of you back home. This is it. This is where we part."

"I don't know how you managed to get all three of us out of here," Edith said, giving him the first hug. "Especially Gabby, our problem child," she added, smiling at her.

"You turned into a very expensive commodity, young lady," Joe laughed as Gabby reached up for a hug. "Flores will do anything for a price. I kept unfolding $100 bills in front of him until he heard footsteps in the hall coming toward his office. Then he scooped up the wad and said, 'Come back tomorrow at 2 p.m.'"

"Sorry," Gabby apologized.

"Don't be! My readers in Arizona were horrified at what had happened to Edith and Jasmine, but when I told them about you, Gabby, they were absolutely incensed. Hundreds of people wanted to know how they could help. They reached into their wallets and gave what they could. Look, here's one of their texts," he said, pulling out his phone. "The text reads 'Please tell Gabby that instead of buying my grandson, Kyle, a PlayStation 2, for his birthday, I told him Gabby's horrific story and asked if he wanted to put that money toward rescuing her. He was all in on helping Gabby. So here's the PlayStation money. It's not a lot, but we hope it helps. Tell Gabby that we are praying for her.' So you see, Pipsqueak, you've become part of a much bigger story about slavery and human trafficking. Arizonans can't wait for the good news that you are home safe and sound, a story I'll be writing on my plane back to the U.S." Gabby gave Joe an extra tight squeeze.

"I think Joe likes you, Jas," Edith said as she buckled herself into her airplane seat. "What about you? Is it mutual? Do you think you'll contact him?"

"If only I had my long, beautiful hair," Jasmine replied, thinking about her damaged self-image. "This," she added, mussing her hair with her hands, "does not say woman. This ugly, chopped up mess," she continued, "says I'm a domestic slave, a nothing."

"This," Edith said, reaching over to muss Jasmine's hair once more, "says you're a survivor, a warrior, one strong W.O.M.A.N. He wants you to call or write, Jas."

"But he lives in America, Phoenix, wherever that is," Jasmine protested. "How will that ever work?"

"It only works if you want it to. Take a chance. God only knows I'd jump at it."

"I guess. Maybe. But what if we're reading him all wrong," Jasmine worried.

"I've been to hell and back with men," Edith declared as the flight attendant was giving the pre-departure speech. "Trust me on this one, Jas, Joe is a keeper."

The droning of the plane put Edith in an ethereal state and she let her mind wander. She tried to imagine her reception at home. Would it be akin to the parable of the Prodigal Son? Would her father rejoice and insist on roasting a pig that he couldn't afford to celebrate her homecoming? Would Luna cry when she tried to pick her up and look to Liezel to be rescued from this strange woman's grip? Would her family be disappointed that her promise of sending her monthly salary home hadn't happened? Would anyone believe that she was actually imprisoned and held as a slave? Were the bodies in the streets, the baby in the bassinet, the rooms with blown-out walls real? Was it all a bad dream?

Edith vacillated between excitement and anxiety as the long flight dragged on. By the time the plane was descending into Manila, Edith didn't know what she was feeling. It was Gabby who named the feelings all three of them were experiencing. "I don't know whether to be happy or afraid," she said as the plane pulled up to its gate. "I'm afraid to go home. I'm afraid I won't be loved."

"I thought it was just me," said Jasmine. "I must be one of the stupidest people on earth to let someone dupe me like they did. Nobody likes a stupid person. Therefore nobody in their right mind will like me. I'm stupid. Stupid. Stupid."

"Stop it!" Edith said. "Stop it this minute. We are not stupid. Let's face it, ladies, we were slaves, abused victims of another's greed and pride. I am declaring, here and now, in front of two of my most valued warrior friends, that I will not let the hell they put me through ruin my future. Let's make a pact. Repeat after me: Although I've been victimized, I am not a victim and I will prove it every day for the rest of my life by the simple act of loving myself." They willingly repeated Edith's pledge and stacked their right hands in solidarity. With that, all three were ready to go home strong.

Part 3

Light at Tunnel's End

*"Yesterday I was clever, so I wanted to change the world.
Today I am wise, so I'm changing myself."*

—Rumi

Chapter 42

Job Hunting

Luna, now almost four, didn't get it. A strange lady had entered her home, and her lola, Liezel, crying and laughing at the same time, had scooped her up from the floor and attempted to thrust her wiggling body into the arms of this stranger. To save herself, Luna twisted violently in her grandmother's arms and put a death choke around Liezel's neck. Nobody was going to pry her away from her lola. She didn't care that all the people she loved including Lolo, Aunt Betsy, and all her other aunts and uncles were celebrating Edith's return with hugs, great noise and tears of joy.

"This is your mama," Liezel was trying to tell the little head now buried in the crook of Liezel's shoulder. "Your mama is home! Go to your mama, little one." Luna bored deeper into her grandmother's shoulder. "It's okay, baby," Liezel consoled, "Lola won't make you go." A few times Luna took a quick peek at the intruder but never let go of Liezel's neck.

Edith was crestfallen. She had suffered a heart-wrenching goodbye to her daughter almost two years ago for the sole purpose of giving Luna a way out of poverty. She had endured imprisonment, verbal abuse, bombings, and had almost gotten trapped in the limbo of an overseas embassy, or worse, a Syrian jail. Both mother and child were having a difficult reunion.

"It's nothing," Liezel said, consoling Edith after Luna had been tucked in for the night. "She was only two when you left. Most people don't have memories from that early age. Do you?"

"I remember the two hikers that came to our house and talked to you about climbing our hill. They said they were students in America and said I should go there someday. I remember they each had a backpack, and that they were happy and that you gave them some yams."

"And how old were you?" Liezel asked.

"Four," Edith said. "I was four because I remember thinking when I turned five I could go to school like those girls. Then I would be able to get a backpack and go on adventures. That's the reason I made you and Papa enroll me in school."

"So you were four when you formed your first memories," reminded Liezel. "Give Luna some time. Teach her that you are Mama. She'll fall for it quickly because she's a very loving little girl."

As always, Liezel was right about children. Within a few days Luna was showing Edith her garden. "But I thought it was Lolo's garden," Edith would tease. "Lolo is teaching me yams," she'd boast, plucking the dirt with the hand trowel she always carries out back. "So it's my garden, too!" she proudly proclaimed.

As Luna scratched the earth with her trowel she burst into her *Os Ps Bees* gardening song and was delighted when Edith joined in and clapped at its conclusion. Before long, Luna was calling Edith, Mama.

Edith went to the library in hopes of getting her old job back but it had turned into a full time job with a full time librarian. Unhappy there'd be no job, she was glad to see that the library had made some much-needed improvements. There were brand new computers at the work stations and the library had added more shelving filled with many new books. Before leaving, she leaned into the low shelves of the children's section and selected a few books for bedtime stories. *Maybe I can turn Luna on to a love of reading like Aunt Agnes did for me,* Edith mused as she picked *Goodnight Moon* from a shelf, signed it out and stuffed it into her backpack.

That evening she told Luna her idea of having story time before bed and Luna was more than willing to get into her jammies early. By now Luna had moved off the cot in the room shared with her aunts, Edith's youngest sisters, and was sharing a bed with her mother. As she bounced onto the bed for their first story time, her foot caught the strap of Edith's backpack.

"Put it on the bed," Edith said, "and get out our first book, *Goodnight Moon*. It's in English. It will be a fun way to start learning a second language." Luna quickly spotted the book with the moon on the cover as well as the notebook next to it. "What's this for?" she asked.

"Oh, that's my notebook," Edith answered. "I write all sorts of things in it, like my thoughts and dreams and ideas. I started my first notebook when I was five, when I learned to write my name. I put a great big letter E on the first page. E is for Everything," Edith said smiling, remembering how she felt when she wrote that first E.

"Will you teach me how to write my name? And then can I get a notebook?" the child asked, delighting her mother. Edith put the notebook on the small table near the bed, then snuggled up with Luna as their first bedtime story began.

Later that night, as she listened to Luna's soft breaths of sleep, she reached for the notebook and it fell open to a page she had written in the embassy basement. "God, no," she said, "I don't need to re-read this crap right before falling asleep. I'll have nightmares for sure." She turned to a much earlier section and smiled as she remembered meeting Michael Peters, the Peace Corps worker, on the bus to Manila and how he had inspired her to think aloud about her pie-in-the-sky dream of becoming a nurse. She put the notebook back on the table, turned off the light and dwelled on pleasant possibilities as she drifted off.

In the light of day there'd be no dwelling on the possibility of going to nursing school. The harsh reality was she needed a job immediately. She was twenty-four, unemployed, and had a child to raise. She who once had been an asset to the Santos' household was now a liability. Her parents would never, ever say she had to move on; instead they'd make sacrifices for her until there was nothing left to sacrifice and she knew it.

"Come on Luna," she said the next morning. "Let's you and I go find Mama a job."

"I can't," the child answered. "I have to grow yams. Lolo needs me."

"I suppose you're right," Edith concurred as she put on a neatly ironed blouse. "Wish me luck."

She needed a lot of luck for there were no job postings in the usual spots and no suggestions from friends or relations. Even Aunt Agnes who usually knows everything in this barrio and in nearby ones as well hadn't heard of any opportunities. The last place on her list to look for a job was one she was trying to avoid: the Gov. Benjamin T. Romualdez Hospital where people in the chronic stages of bilharzia, commonly known as snail fever, come to get well, or to languish, mostly languish.

Every Filipino knows and dreads snail fever because it's so easy to contract yet so difficult to get over. People are infected when the larval form of the schistosoma parasite passes through snails into fresh water where it penetrates the skin of swimmers, fishermen, even farmers and then grows from its larval form into flatworms called flukes. Edith knew that once in the bloodstream the flukes make their home in the intestines or urinary tract. No one, except the saintly nurses and the inquisitive research doctors who are hoping to find a fast cure for snail fever, would eagerly apply for a position here. But Edith was desperate.

"You've worked as an overseas housekeeper!" The lady in personnel rejoiced when she saw Edith's credentials. "Perfect!

That means you've been well-trained and will know exactly how to handle the details of this job. I'd hire you on the spot, but you need to be interviewed first by our head physician, Lorynn Hunter. Let me see if she's available now."

"Hello, Edith, I'm Dr. Hunter. I hear you've applied for a housekeeping position here and it looks you are well-qualified. Do you have questions or concerns about the job?"

"Well, yes. I have a four-year-old daughter and live at home with my large family. I can't afford to catch any illness here."

"I appreciate your concern; however, schistosomiasis is not contagious," the doctor quickly assured, recognizing the look on Edith's face. "It's never passed from person to person. Those who get it have been in contaminated fresh water."

"I know. That's what everyone says," said Edith, "but this housekeeping job requires handling the contaminated bedding of patients. This could easily release more parasites into the wash water, the water *my* hands will be in. I don't know about this job," she worried aloud.

"No one on our staff, including housekeepers, has ever come down with it," the doctor reassured. "Trust me, it is not contagious."

Dr. Hunter spent time talking about the work being done on behalf of the afflicted patients. "Our research doctors are second to none and I'm proud to say we are making significant progress in treating and often curing this disease."

By the end of the interview Edith decided she could trust this smart, compassionate, and dedicated woman. "I can do this," Edith said with confidence. "Better yet, I would *like* to do this."

"Fantastic! We're in dire need. Can you start tomorrow?"

She left the hospital as a new employee with a salary of $89 a month.

Chapter 43

Looking for Love

Everyone was about to give Edith a congratulatory hug when she announced she landed a job, but when she added "at the Gov. Romualdez Hospital" they all took a step back as if she already had a plague.

"Come on," she scolded. "It's not contagious. You have to swim in contaminated water to get it. Doubting Thomases, all of you," she chided, but added that she intended to take precautions like wearing latex gloves, washing her hands frequently and changing out of her work clothes before coming home. That seemed to mollify her dubious family and they conceded they were happy she had found work in these difficult times.

Even though the snail fever hospital was small with only about twenty-five beds, the job was huge. The unending cycle of stripping beds, hauling, washing, drying, folding and remaking beds six days a week was mindless, demoralizing and hard. If it wasn't for the grateful nurses and doctors who constantly told her that the patients never looked so refreshed and the place had never been so clean, she probably would have quit before her first paycheck but, by the end of the first month she was already feeling she was an integral part of this dedicated team. It all seemed so worthwhile until the first paycheck arrived. "Eighty nine dollars! What was I thinking? I can't raise Luna on $89 a month! After story time tonight," she told herself, "I need to have a little chat with my notebook."

Do you see a way out? she asked the notebook. *Come on! Think!* She twirled the pen between her fingers but no words were willing to fall from it.

Edith had been at the snail hospital for six months and was no further ahead financially, when on a Sunday after church Betsy came to the house in extremely high spirits. "Guess what everybody?" she said twirling around her mama's kitchen. "I'm in love! I'm in love! I'm in love!"

"You fall in love too easily," Liezel winced, shaking her head and rolling her eyes. "Who is it this time?"

"Nobody you know," Betsy replied. "And, guess what! We're getting married!"

"What?" screamed Edith from the next room. "Married? We know everybody in this town,, so don't pull that 'nobody you know' on us. So who is he?"

"He's not from around here," Betsy teased.

"Then where's he from? France?" Edith snickered.

"As a matter of fact, yes, from France," Betsy bragged.

By now a crowd of family was forming around Betsy and her nonsense talk. They all shouted their questions at once. How could she possibly marry a guy she hadn't brought home for Papa's approval, how could she possibly have met a guy from France, and would she be moving to France?

"Whoa," said Betsy. "One at a time. I'll answer Mama first: of course I'll get Papa's approval. Jacques is coming next month to meet everyone and ask Papa for my hand. Tomás, I don't know if I'll be leaving Palo, but it's possible because Jacques is a wine distributor and has a good job in Burgundy. And Edith, you won't believe it, but I met Jacques on this," she said as she pulled her iPhone out of her pocket.

"What?" Edith said shocked. "That's crazy. How do you meet a guy on a phone?"

"Online dating, sis. You gotta catch up to the 21st century."

There were dozens of more questions; and as other family members joined the foray, the news had to be repeated over and over. Finally Edith had Betsy to herself. "How does that work, this phone dating thing?" she asked.

"I just downloaded a dating app, wrote up my profile, took a selfie …"

"Let me see your selfie," Edith butt in, wondering how her plain jane sister could entice a Frenchman. "Wow!" she whistled, when Betsy enlarged her picture, "you look really awesome."

"Well, a girl's gotta do *some* enhancement," Betsy admitted. "Hey, if you want to try, I'll give you some tips."

"No, I could never do that. Who shops for a guy online? Uh uh, that's just not me."

That night after Luna was dreaming sweet dreams, Edith was still thinking about Betsy, her saucy profile photo, and her online dating success. *Is it possible I'd have similar luck?* she mused. Edith went to the mirror and started playing with her hair. Then she took off her shirt and shorts and studied her figure in the looking glass. She went even further. Now nude, she stuck out her butt and pushed up her breasts. She tilted her head while still holding her hair aloft and began a routine of sexy poses. "Not bad," she admitted. Then grabbing her granny nightie from under her pillow and wrapping herself tightly in it, she said, "No. I could never."

Chapter 44

What's in a Name?

Edith's sleep that night was interrupted by some very horrible dreams, brought on by Betsy's shocking news. The dreams were populated with the unscrupulous men Edith had met in real life. In one of the dreams, lustful Wa Chin was playing footsie with her under the table at the Chin's Sunday dinner, a move that his wife quickly noticed. Maria grabbed the steak knife and thrust it into her husband's neck, screeching, "You'll never cheat on me again, you bastard!" Then as blood spewed out of Wa's artery, she turned to Edith with the meat fork in her hand. Edith awoke in a sweat just in time to avoid the bludgeoning.

Shortly after she fell into an uneasy sleep, Jun showed up. In this dream, she had just told him that she was pregnant because he had raped her. Instantly, his handsome face transformed into pure evil and ugliness. Horns popped out of the top of his head. In fury, he jumped on his motorbike, yelling, "This is goodbye, you gullible fool," as he gunned the engine and aimed the machine at Edith's pregnant belly. Edith woke up screaming, "No-o-o-o!"

Edith lay awake for quite some time after that. Eventually sleep came again with yet another dream. This time it was the deceptive lying salesman, Mr. Arno, convincing the roomful of young Filipina women how wonderful their new jobs in Syria would be. He was making one false promise after another. As he pushed them into the jetway at the airport, the point of no return, he stood there laughing hysterically. "So long, suckers!" he shouted after them. Edith woke up in shame and in tears.

Just before dawn, Mr. Habib showed up in her dream. He had one hand on her passport and the other hand on her elbow, pushing her into the home of the nasty Saleebs in Damascus. She wrenched her arm away and started running. And running. And running. Mr. Habib was on her tail. She could not escape.

Liezel took one look at Edith at breakfast that morning and said, "What's wrong? You look like you've seen a ghost."

"Uh, I didn't sleep well last night. Must have been that late coffee I drank," Edith answered, trying to shake off all the ghosts with whom she had actually spent the night.

She was feeling very unhinged as she headed out to work that morning. Once she began her mindless job of changing bedding, she began to wonder if she ever wanted to have anything to do with men. But things changed when she entered Room 14, where her favorite patient lay bedridden. "I'm so used to seeing you happy and smiling," the woman said, "that I almost didn't recognize you! Whatever's troubling you, just change your mind. It's as easy as changing sheets," she said with a laugh.

Edith couldn't help but laugh also. That was enough to change her mind about how she was thinking about men. *There are some really good ones*, she thought, as the good ones popped into her mind. She thought about how fun and interesting Michael Peters had been on the bus ride to Manila; how generous and kind Jun's father had been when he showed up at her door with a magnificent check for her baby; how helpful and caring Joe Voltz had been in securing her escape from slavery. Most important of all, she thought of how selfless and loving her own Papa was. By the end of her shift, she was beginning to think that online dating might be for her.

That night, she excitedly rummaged around in her backpack looking to see if she still had Abeena's cellphone. There it was, snugged down in a zippered pocket. The sight of it immediately conjured up images of Abeena lying prone on the floor after she had kicked away the housekeeper's crutches during their escape from the Saleeb household. She said a quick prayer that Abeena survived the ordeal, but having the phone in her hand removed any regret.

"This is a really old phone," Betsy said the next day, "but I know a guy who might be able to get it up and running." With Betsy's help, Edith soon had the phone she needed to begin her online dating life. "I need your help with something else," she confided in Betsy. "I've been thinking about my name. I really don't like it. It sounds old-fashioned and not very sexy at all. Do you think Mama would be upset if I changed my name to Soleil?"

"Soleil? I love it!" Betsy proclaimed enthusiastically. "It's so you! Let's go play with makeup and dress you up to match your new sexy name. Do you still have some of Aunt Agnes' exotic outfits? You do? Great! We're going to get some gorgeous photos, Edi…. Oops, I mean, Soleil."

"I'm Soleil, Exotic Beauty with Good Temper" was how Edith titled her profile. It took her nearly a week working late at night to fine-tune her honest and interesting profile story. Betsy agreed it was perfect. "You're ready to meet your match. Let's get this posted right now," she insisted.

That night Edith had another very fitful slumber. It wasn't nightmares that woke her this time, but a consistent ping-ing. It was hours before she realized the sound was coming from her cellphone and every ping was a notification of a message from the AsiaMe.com dating site. She turned off the phone, and fell asleep, excitedly looking forward to the morning.

"Forty-seven messages! Wow!" Edith was astounded. "Wait 'til I tell Betsy!" she said before charging out the door, late for work. Her day at the hospital couldn't go fast enough and she spent it humming and smiling. Rosa in Room 14 immediately noticed. "Your smile is back! Now that's how to live your life. What a nice change you've made," she told Edith.

Even Luna noticed a change in her mother when, after dinner, Edith told her she was sorry, but a bedtime story wasn't going to happen tonight. "Go play cards with Lolo," Edith suggested.

Edith was alternately intrigued, disgusted, interested and put off after reading the profiles of the men who had messaged her. At last count it was seventy-four. She was surprised to find a message from Mateo, the local Palo boy who had been besotted with her years ago at the market stand. She remembered him planting that wimpy first kiss on her and wasn't too surprised he was still single and looking. She didn't respond to his beseeching and weird message.

Twelve of the other messages had piqued her interest and she decided to respond to those. One was a handsome fellow Filipino named Angelo who lived in nearby Tacloban. "Searching for my Soulmate" his profile said. Another was Luis Rivera of Manila, "a very successful businessman" his profile claimed. She dashed off responses to both of them. She was about to respond to a tall, rugged-looking "medical tech/salmon fisherman" from Alaska, but noticed this Ernie guy was twenty years her senior. *Too old*, she thought, and passed him by.

Angelo of Tacloban was quick to respond. By midnight, they had exchanged many messages and made plans to meet up in Tacloban's better restaurant on Saturday evening. In between, she had also received a response from Luis Rivera who said he had business on Leyte the following week and he'd love it if she'd join him for drinks. She agreed to that also.

"Would you believe I already have two dates!" Edith excitedly told Betsy. "I can't believe how cool online dating is. I might be older than you, but you always give me great ideas and wise advice. You're the best!"

Chapter 45

Red Flags Flying

What she thought would be so much fun took a weird turn by Saturday night. As the week wore on, she had become increasingly anxious about her upcoming date with Angelo. *What if I'm not pretty enough? Sexy enough? Smart enough for a "very successful businessman"? What should I wear? What should I talk about? What if I forget my new name?* Her worries were filling her notebook pages.

She called Betsy who came to her rescue, helping her choose the right outfit, apply the right makeup, and tousle her hair into a seductive coif.

"You look even better than your online photo," Betsy exclaimed when she'd worked her magic on the nervous Soleil. "Just be yourself. Have fun," Betsy advised. "And remember, you have to kiss a lot of frogs before your prince appears."

"Yeah, yeah, I know. But I'm still very nervous. What if he doesn't like me?"

"That's not the question to ask. What if you don't like *him*? You'll know. Red flags will be flying. Pay attention, that's all. Have fun and good luck," Betsy said, hugging her sister as Edith headed out for her first date in years. Edith was quite relieved to see Aunt Agnes in her 1968 Chevy Biscayne pull in front, exactly on time. "You're a life saver, Auntie," she said. "Thanks for taking me to meet my date."

"My, my, my! Don't you look quite beautiful! Any man who doesn't see that has got to be blind," Agnes said enthusiastically. "Now let's say a quick prayer that this old clunker makes it to Tacloban. 'Dearest God, we hope and pray / That this old car survives the day / Cause if it dies along the way / There's going to be some hell to pay.'"

Soleil couldn't help but laugh. "Aunt Agnes, you've been saying that exact same thing since the first time you drove me to the library when I was six!"

"And this baby's still purring," Agnes said. "See? That's the power of prayer, my dear girl."

"If it works so good, wanna hear my prayer?" Soleil asked. "I pray this guy is not a creep / Don't want no man who makes me weep."

By the time they safely arrived in Tacloban, Edith was giggling and in high spirits, ready to meet her man. "Um, Aunt Agnes, would you mind dropping me off down the block a bit?" she asked.

"Of course. I get it," Agnes said knowingly as she pulled the rust bucket to the curb and wished Soleil good luck.

Angelo was waiting near the entrance to the Ocho Seafood & Grill. He was on the phone as Edith approached. She could tell from his expression that he was angry, raising his voice in argument. He abruptly ended the conversation when he recognized Edith walking toward him. "What a cheap-ass brother I have," he said aloud, by way of greeting Edith. "You must be Soleil. Geez, you're even prettier than your photos. Shall we?" Angelo said as he opened the door for her. Soleil was quite pleased by his compliment and his manners. *What a gentleman*, she thought.

The restaurant was very busy and the hostess was doing her best to get everyone seated. "I'm Angelo Ramos. I've a reservation for two at 7:30 p.m.," he said when he reached her podium.

"Oh, I'm sorry, Mr. Ramos, I'm afraid there will be a ten- or fifteen-minute wait for a table. We are unexpectedly busy tonight because of the ball game. I'll seat you the minute a table becomes available," the hostess said kindly.

"Why did I bother making a reservation if we still have to wait?" Angelo snapped at her. "I am a valued regular here, but this will be the last time I'll ever patronize this restaurant again. Such slipshod scheduling!" he huffed.

"Again, I apologize, Mr. Ramos," the flustered hostess replied. "Please accept a complimentary drink at the bar while you wait."

Angelo harrumphed, then guided Soleil by the waist toward the bar. As Soleil climbed onto the bar stool, Angelo looked her over appreciatively, saying "You really are an exotic beauty. Your profile doesn't do you justice!" Although Soleil was embarrassed by the kerfuffle at the hostess stand, his compliments once again snagged her full attention. *I can do this*, she thought to herself.

"So tell me all about Soleil Santos," Angelo prodded. "I want to get to know you better. Much better."

Soleil began telling him the slightly edited story of her life. She was just in the middle of describing her job as a pattern maker in Manila when she was interrupted mid-sentence. "Hey! You! Yes, you!" Angelo shouted over her words to the harried barmaid. "What's it take to get a drink around here?"

In the midst of pouring drinks for a table of six, the barmaid indicated she'd be there in a minute. "A man could die of thirst in this place," Angelo grumbled at her as they placed their drink orders. "Just messing with her," Angelo said to Edith by way of explanation, raising his glass to hers. "Here's a toast to the sexiest woman in this place," he said jovially.

Ten minutes went by quickly and soon they were seated and ready to order. "I'll have the calamari special and the lady will have your sinigang shrimp with garlic butter," Angelo said. "And make it fast. We're hungry." he barked unpleasantly.

Hmmm, Soleil thought. *He ordered my food. He didn't even ask if I like shrimp, or if I was allergic to it. Hmmm. That was kind of presumptuous.*

By the time their dinners were finished, Soleil was tired of him talking about his businesses nonstop throughout the entire meal. She was relieved when the check arrived until Angelo spotted a small error on it. "Miss! Come back here, miss!" he shouted loudly. "Look, you screwed up. You trying to scam us by overcharging for the breadsticks? This is outrageous. There goes your tip."

Suddenly Soleil realized she was seeing red. Red flags, as Betsy would say. *I may be sitting across from Angelo Ramos, but I'm now seeing Mr. Arno, Mr. Habib, Jun and others like them who treat people like trash. I want to go home.* She excused herself to go to the restroom where she made a quick phone call.

Outside the restaurant, Angelo guided Soleil toward his car and was opening the door for her. "Let's stop at my place for a nightcap, beautiful," he was saying, oblivious to Soleil's changed demeanor.

At that moment, Edith faded away and Soleil finally took charge. "No. No way. I really don't like you. At all," she said just as a motorbike pulled up alongside.

"Thanks, sis," she said, wrapping her arms about Betsy's waist, leaving Angelo Ramos spewing abuse as the two women fled the scene.

"I just couldn't believe how nasty and demeaning he was to every worker in that restaurant. I just didn't see the red flags because he was so sweet to me," she complained to Betsy. "But something weird happened to me just after I called you for a ride. I was no longer meek, agreeable, long-suffering Edith. I saw myself as a feisty, grown-up woman who was finally figuring out who and what she wants in her life. I'm not taking any kind of shit from anyone, anymore, Betsy. I am now Soleil ... mind, body and soul!"

"You go, girl!" Betsy exclaimed. "I finally have the no-

nonsense, feisty kind of sister I always wanted!"

Soleil was more than prepared for her date with Luis Rivera. Gone were the first-date jitters and she arrived at the bar cool-headed, confident and on high alert for red flags.

Well, he looks just like his profile photo, that's a good sign. And, he is hot! I hope he's as polished, polite and professional as he looks, Soleil thought to herself as she approached Luis standing near the entrance. As they ordered some drinks at the bar crowded with young partiers, she thought *he's being polite and pleasant to the bartender, too. He might be okay.*

"Tell me about yourself, Soleil," he said. "Your profile mentioned that you've lived in Manila for a while." Soleil launched into a watered-down version of her experiences in Manila and they had some great conversation about their favorite Manila haunts and other places they would like to visit someday, "hopefully together," Luis said suggestively. Soleil was feeling very relaxed and comfortable. *Not a single red flag!* she thought with a happy smile. She was interested in knowing more about him.

"So, Luis, you say you are a very successful businessman. Tell me, what do you enjoy about your job?"

He laughed. "Most women I've met, their first question is: 'how much money do you make?' That makes you special, Soleil," he said brushing his hand against hers. "But the fact is, I do very well for myself. Anyway, here's my story. I am an unofficial government official and I work as a sales rep. I am in the people business. What I like about my job is that it involves traveling and giving seminars to Filipinos who want to improve their lives. I tell people about all-expense-paid travel opportunities and fantastic job openings in foreign countries. Most people sign up with me right at the seminar, because the money-making opportunities are enormous. By the way, Soleil, you like to travel and who couldn't use more money, right? You should come to my seminar at the library in Palo on Thursday.”

Before Luis had even finished his spiel, Soleil was horrified to discover she had been yukking it up with a despicable slave recruiter. But she willed her composure to be cool and collected. “Do you know if there are such opportunities in Syria?” she asked, nonchalantly. “I’ve always dreamed of visiting Damascus.”

“Why yes!” Luis excitedly announced. “That’s one of our most popular destinations.”

“By any chance do you know Mr. Arno? I understand he’s in a similar business.”

“Why, yes, I know him well. He's my sales partn…”

While those words were coming from his mouth, Soleil’s arm was stretching back. With all her might, she executed a powerful slap across Luis’ face. “You and Mr. Arno can go to hell!” she shouted, jumping off the barstool before the shocked Luis could recover from the assault. The bar full of partiers immediately stopped partying and were watching as Soleil charged toward the door. Then, a parting shot as she turned, looked at the crowd, and pointed at Luis: “I do believe I just gave that lying slave trader exactly what he deserved.”

The very next day, Soleil called in late to work and hurried over to the library.

“Hey, Edith, what are you doing?” the librarian demanded sharply as she watched her rip down all Luis’ seminar posters.

“I’m Soleil now,” she answered. “This man and his seminars are pure evil. Promoters of slavery and cruelty. I should know. Thursday’s seminar is hereby canceled. I don’t want this man to steal any more of our young women.

“I ran out, leaving a huge red mark and a beautiful gouge on his face where my ring snagged his skin,” Soleil said laughing as she replayed her date to Betsy. “I could say he never knew what hit him, but that wouldn’t be true. He wasn’t looking so hot any-more!” The sisters laughed and laughed until their sides ached.

Chapter 46

Mystery Man's Box

Now that Soleil believed she had eliminated any remnants of Edith, she was much wiser about the men she was willing to meet. For every thirty men she rejected based on their profiles, she accepted dates from only one or two after interrogating them via messages for several weeks. Two months later, she still hadn't met anyone she wanted to spend her time with.

Meanwhile, she'd been spending quite a bit of time with her notebook, recording her dating experiences, the crazy things she read in profiles, her disappointments and her thoughts about the future. *I know I'm being really picky. Maybe too picky. What if there will never be a man in my life? What if I never find a loving husband for me and an awesome papa for Luna? Oh, gosh, that sounds just like Edith. She keeps trying to sneak back into the Soleil I've become. Shut up, Edith. Just shut up. I must always remember that I am Soleil. I will get what I want. I will find that loving husband and Luna's awesome papa. I feel it deep in my bones. He's out there and I will find him. I just wish it could be sooner rather than later.*

She was thinking about this particular notebook entry at work the next day. As she delivered fresh bedding to Room 14, her favorite patient was out of bed and sitting in a chair by the window.

"You're out of bed, Rosa!" Soleil said, surprised. "How wonderful! You look like you're ready to take on the world. You must be feeling better at last!"

"I really am feeling so much better. Dr. Hunter said I'm showing great improvement. You know, my dear, I am proof that you can get what you wish for," the woman responded with a smile that lit up her whole face.

Soleil was happy for Rosa and was thinking about their brief conversation as she headed to the laundry room. She saw Dr. Hunter coming down the hall. "Hey, Dr. Hunter, I hear Rosa is showing some improvement. That's great news, she's one of my favorites."

"Mine, too," the doctor agreed. "You know, it is her positive attitude that is helping her. And if she's lucky, she'll have no chronic after-effects." Before stepping away, Dr. Hunter added, "Oh, by the way, sorry for the condition of the laundry room this morning. We had some big shipments come in today with nowhere else to put them. They ended up in your workspace. We'll get them put away on the next shift. You're doing a great job here. Thank you, Edith!"

"Uh, er, one little thing, Dr. Hunter. I don't want to be Edith anymore. I've just changed my name to Soleil and hope that's okay with you and the staff."

"That's a beautiful name. It suits you well. I'll let the others know."

The laundry room indeed was piled with a dozen or more boxes. Soleil had to move a few to get the dryer door opened. As she did, she idly scanned the shipping labels. Shipments had come in from Manila, China, Alaska and more. The Alaska label captured her attention. *That's funny*, she thought. *Alaska? Alaska? Why is that ringing a bell?* She inspected the label more closely. It was from Ernie McDowell. *I know that name from somewhere. But where? Of course!* she recalled, slapping her temple. *I saw that name on an AsiaMe profile a while ago. I can't*

*wait to check this and see if it's the same person. If so, what could
he be shipping to this little hospital in Palo?*

Ernie McDowell was a medical technician in a hospital in Anchorage, Alaska. His two passions were salmon fishing and his
one-man philanthropy of sending surplus medical supplies to hospitals in poor countries. This passion had begun unceremoniously.
"Are you going to throw that away?" he asked a scrub nurse after
a procedure. He had just seen her send an unopened suture kit air-
borne toward the medical waste receptacle. "That kit was perfectly good," he remarked. "I know," she responded, "it's a pity we
can't reuse it once it's been on the OR tray."

"That's not right. There must be something we could do about
such waste," he mentioned as the nurse turned to other duties.
"There must be something *I* can do about it," he reasoned as he
gave it some real thought. He started collecting usable medical
supplies. Word got around the hospital about the tech who was
willing to stop the waste and find a need. Soon a collection of unopened scalpels, forceps, syringes, and suture kits began filling
his donation box. Thus began his one-man mission to fulfill medical supply needs in hospitals around the world. In the last five
years, he'd sent packages to such faraway places as Bolivia, Gua-
temala and Fiji.

Ernie had just filled a large boxload of supplies when he
learned of a need at Governor Benjamin T. Romualdez Hospital
in Palo, Leyte. This would be the first time he had shipped to the
Philippines, so he wrote a note of explanation and put it in the
box. A few days later, he took the box to the post office, paid the
$150 postage, and put the now empty donation box back on the
floor in the nurses' station.

Meanwhile in Palo, Soleil couldn't wait to get home and look
up the Alaskan guy's message on AsiaMe. When she finally
found it, she remembered him. *Oh yeah, that's the old guy.* This

time she didn't pass his profile by, but read the entire thing and was quite impressed. He had only posted three photos, but in all of them, he looked fit, rugged and happy. She most favored the shot of him smiling boyishly while holding what she viewed as a gigantic salmon. *He's a mystery man,* she thought. *What could be in that box he sent?*

At work the next morning, she was a little miffed to see that the second shift had not removed yesterday's shipment from her laundry room. But her miff turned to mirth when Dr. Hunter popped her head in, apologizing, saying they were short-staffed last evening and asked Soleil if she had any extra time today, would she open and disburse the boxes' contents. "I'd be more than happy to!" Soleil said with great enthusiasm, as she grabbed a boxcutter from the toolbox and started on the Alaska box first.

She was astonished when she read the note inside the box that was filled to the brim with much-needed supplies.

Dear Fellow Healers of Palo, the good nurses at our hospital in Anchorage, Alaska, have collected these medical supplies in the hopes that your hospital will be able to put them to good use. Since we no longer need them, we are happy to share our over-ages with fellow healers. If your need is ongoing, more supplies can be available in the months to come. Yours truly, Ernie McDowell, Med Tech, Emil B. Straub Hospital, Anchorage.

As excited as she was by these much-needed supplies, she was even more excited to realize that this Ernie McDowell was the same Ernie McDowell who had messaged her. *How many Ernie McDowells could there be in Alaska,* she wondered? *So, he likes to brag about his fish, but says not a word about being a humanitarian. He sure is a mystery man. A rather intriguing one.*

Long after Luna was sound asleep and the household had quieted down, Soleil had written-and-deleted more than twenty messages to this Alaskan Ernie. He had messaged her more than two months ago. By this time, he could already be married, she worried. Finally she settled on messaging an apology for not getting back to him sooner and told him she loved the photo of him with the salmon. She ended her brief message with an invitation: "I'd be interested in learning more about you and life in Alaska," she wrote, which she quickly edited to read "*very* interested" before hitting Send.

"Well, has he responded yet?" Betsy had to know when Soleil told her the strange story about the mysterious Ernie and the serendipitous shipment from Alaska.

It had been four days with no word from the frozen north and Soleil was doing her best not to sound disappointed. "Not yet, but four days isn't all that many considering it took me two months to answer *his* message!"

"Not to worry," Betsy assured her. "I've found that men don't check their messages very consistently. Women, on the other hand, sit by their computers and respond instantly to every single ping. I know. I did!"

"Maybe." Soleil was unconvinced.

Betsy had more to suggest. "Hey, maybe his computer is broken, or his phone is lost. Perhaps he's on vacation in a remote place with no cellphone service. It's also possible he's out testing the waters."

"Meaning?"

"Meaning maybe he's dating someone and is still trying to find out if she's the one he'd like to hook," Betsy postulated.

It turns out that none of Betsy's best guesses were true. Ernie had read Soleil's message right after she sent it. He discovered that he was totally intimidated by this 'exotic beauty.' He'd spent the last four nights composing-and-deleting messages. "Why did I ever let Moose talk me into this?" he moaned. "If I hadn't gone fishing with him that day a few months ago, I wouldn't be such a wreck."

Chapter 47

Moose's Crazy Idea

Many months earlier, Ernie hadn't given online dating any thought at all. This changed one auspicious day in May.

"No way, not me, I'm happy. Couldn't be happier," Ernie said as he whipped his line into the air ahead of the skiff. He and his best bud, Moose, were drifting the Kenai River fly fishing for sockeye. Fishing with Moose was one of his favorite things, but today Moose was downright annoying. "I don't need a woman," Ernie insisted, "I've got my hands full just raising my boys. Besides, it's been just me and the boys for more than thirteen years now. A woman would have us lifting our feet to vacuum under us or picking my Coors off the mahogany to wipe the drips while I'm trying to enjoy a cold beer."

"That's what I mean," Moose replied, not letting the topic drop. "You've got socks laying around the floor in every room in the house. The boys snack in their bedrooms leaving you to retrieve the silverware. What's-her-name ran off to the lower 48 with that wildlife photographer thirteen years ago! That's a long time to be without a woman. A man needs a woman. A man needs a *good* woman."

"Her name was Cindy," Ernie said sadly, softly. "Drop it, Moose."

"Okay, okay," Moose said, realizing he had gone too far.

"Just let me say one more thing and then I'll shut up. The whole point of me bringing up this subject was because Chops—you know Chops, runs a charter out of Clam Gulch—he just got married. He went online and found himself a wife, a Filipina, and now he's as happy as a pig in mud."

"That *is* news," Ernie admitted as he reeled the line back in. "I hear a lot of guys are looking online for romance. A woman would have to be crazy to leave one of the world's favorite tropical paradises to come live in one of the world's coldest, darkest winters." Ernie laughed just thinking of its absurdity as his whipped line whizzed over his head into the river.

Moose was on a roll. "Chops said it was fun looking at pretty faces all last winter, reading profiles, answering a few. Tense but fun. Look what it got him! Why not look at pretty faces all winter, Ernie? Beats all those damn who-dun-its you read."

The sockeye almost yanked the pole out of Ernie's hand. "Holy shit!" Ernie yelled, standing suddenly to get a better grip. Moose grabbed the net. No more silly girl talk, serious fishing had begun.

When they finally pulled the skiff ashore Ernie held his thirteen-pounder front and center so the lookie-loos milling about the ramp could get an eyeful. Moose snapped a photo. "Hey, this would be a great photo for your online profile," Moose chided.

Ernie looked at his friend's phone. It *was* a damn good photo. "I am *not* going online," Ernie emphasized, "but send it to me anyhow. I want to show my boys." Moose could feel it in his bones: his bud was going to go online, maybe as soon as tonight.

"What are you doing, Dad?" fourteen-year-old Danny asked after dinner when his dad plunked himself in the Barcalounger, and, instead of picking up his recent Baldacci novel, opened his laptop.

"Nothing. I'm just looking up something Moose told me about today."

"Dad, that's a dating site," Danny chortled, coming up from

behind and looking over his father's shoulder. Ernie snapped the laptop shut.

"Are you looking for a woman?" Danny teased.

"Whose looking for a woman?" sixteen-year-old Brian overheard and wanted to know.

"Dad is."

"It's about time," Brian stated.

Ernie was flabbergasted. He thought the boys would strongly object to the idea of 'Dad finding a woman to love.' He thought they'd see it as a replacement for their own mother and that it might change their relationship.

"Dad, I was a baby when she left us," Danny reminded. "All I've ever had is you and that's always been enough."

"I was three," Brian added. "I barely remember her. You would stick me in front of the TV in those days, Dad. I used to think Vanna White was my mother because she always looked right at me and smiled just before I went to bed."

"Oh God," Ernie said, pulling his hands through his hair. "You guys are so silly. Now, go to bed, boys. I'm busy."

"It's only 8 o'clock!" they laughed.

"Then go do your homework or something. Wait! Maybe you can show me how to create a profile."

The boys cracked up. "You're really gonna go online? If you're gonna do it, you gotta start off with a catchy headline. How about 'Old Man and the Sea?' or 'Sexy, Hot Old Guy in Search of Love? All offers accepted.'" When Danny thought of his old man trying to hook up, he laughed so hard that he began to snort and Brian doubled over with tears of laughter rolling down his cheeks.

Ernie didn't appreciate their old man jokes. "How about I write, 'Dad of two feather-brained teenage boys needs to escape home.' Now disappear, boys."

Now that he was alone, he began to think about what he would really write in his profile. This was new territory for him and he was both nervous and excited. "This isn't easy," he said after looking at a blank screen for fifteen minutes. He grabbed a pen and made a list of his attributes: only a few pounds overweight, has a good head of hair, goes to church on Sunday, has a good job, enjoys helping people, likes to fish, willing to learn to dance.

"Cripes! I'm boring!" he said, throwing the pen down and grabbing Baldacci. But he couldn't concentrate. He opened the computer again and this time he actually downloaded the dating app and signed up. His fingers were sweating all over the keyboard but he pushed on. "Wow," he said as the AsiaMe site started popping up pictures of beautiful women. "These girls aren't going to be turned on by a ruddy-faced fisherman. No way." Then he thought of Chops. "How did Chops get so lucky?" he wondered. As he continued browsing profiles, he thought maybe Moose was right. This *would be* an entertaining way to spend long winter nights. He continued to browse when eventually a headline caught his eye: "Exotic Beauty with Good Temper." The beauty's name was Soleil and he couldn't resist reading her brief, but intriguing profile. In it, she said she was interested in meeting a man who was kind and honest, had a good sense of humor, was loyal and dependable.

"That sounds like me," he said with bravado, before admitting to himself it was probably a waste of time to message such a pretty woman. Instantly, he could hear Moose saying, "What are you, a chicken?" The thought of Moose's harassment was all it took.

"Hi there. I really liked your profile. Your beautiful name and enticing headline caught my eye," he typed. "Would love to hear from you." His fingers were aching to hit the delete key, but with Moose in mind and with great resolve, he hit Send.

In the next few days he got tons of responses to his profile but not a word from Soleil. Days turned into weeks and finally he stopped looking. He was sick of all the "I make you happy, Big Daddy" rubbish that filled his mailbox. "I'm done with this online dating crap," he told himself but he didn't delete the app, just in case.

Chapter 48

Cold Beer To The Rescue

"What do I do now?" he nervously asked Moose. "That woman I messaged two months ago finally responded. Soleil. Remember? It was quite a short message. But she wrote that she is very interested in knowing more about me."

"Did she actually say *very?*" Moose wanted to know. "She did? That's a good sign. You need to respond quickly while the iron is hot. Tell her a bit more about yourself and let your personality show through. If she really is *very* interested, she'll respond right away. I hear this is where it gets fun and exciting. Least that's what Chops said."

Hope Moose is right, he thought as he typed his response to Soleil. "Hi, Soleil, I'm new to this dating scene and to be honest, this is a little scary for me. I haven't been tempted in a very long time to look for a partner. I've been quite busy the past thirteen years raising two sons as a single parent. Two teenagers can be a handful but I'm proud to say that they have turned out well and I love them intensely. I work in the medical field as a med tech in a hospital here in Anchorage. I absolutely love my job. As you might have guessed from my photo, I also love salmon fishing. Maybe someday I could tell you the story behind that photo and how that day of fishing led to my joining this online dating site.

You probably already noticed that I'm almost forty-six. That only means that I've had time to mellow, to grow up and to know who I am and what I want. I think you and I might hit it off because I, too, am looking for someone kind and honest, with a sense of humor who's loyal and dependable. If our age difference doesn't ruin it for you, I'd love to hear from you again soon."

What had started in the beginning as bashful and simple email exchanges for both Soleil and Ernie, in a few months had progressed into daily email contact. Each message led to revealing more of their personalities and histories that had initially been well-guarded. She confessed to him that it wasn't until the day she opened the shipment he'd sent to her hospital, that she finally decided to respond to him. "Ah, so that explains why I was on pins and needles for weeks on end! LOL!" he teased. He revealed that his wife had run off with some other guy leaving him with two babies. "Ah, I was wondering about that," she replied. To which he responded, "I blamed myself and I was embarrassed. Her taking off left me with a heart that has taken forever to heal, until now." Soleil thought it was about time to tell Ernie about her enslavement in Syria. About how she escaped only because war broke out. *I'm afraid he will think I am stupid, or worse, that I'm just an easily-conned poor waif from the Visayas.* "Why didn't you tell me before now?" he questioned. "I would have fallen for you that much sooner." They had settled comfortably into an online relationship that had no secrets.

"He wants to come and meet me!" Soleil giddily shouted when she opened his latest message. "Ernie is coming to Palo! Oh my God!"

Soleil's next text was "When???" with a long string of question marks.

"ASAP!!!" was his immediate response with a long string of exclamation points. "I'll ask for the time off tomorrow, check airline schedules and let you know. XOXO!"

"I'm scared shitless," he told his boys who were watching his reaction as the texting unfolded. "Am I crazy for falling for a stranger and going halfway around the world to meet her? God knows I don't travel well. I'm sure I'll need the barf bag. What have I done?"

"We're getting a new mom!" the boys teased as they danced around the living room laughing, and when they pried it out of him that 'mom' was only twenty-five, they laughed even harder. Both the boys grabbed their big wooly-bear dad in a group hug and assured him that he would do fine, and they would all live happily ever after just like in a fairy tale. "I'll leave breadcrumbs, boys, so you can find your way back home in case your new stepmom wants to drop you off in the woods." Ernie had the last laugh.

Luckily Betsy was still in Palo getting ready for her own big move with Jacques. Soleil thought Betsy would know what to do, what to say, how to plan, so Betsy was the first to hear the exciting news. Her reaction surprised Soleil.

"Alaska, no less!" Betsy whooped, wrapping her arms around her sister. "And I thought my move to Burgundy was far away! I can't wait to meet him. But I should warn you: when Ernie arrives, you're likely to have some competition."

"Competition?" Soleil asked incredulously. "I don't have any competition."

"Oh yes, you do," Betsy informed. "I've been there, done that. Here's how it goes."

Betsy explained how online dating has become a windfall for Filipinas. According to her, guys across the globe are looking for long-haired beauties who are known to be loyal, loving *and* willing to cook, clean and do laundry. "It seems French girls won't clean, American girls can't cook and the Brits won't do either. But we will," Betsy touted, "and we're prettier.

"You'll be amazed at the chicanery that goes on at the airport when the afternoon plane comes in from Manila, but I have a plan," Betsy assured. "When that day comes, he will only have eyes for you."

"I hope you're right. By the way, Betsy, I need your advice on something else. Should I get some of that whitening cream for my face? He may be shocked to see my real skin color because Albert helped me lighten up my profile photos. I've heard that Americans, especially, often think of darker-skinned women as poor and less attractive. Did you lighten your skin when you first met Jacques?" Edith inquired.

Betsy burst into laughter. "No, I wouldn't have dreamed of doing that. I haven't told anyone yet, but Jacques is black."

Edith's eyes popped open to twice their size. "Wow!" was all Edith could think of to say, so she repeated it. "Wow!" She took one look at Betsy's beaming face and said, "I can't wait to meet this man who is making you so happy. He must be very special. I'm so thrilled for you and Little Carlos."

"I know you are. I still haven't answered your original question, though. So here it is. Soleil, don't you dare go slopping crap on your face to whiten it up. If Ernie's as wonderful as you say, he will love you in any shade. You can't have a great relationship if it starts off by trying to fool him. Deception leads to disappointment. Disappointment leads to trouble. Besides, I know you too well. If you marry him, I just can't see you for the next fifty years rising an hour early to whiten your skin before he awakes. Face him just as the bronzed beauty that you are."

Soleil reached out to her sister and they embraced in an affectionate bear hug. "I'm really going to miss you, Bets," she whispered, thankful that Betsy couldn't see her eyes getting misty. "You may be younger than me, but you are wise beyond your years. I want you to know how much I appreciate you. You've always come to my rescue when I needed it most."

"Hey, that's what sisters are for."

Liezel was beside herself. "An American coming here, to this house?" she cried. "Please no," she begged as her eyes scanned her meager surroundings. Until this moment Liezel felt she had everything she needed to be happy. Now, suddenly she realized how poor she really was. "Why is he coming here? You should go there," she implored. She called to her husband. "Carlos, tell our daughter she should go to America to meet him. Not here in our poor barrio."

"Mama," Soleil said softly, taking her mother by the shoulder, "I want Ernie to meet you and Papa, Luna, our whole family, and Aunt Agnes and our neighbors, too. I want Ernie to really see who I am, and he can't know me without knowing you, all of you."

"But we have nothing to offer," Liezel fretted.

"But we do!" sang Carlos who loved the idea of inviting an American into his humble home with its incredible garden. "We will roast a pig in his honor. It will be the biggest one we can find!" His delight for the event stopped suddenly when he realized he probably couldn't converse with the gentleman from America. "Does he speak Filipino?" he asked Soleil.

"I don't know," she answered, hoping Ernie might find his introduction to her family more fun than strange.

"How do you say 'malamig na beer' in English?" Papa wanted to know.

"Cold beer. Why?"

"I hear Americans love 'malamig na beer.'" Carlos proclaimed. "It will be quite a feast! He will love us!"

"What's a Filipino celebration without roast pig and cold beer? You're such a guy, Papa. I'll tell him of your plot to have him love us," Soleil laughed.

It took Ernie a month to get his vacation scheduled and his anxiety under control for he had never contemplated such a crazy idea before and now he was at its starting point. Soleil was in a similar state of anticipation; at least she had the home advantage, but she had taken chances before which had ended badly. She sought her father's advice.

His wisdom was as simple as the man himself. "Don't look back," he said. "You're not going that way."

"I'll pick you up tomorrow before 3 p.m. for a dry run to the Tacloban airport," Betsy texted Soleil. "I want you to see your competition. There's a 100% chance somebody's online guy will be stepping off the 3 p.m. flight from Manila and into the arms of a girl he has never communicated with. He's about to be hi-jacked! I'll pick you up on the scooter. Be ready."

"I find this hard to believe," Soleil said, putting on the passenger helmet the next afternoon. "Are women that aggressive?"

"You'll see," Betsy said as they sped away.

There was about a dozen very pretty Filipinas at the passengers-only-beyond-this-point rope on the tarmac that separated visitors from the arriving travelers. Each of the girls seemed to be holding a paper. Soleil and Betsy watched as the girls became edgier as the plane taxied in. It stopped on the tarmac a hundred feet away. The girls began elbowing each other for better positions. At last the door opened and passengers began to disembark nonchalantly as if they were frequent travelers to this airport. Finally, a bewildered guy stood at the top of the portable stairs. He reached into his pocket and unfolded a paper with one word on it: CHARLENE.

At once, all the young women behind the rope scribbled one word on the papers they held: CHARLENE. Suddenly the word CHARLENE began waving and bobbing from dozens of lifted arms attached to the beauties behind the rope. When the rope that was holding them back was officially removed the girls swarmed the bewildered passenger. "I'm Charlene. I'm Charlene," a chorus rang out. He scanned the sea of beautiful faces and realized they all looked alike to him. He ended up leaving with the fastest, the loudest, the boldest among them who had gotten her arms around his neck first.

"This is going to be you in two weeks," Betsy explained.

"How is Ernie going to know it's me? I'm not that pushy," Soleil worried aloud.

"You're smarter than the others," her sister assured her. "You and Ernie are going to have a secret word. When he holds up his Soleil sign, you will hold up your secret word."

"You are just too clever," Soleil proudly admitted.

The next text Soleil sent Ernie was about a secret word. They batted around a few possibilities until they finally came up with a good one, one that made them send a bunch of LOLs back and forth.

The next two weeks were both bitter and sweet. Sweet because the pig was ordered and the pit constructed. Papa didn't think he could make good on his cold beer idea until Albert said he knew a guy who had a Beer Below Zero freezer. His father was skeptical.

"It's true," Albert explained. "Three clever beer-drinking Filipinos perfected a freezer to keep beer ice cold. Leave it to us Filipinos to solve one of the hot world's most serious problems," Albert laughed. "Anyway, I can rent one."

The bitter part of those two weeks was due to Luna's reaction. She was stomping about and pouting over the arrival of this visitor. She had been tuning in on the family conversations and was fretting that Mama might leave her again.

Liezel was particularly quiet during this two-week interval. Her feelings were mercurial. At times, she felt the sadness of losing not one, but two daughters to faraway places. Then her spirits would soar realizing that both Edith and Betsy would have opportunities not found in the Visayas. In between, she kept hoping that Ernie would be Edith's forever man. Liezel was the family worrier. Her cup always seemed half empty.

As the days sped by, Soleil's anxiety ramped up. The old "what ifs" from her Edith days returned to plague her. "What if he's only five feet tall? Or two hundred pounds heavier? I hear that happens with this online stuff," she wailed to Betsy a few days before Ernie's arrival.

"Get over yourself, prima donna," Betsy retorted.

"Well, I'm sure of one thing. I'll be checking him out very carefully. I'll scrutinize every hair on his head, every pound on his body, every word he says. If I notice anything, *anything,* I don't like, he's history," Soleil declared.

"As if you're the queen of England," Betsy said with a laugh. That broke the "what ifs" spell.

The Philippine Airline passenger in the seat in front of Ernie kept looking through the slit between seats to the row behind to see who was so violently tapping his foot and making the seat vibrate. When he saw that it wasn't an annoying kid, but a grown man with sweat on his brow, he let it go. Ernie had flown before but not like this, not into his future. He thought maybe he should have stuck to the life he was leading, just him and the boys. It was a good life. *Damn you, Moose, you made me screw up my perfect life,* he cussed. In reality, life hadn't been that perfect. Raising two boys alone for the past thirteen years was the most difficult thing he had ever done. *If I have a heart attack before I land, it's on you, Moose.* That was the old Ernie talking, the one he left on the Kenai Peninsula yesterday at dawn.

The new Ernie was on his wings of love, flying to the one person on God's sweet earth who made him feel as if he was handsome and strong. Adonis. Hercules. She was his missing piece. He was already in love with the idea of his Soleil but that didn't stop his jitters.

I hate change, he told himself as the flight attendant made her last pass through the cabin collecting trash. "Do you need some napkins, sir, to mop up the Coke you spilled?" she asked kindly as she collected his plastic cup. "Yes," he muffled in embarrassment adding, "and if you wet it a bit I might be able to get the stain off my pants."

"Of course," she responded. "Is this the first time you'll be meeting her?" she asked sweetly, knowingly.

"God! Is it that obvious?" he said, fidgeting.

"She's going to love you," she whispered close to his ear. Nearby passengers looked his way, some smiled empathetically, some winked and the elderly lady sitting next to him said something in Filipino and patted his hand.

Damn it, Moose, he said under his breath. *I'm a wreck and it's all your fault.*

The plane landed. He checked his pocket to make sure it still held his Soleil sign. It did. He willed himself to a standing position as his sweat turned cold and made him shiver. It was 90 degrees when he stood at the top of the portable stairs and unfolded his sign. Dozens of signs reading 'Soleil' began waving in the air before him. Then an airport worker dropped the rope that separated him from the lunging ladies. His eyes scanned from left to right and right to left looking for the secret code word. At last he saw it. COLD BEER. He bounced down the stairs two at a time and ran toward COLD BEER. Soleil dropped the sign as he swooped her up and swung her around and around. He set her down and panicked. *What happens next?* he fretted. *Do I kiss her? Do I not kiss her? What would Moose do? He'd plant a wet sloppy one right on the lips. She won't go for it. Look how classy she is. Oh God!*

As she was being swung around she was agonizing. *What happens next? Do I let him kiss me? What if he plants a big sloppy one on me? I'd run. What would Betsy do? She'd kiss him back. I can't. I only know him by his texts, not his body. But wait! Wow!* she thought, collecting her wits and taking a good look at him. *Now that's a great body!*

"You're beautiful," was all he could say.

"And you're more handsome than your selfies," she replied, staring into his face.

He blinked first. "Honestly, I don't know what to do next," he confessed.

"Me neither," she admitted. They both laughed and hugged in a welcomed truce.

"Let's get your stuff," she said, taking his hand and pulling him toward baggage. His fingers encompassed her whole hand. Touching this man felt wonderful, *a good sign*, she mused.

As they got into the taxi she suggested a stop at her hospital before going home. Dr. Hunter wanted to meet him. "It's on the way," she added. Indeed, Dr. Hunter kept pumping Ernie's hand thanking him over and over for the supplies he had sent. "You can't possibly know what this means to us. We were desperate for supplies and God sent *you*."

"One more person to meet before we leave," Soleil told Ernie. "Rosa in Room 14. She's a character!"

"Rosa, this is Ernie," she announced as they entered the room.

"Come closer," Rosa said, curling a bony index finger toward the American. When she could reach his hand, she grabbed it and wrapped her frail fingers around his. She studied his sapphire blue eyes for a long minute. "Yes, you're the one!"

He didn't understand a word she was saying and looked toward Soleil for help. Had he understood he might have blushed bright pink.

"Yes, he's the one," Rosa repeated, looking directly at Soleil.

"Rosa!" Soleil grimaced. "Shh. I just met him thirty minutes ago. You shouldn't say that."

"I'm always right, dear," she added. "Now plump my pillow and get out of here, you two."

"It's going to get worse," Soleil admitted when they got back in the cab. "My family is Rosa times twenty." They rode the rest of the way holding hands, anticipating. She was right. A crowd had gathered. Her family alone looked like a crowd but there were also relatives and neighbors at the gathering. "You're big news in this barrio," Soleil laughed, "just smile."

"Okay," he answered. "Here goes nothing."

Carlos tried to put his arm around Ernie's shoulder to guide him to the Beer Below Zero freezer but he was much too short. He settled for grabbing the Alaskan's arm and dragging him to the freezer that Albert had rented. "Cold beer? Cold beer?" he said bobble heading, "Yes? Yes?"

"Yes!" replied Ernie, "I badly need one."

"Yes! Yes!" exclaimed Carlos, pleased but with no clue.

"Hi, I'm Edi... Soleil's brother, Albert," said Albert as he stuck out his hand, adding, "and I speak English. It may come in handy around here," he joked. "We're glad you're here. Soleil's been talking non-stop about you. We didn't think you'd really come all the way from Alaska to meet her. Either Soleil's special or you are."

"It's her," Ernie answered. "Honestly, I'm just a tech in a hospital who loves fishing. Not much to write home about." That last part didn't make any sense to Albert and he quickly gave up trying to figure it out.

"It's absolutely her," Ernie repeated. "From our emails over the past few months I've come to know your sister as a beautiful soul. I had to come and see for myself what a beautiful soul looks like in person."

Albert was impressed. "And for the past several months," he said, "Soleil's been talking about you so much you already seem like part of our family. I really wanted to see what it was about you that makes her so ga-ga. I see it now. By the way, I hope you don't mind sleeping in the backyard tent. As you can see, our house isn't equipped for extra sleepers."

While Albert was talking, Ernie could see a little girl darting from behind one person to another in hopes of not being seen, peeking at him. Luna thought she was invisible but he caught her eye and she ran away to the back yard where she sat with her yams, pouting.

Ernie disappeared into the house where he opened a suitcase and pulled out a Beanie Baby. He went looking for Luna and found her moping in the yams. "I see you," he said. "You can run, but you cannot hide." She covered her eyes to make him disappear. "I brought you something all the way from Alaska," he teased hoping she'd look at him. It took a minute, but she was a curious child and couldn't help but look. "Which hand?" he said, holding both behind his back. More curious than ever, she stood, came close and made her selection. Ernie handed her the plush toy, a puffin, and she immediately did what every American kid does when she gets a new Beanie Baby, she cuddled it to her face.

As much as she loved the present, she was still unsure of the stranger who had given it to her.

"Puffins only live in cold climates like Alaska. We have lots of puffins," he explained.

"He's so cute," she said, still holding it to her face.

When Soleil didn't see Luna darting among the guests any longer, she became concerned. She noticed that Ernie, too, had disappeared. She found them behind the house in the garden, seriously discussing yams.

"I have a garden, too," she overheard him telling her daughter. "I grow tomatoes and lettuce."

"Do you sing the garden song to your lettuce to make it grow bigger and fatter?" Luna asked, amazed, still clutching the puffin.

"No, as a matter of fact, I never heard of that," Ernie replied.

"It's easy. I'll teach you," Luna said, and she started singing her *Os, Ps, Bees* song.

"Look, Mama!" she squealed when she noticed her mother. "Ernie gave me a puffin! Isn't he cute?" Then she remembered: puffins live in Alaska. "I don't want to go to Alaska," she cried and ran into the house still holding the puffin to her cheek.

Ernie was getting more at ease as cold beer caps kept snapping off. With Soleil or Albert or Betsy by his side as interpreter, he worked the yard with charisma. The family and friends liked him. He liked them.

Tomorrow, though, might be a different story. Tomorrow was the pig roast and the whole barrio would be there to gawk at the tall Alaskan. He wondered when all these festivities would end. He wanted to be alone with Soleil. It wouldn't be tonight, though. He was exhausted. Soleil politely shooed the neighbors home and Ernie was asleep, alone, in the tent in minutes.

Chapter 49

A Slip of the Tongue

The pig roast had been a huge, happy and exciting success. The next morning when they had a moment alone, Ernie admitted maybe he'd had a bit too much to drink. "Every time your papa looked at me, he'd say 'Cold beer?' I didn't want to seem rude."

Soleil explained, laughing, "That's the only English he knows. He's been practicing for weeks!"

"Oh, that's so funny. I think your family is wonderful! But, right now I could use some fresh air. I'm just not used to this heat," Ernie said, taking Soleil by the hand and leading her to the backyard. There they stood awkwardly for a few minutes, neither of them knowing what to say now that they had some privacy. "Everybody has made me feel very welcome, Soleil," Ernie said. "I really loved meeting everyone you've been telling me about. And that pig roast! Wow!" Ernie was never very good at small talk and searched his brain for something else to rave about. He had been quite surprised when the taxi had dropped them off at the Santos' home yesterday. It was little more than barebones shelter with its corrugated roof and windows without panes. He'd never experienced such poor living conditions anywhere he'd ever been. There was no good small talk to be had about her surroundings. But one look at the beautiful woman who had beckoned him here, and the small talk got larger.

"Soleil, I'm still a bit nervous being here with you. I've imagined this moment a thousand times and yet, I never imagined it would be quite so wonderful. That you'd be quite so beautiful. That I'd be quite so lucky."

Soleil smiled and said, "I've done my own share of imagining! I feel like we're on a blind first date! I'm really glad we have all week to get to know each other. Tomorrow we'll go into Palo and I'll show you where I sold veggies when I was fourteen. Won't that be exciting?" she teased. Then she had another idea. "Do you like to hike?"

"Love to hike. I think I've hiked every trail on the Kenai Peninsula."

"Perfect. Then the day after tomorrow, we'll hike up what's known as Hill 522. It's where the …"

Excitedly, Ernie interrupted her. "Hill 522? You're kidding! It's around here?"

Soleil spun Ernie around and pointed. "That's the backside of it right there. You know about Hill 522?"

"Boy, do I know about Hill 522! My grandfather was with General MacArthur when the Americans routed the Japanese on that hill during World War II. Grandpa spent many long winter nights telling me stories about that victory. Trust me, the way he told it, it was more exciting than any book he could have read to me. He died when I had just turned twenty and I remember saying to him on his deathbed that someday I would visit Hill 522. I never thought I'd have the chance. I will be honored to hike Hill 522 with you."

"Then I must confess to one little secret you don't yet know about me," Soleil said. "The Filipinos were, and still are, so grateful for the Americans' help, that they've been giving their babies American names for generations. Bet you didn't know I was born Edith. I became Soleil when I started looking for someone. Well, actually, looking for you. Just wondering, would you be here if I was still named Edith?"

"Hmmm," he said with a teasing twinkle in his eye, "that's a tough one."

Soleil playfully swatted at him and loved knowing he could make her smile.

Ernie and Soleil had been inseparable since his arrival. One night after having dinner in one of Tacloban's nicer restaurants, Ernie asked her if she'd mind if they didn't make plans for tomorrow. He had something he wanted to do. This surprised Soleil and she teasingly asked, "Getting tired of me already?"

"Never!" was his response. He explained his plan. He wanted to spend some time with Luna, just the two of them. "I get the sense she's not sure of me. That I might be trying to steal her mama away. Which I am, by the way." There was the teasing twinkle again. "I want to take her to Palo. We'll visit the library, and have lunch at that little place we went to the other day, or even better, have a picnic in the park. How's that sound?"

"I can't think of anything nicer."

Luna was shy and withdrawn on the walk to Palo, but it was not long before she warmed up. Ernie told jokes and shared stories about his home. She became inquisitive, asking all kinds of questions about Alaska. "What does snow feel like? Are there puppies in Alaska?" She wanted to know if Alaskan rainbows were pretty. "I love rainbows," she announced. Ernie had a good answer for that one. "If you think rainbows are pretty, you'd be amazed by the Northern Lights. At night, sometimes the whole sky lights up in red, green, blue and purple colors. Even bigger and better than rainbows," Ernie explained. "Oh, I love purple," Luna announced.

"Do you know what, Luna?" Ernie asked. "I think you are the prettiest and smartest little girl I've ever met. You're just like your mama." Luna beamed.

It was warm on the dusty road home. "Hop on my shoulders, little one. I'll give you a piggyback ride." Luna was still giggling when they reached the front yard where Soleil felt as if a miracle had occurred. "Mama, Mama," Luna shouted out. "They have colorful sky lights at night in Alaska. Prettier than rainbows! Can we go there?"

Luna's question stirred Soleil. Her daughter's giggles and excitement were what Soleil had been waiting for. *Now that Luna's on board, I feel so much better,* she thought to herself. *I wonder why he hasn't proposed yet. Heck, he hasn't even kissed me yet.*

Ernie was also deep into his own thoughts. *Time is running out, buddy boy. It's time to pedal or get off the bike. I would love to marry this woman, so I don't want to screw up by acting too fast. Best to just give her time. Let her call the shots.* A final thought worried him: *I'm definitely in love, but ... is Soleil?*

Luna dove into bed early after her adventure-filled day. Soon after, the house grew quiet. "Let's take a walk," Ernie said. "I want to talk about my day with Luna, and a few other things."

"Oh my!" Soleil exclaimed when they stopped in the corn field. "Look at the gorgeous full moon! They say many unusual things happen during full moons. So it seems especially interesting that you and Luna seemed to bond today. When she was born, the midwife predicted that, like the moon, my Luna would light up my darkest times."

"Well now that I know her better, she has certainly lit up mine! Just as you have," Ernie confessed, opening wide his arms and inviting Soleil in for an embrace. Then he leaned over and shyly, tentatively kissed her. "I am so in love with you, Soleil. Will you marry me?" he asked.

There was a long pause. The silence, the lack of an immediate response, made Ernie very uncomfortable. He had been envisioning that she would be jumping for joy at his question. When she finally broke the silence, Ernie wished he could shrivel up and disappear. "Ernie, no, I'm not going to marry you."

Ernie wasn't one to plead or beg for reasons. Rejection was rejection. "Well, okay then. I've had a really long day. I think I'll turn in."

Soleil didn't mean for the evening to end in ruins. She didn't want to reject him, but she had a reason, a damn good one, she thought.

When Soleil could hear serious snoring coming from the tent in the yard, she went into the kitchen where her mama was putting the last of the dishes away. "Mama, Ernie proposed to me tonig …"

Before she could finish the sentence, Liezel dried her hands and rushed with mad excitement to embrace her eldest daughter.

"But I told him no."

"You what? You said NO???" Liezel couldn't believe what she was hearing. "He seems perfect for you, Soleil. The whole family loves him. Tell me what happened?"

Soleil hated to tell her mother her reason, but she knew she had little choice. Her mama would never let that go.

"Well, um, this is kind of personal. I'm really embarrassed to talk about it. But the thing is: Ernie is not a good kisser."

This time mama's shout of "what?" would have awakened the chickens, if they'd had any. "You decided to throw away a good life because your man's not a good kisser!!!" Liezel shouted in disbelief. "Is it really *that* important to you? Silly girl!"

"Here's what I think, Mama," Soleil began, sputtering. "My dream has been to have two, maybe three more children. Growing up in a large family like ours has been wonderful. I wanted that for my own family. I couldn't help but notice over the years that you and Papa did a lot of serious kissing. Nothing wimpy about those kisses, ever! The result was often another baby on the way. Since Ernie's not a good kisser, what are my chances of having lots of babies?"

Soleil had never surprised Liezel so much, ever. Her surprise led her to double over in laughter. Liezel was snorting, holding her sides and howling unstoppably.

"Oh, my sweet Edi ... Soleil," she said when she finally caught her breath. "Did you ever think that maybe it's *you* who's not a good kisser?"

"Mama!" Soleil shrieked in disbelief.

"Mama thinks I might be a bad kisser," Soleil confessed to Betsy when she called her around midnight and explained what had happened.

"Boy, you are more naive than I could ever have imagined," Betsy said, now wide awake and trying to hold in giggles. "Don't you know *anything* about kissing?"

"Well, I haven't had as much experience as you, *obviously*," Soleil began, a little miffed that Betsy thought this was funny. "I got my first kiss from Mateo at the market when I was fourteen. It was very disappointing. Sloppy and wimpy. But when Jun kissed me in Manila, well, *that* was a kiss! At the time, I never thought it would lead to pregnancy, but it did. I see a real connection."

"For a very smart sister, you're an idiot," Betsy proclaimed. "Let me tell you some things about kissing. If your goal is to make some babies, it all starts with good kissing. And good kissing starts with the woman. When a woman has desire, she signals it by delivering deep, wet, longing kisses. She plays with his tongue, breathes heavily, moves her body suggestively. He will take his cues from her and return kisses that are even better. Very quickly, the poor fellow loses all control. That's how you make babies!"

Soleil sat alone in the kitchen thinking about Betsy's words. She had never realized that kissing might be an art, one to be learned and practiced. What if Betsy was right? She finally admitted that she really loved everything about Ernie, except his kiss. *If it's true that good kissing requires practice, it's all up to me to fix my little hangup. I can do this.*

It was nearly 2 a.m. when Soleil lifted the flap to the backyard tent and dropped her nightie on the hard-packed dirt. She slipped onto the thin mattress next to the sleeping Ernie and gently draped her leg over his. She was amazed that the feel of his bare leg touching hers elicited such surprising sensations. He didn't stir. He was dreaming she was lying beside him, wanting him. He could almost sense the warmth of her body and the soft touch of her fingers. He was afraid to awaken.

Abandoning any trace of timidity, Soleil leaned over and kissed him, teasing his lips open with her tongue. Within seconds, his surprised and welcoming lips responded with pent-up passion and soon two hot fires were raging. Their hands began exploring and caressing and canvasing each other's bodies. *Betsy was right* was Soleil's last thought of anything except the wonderful moment she was in.

Later, as their bodies melted into each other's afterglow and her silky black hair fell softly across his chest, she whispered, "Please, please ask me again."

"Soleil, will y…"

"Yes! Yes!" she cried, smothering his question with kisses. "Yes, I will marry you, Ernie McDowell."

Epilogue

Soleil. Three months after their first great kiss, Soleil moved into Ernie's spacious cabin in Alaska. An outdoor wedding photo on their credenza shows Soleil in a white sleeveless gown and Ernie in a suit and tie with snow whirling all around them. Before her first year in Alaska was over, Soleil began pursuing her recurrent dream, that of becoming a nurse. After three years of struggling to read medical textbooks in a language other than her mother tongue, she did it: she got her RN. She is currently on staff at the local hospital. She is, according to her, now living the best chapter of her life.

Mama and Papa. When the last of their ten children went off on their own, Liezel and Carlos accepted Ernie's invitation to come live in Alaska with them. Eager to work, they quickly found jobs at the local McDonald's. Their combined wages of $30 an hour in Alaska is a far cry from the $30 a month they struggled for in Palo. They are grateful to feel so rich.

Ernie. Ernie says: happy wife, happy life. He is quite content having a new daughter and in-laws under his roof. His house hums with activity, a cacophony of languages and, a cornucopia of foods and aromas. Ernie goes with the flow. He still collects medical supplies and sends them around the world.

Luna remains close to the earth. Ernie has taught her tricks about gardening in Alaska. She starts her lettuce from seed during the dark days of late winter and she marvels at how enormous her crops grow when the sun shines almost 24/7 in summers. The boys have taught her the fun of snowmobiling and the intricacies of fishing. She loves having older brothers.

Betsy is happily married to Jacques. Little Carlos now has three siblings with another on the way. A stay-at-home mom who used to rake up weeds in Palo, Betsy now is raking in money with her successful online advice podcast. She has thrived living in France, dresses in couture fashions and never misses her hair and skin appointments. In 2023 there's nothing plain about Betsy.

Jasmine hemmed and hawed for three years before she wrote her first letter to Joe Voltz in Arizona. He'd been waiting for it. When she stepped off the plane in Phoenix with long black hair cascading down her back, Joe was as smitten as ever. Not long after, he took her out for ice cream and, with cones in hand and a knee on the floor, he proposed.

Gabby returned home to an overjoyed and forgiving family. Her mother's hug had healing power. She landed a job at a nearby call center for a US telecommunications company. Now Gabby talks all day solving problems for Americans who call the 1-800 help-line. She loves her job.

Abeena, who was left crutch-less on the floor when Soleil and Jasmine escaped, wailed incessantly in her distress, attracting the attention of widower Agi, the bored codger who lived next door. He took her in and suddenly found himself with plenty to do, caring for the ailing Abeena. Their companionship softened both of them and became something more. They moved out of Damascus to the countryside. They seem to be quite content.

The Saleebs didn't come back the next day to rescue the help like they had promised. When they did return a few weeks later, they found the door unlocked and everything of value gone. All that was left were footprints in grandpa's ashes. Mohammad's bank had been destroyed in the bombings and he was reassigned to a bank far from Damascus in a poor area. He no longer wears his Rolex; it just wouldn't impress the bank's clientele of herders and farm workers. Layla is despondent. With no help to cook and clean, she eats junk food in their tiny apartment and the place is a mess. Some days she never gets out of bed. Once svelte, Layla has put on thirty pounds. She whines incessantly. Mohammad ignores her. This family was always a house of cards; now it has fallen apart.

Ahmed never reconnected with his family on the day of the initial bombings. No one has heard from him since. He could be a rebel. He could be dead.

Fadi kept honing his artistic skills and by the time he was eighteen, had amassed an impressive portfolio. He brought it to an instructor at the art school in Damascus that he hoped to attend. The teacher looked through the portfolio, told Fadi there was nothing more school could teach him and instead recommended him for a position as an illustrator for a high-tech company. Fadi often thinks of his life before the war, and never forgets to say a prayer for Edith.

Nadia is the most severely devastated by the family's changing circumstances. With no enslaved servants to abuse, she turns her venom on her mother, calling her the sloth. Mother and daughter argue incessantly. At sixteen, Nadia quits school and leaves home. Because she is pretty she finds jobs quickly; because she is lazy she gets fired immediately. To survive, Nadia does what most spoiled and angry sixteen-year-olds do: they make bad decisions.

About the Storytellers

Carol LaDuca, Merry Carroll, and Victoria VanHorn, sisters, were raised in a middle-class 60s environment by parents who encouraged creativity. Both Carol and Merry developed a life-long interest in writing. *Bamboozled* is Carol and Merry's first joint writing project, where chapter after chapter, they endeavored to mesh their individual writing styles.

Carol obtained a degree in Journalism and has worked as a newspaper editor, a feature writer and advertising copywriter. She has published cookbooks and, with a passion for photography, she has produced several story-line photobooks.

Merry's writing career began in fourth grade when she won a diocese-wide writing contest. After earning a B.S. in Biochemistry, she became a technical writer, a copywriter, and owned an advertising agency. She is ready to publish her second novel called *PlastiSized,* which brings awareness to the health dangers of plastic pollution.

Victoria is this story's plot facilitator, fact checker and critic. Because Victoria read as the writing was in progress, her critiques and ideas for plot maximization provided real-time strengthening of the novel's structure. A career art teacher, her eye for continuity, perspective, and creativity all came into play.

Acknowledgements

We thank Soleil, formerly of the Visayas, Philippines, and currently an RN in Kenai, Alaska for sharing her experiences as a domestic slave in the Middle East and her daring escape. She was the real inspiration for this novel and is featured on our cover. She hopes that even fictionalized stories like this will shed light on the problem of domestic slavery that still persists in the poorer regions of the Philippines.

We also thank Julie Peters for scrupulously reviewing the manuscript before publication.

www.ingramcontent.com/pod-product-compliance
Lightning Source LLC
Chambersburg PA
CBHW031001260626
47169CB00002B/637